ESPRIT de CORPSE

EF DEAL

NEO PARADOXA

PENNSVILLE, NJ

PUBLISHED BY
NeoParadoxa
a division of eSpec Books LLC
Danielle McPhail,
Publisher
PO Box 242,
Pennsville, New Jersey 08070
www.especbooks.com

Copyright © 2023 Ef Deal

ISBN: 978-1-949691-83-2
ISBN (ebook): 978-1-949691-82-5

Copy Editor: Greg Schauer, John L. French
Interior Design: Danielle McPhail, McP Digital Graphics

Cover Art & Design: Mike McPhail, McP Digital Graphics
Interior Art: Jason Whitley

Limited Edition Cover Art: A beautiful girl in a steampunk-style suit is sitting on the train tracks and waiting for the train © Darya Komarova, www.shutterstock.com

DEDICATION

To Arlene and Bud, who would never understand.

1.

"Jacqueline Marie-Claire Duval de la Forge-à-Bellesfées."

Jacqueline ducked her head to avoid the Paris prefect's cynical gaze as he examined Jacqueline's papers. The platform of Gare d'Austerlitz teemed with travelers anxious to board. They glared at Jacqueline, blaming her for the delay. Even the shiny green locomotive's blasts of steam accused her with each passing minute.

She reached down to scratch behind the ear of the she-wolf beside her. The wolf's eyes closed in delight. Jacqueline squatted down to whisper, "This is the third time this year I've had to rescue you from your own indiscretions, Angélique. Next time, I'll let you sit in jail."

"What was your business in Paris?" the prefect asked.

Before she could answer, a man stepped between Jacqueline and her inquisitor and addressed the prefect too quietly for Jacqueline to hear. Angélique snorted a laugh. Her lupine sense of hearing must have caught the exchange. The man strode away, and the prefect offered Jacqueline a hand to help her rise.

"I apologize, Madame Duval. I did not realize who you were." The prefect returned her papers, spun on his heel, and left.

The conductor blew his whistle. As second- and third-class passengers boarded their coaches, he opened the door to Jacqueline's first-class carriage and lowered the steps for her. Angélique leapt in and Jacqueline followed. The conductor closed the door, only to quickly open it again to allow another man to join them. The man removed a silk brocade fez and set it on the seat beside him, then opened the sketch pad he'd brought and lost himself on the page.

Once again Angélique snorted her amusement. Annoyed, Jacqueline turned her gaze out the window, chewing the inside of her cheek. Her sister seemed to know every man in Paris: artists, musicians, writers, expatriated nobles, owners of all the bar-tabacs and taverns in the Latin Quarter, and purveyors of opium along the Boul'Mich.

With a soft whine, Angélique lay her head across Jacqueline's lap, one paw on her knee. Jacqueline stroked her sister's tawny brow until the amber wolf-eyes closed, then tucked herself deeper into the corner of the carriage further from the strange artist and leaned against the window, staring out over the farms, brick factories, and slaughterhouses of southern Paris. Once the train chugged away from the station, she could breathe a sigh of relief. Angélique was safe. Again.

"Your dog loves you," the artist said.

"She is not a dog, monsieur," Jacqueline answered.

Peering closer, Delacroix slowly grinned. "So I see." He twisted his thin mustache. "Intriguing."

She wanted to scream, 'She's my twin sister who is determined to destroy herself, body and soul, because she despises the beast she's become through no fault of her own, leaving me to clean up her messes, bail her out of jail, collect her unconscious body from some hashish den, or smuggle her out of town before the police track her down.'

Angélique whined once more and licked her hand. Jacqueline tempered her anger. She would not allow her sister's antics to ruin the flush of good fortune Jacqueline had enjoyed the past three weeks. Four buyers had purchased her design for fuel conservation, and a fifth bought plans for a cooling system for his metalworks. She had also secured a commission to do a chemical analysis of a vineyard and develop a nutrient-rich fertilizer. The last elicited a nostalgic smile; the task essentially replicated the same project she had completed for her chemistry thesis at the Polytechnique when she was fifteen, allowing her to graduate with four doctoral degrees.

Jacqueline folded her arms and snuggled down, her good humor somewhat restored. The trip to Orléans would take eight hours. She dozed off and on with the rocking of the carriage, waking at each thin shriek of the locomotive's whistle, then settling comfortably again on her travel cushion. When she glanced out the window of her carriage, billows of gray smoke from the locomotive lent a misleading gloom of clouds obscuring the view to the countryside despite the midday hour. Every so often, the smoke parted to reveal a shaft of summer sunlight piercing the woods or glittering on a distant farmhouse. Not yet accustomed to the new railroad's daily passages to and from Orléans, goats and sheep scattered at the thundering noise. Down on the streams and canals, mule drivers and punters shook their fists and cursed the infernal iron invader.

Angélique grew restless, confined to the little coach in the stifling mid-July heat. Jacqueline could scarcely blame her. If they had taken the road coach from Paris, her sister would have been free to run about on the frequent stops. Never mind the trip would have taken two days and would have left them both filthy with road dust. Of course, Angelique and her antics held the blame for their manner of transport. Not that Jacqueline minded, as a polytech and master of the forge, she felt it her duty to give her patronage to the industrial marvel that was the new Paris-Orléans Railroad, particularly since she made frequent clandestine use of its rails.

"At least we're not locked into a compartment car, like the unfortunates in the Versailles disaster last year," Jacqueline said to her sister.

The man looked up from his sketch pad. "Indeed, madame. What a horror, unable to free themselves as their train caught fire. These new coaches are much safer and a relief to my rheumatic bones."

Jacqueline turned her head and chewed the inside of her cheek. She had meant her comment to reassure Angélique, not initiate conversation with a stranger. Angélique pawed lightly at her leg, teasing her for her social inhibitions. Jacqueline ignored her and returned to her nap.

The locomotive suddenly lurched with an ear-piercing squeal. Gasping, Jacqueline pitched forward as the brakes dug in. Angélique yelped as she fell to the floor, growling her displeasure as she climbed back up on the cushion. Cries of alarm rose from the adjacent first-class coaches, the Versailles tragedy uppermost in everyone's thoughts. Jacqueline peered through the dissipating smoke. The train had halted in the middle of a vast meadow. Frightened goats darted forward, charging the invader, some stiffening and dropping to the ground, others bounding to hide behind the stolid cows. Off beyond the fields, a simple church spire rose above gray roofs.

She looked at Angélique and shook her head. "Not yet."

"Probably cows on the track," said the man seated across from her. He set his sketchbook down and stood stiffly. "Just in time." He opened the carriage door and peered about. "I could do with some fresh air."

He turned back to retrieve his fez from the corner of his seat. As he set it on his head, he turned to Jacqueline to offer a hand. When she recognized Eugène Delacroix, she suddenly realized why Angélique had found their situation so amusing. Delacroix counted among the coterie of artists whose salons Angélique frequented. Jacqueline demurred, looking away.

Delacroix turned and stepped down, then jumped the remaining meter to the tracks through hissing billows of steam. As he descended the rail bed, he drew a silver cigar case from his vest pocket and placed a panatella to his lips.

Jacqueline chuckled. "Fresh air, indeed."

Angélique growled.

Jacqueline stroked her sister's brow. "If you didn't have half the Paris prefecture looking for the notorious Angélique Laforge, you could have ridden in your human form, so you can very well quit your growling. And no, I have no wish to engage with your friend." She rubbed Angélique's ear to calm her. "Patience, mon Ange, we'll soon be there. And I wired ahead for a diligence to convey us to Bellesfées, so it will await us. We should be home in time for supper."

Her smile turned to a determined pout. "Time for some new designs."

Thinking of her draughting board, Jacqueline leaned over to see what the artist had been sketching. To no surprise, she saw her own face in several casts of repose or gazing out the carriage window, along with various poses of Angélique, maw to paws or head resting on Jacqueline's lap. Delacroix had focused on Jacqueline's curls and the roundness of her eyes, but she wasn't happy with his depiction of her wide cheeks or her strong jaw and mouth. The sketches accentuated her less-than-feminine features. He had also insisted on portraying her bosom rather décolleté, despite the fact she wore a travel coat. Thank goodness he hadn't seen her without her coat: Her arms, large and firm and muscular from years at the forge, would have made him wonder if she were a woman at all.

"Delacroix is probably on his way to Nohant to referee the bouts between Madame Sand and Chopin." She chuckled drily. "Shall we demand payment if our likenesses end up on display in a certain someone's salon?"

Angélique's ears perked up and flickered; she pawed at them and whined. Sliding from the seat, she panted her sudden anxiety. Jacqueline stood to leave their coach, watching as several second- and third-class passengers, mostly men, passed the forward first-class cars to see what had stopped the train. None of the other first-class passengers seemed curious enough to leave their coaches. Angélique leapt from the car. Jacqueline was about to step down but halted when her poised foot knocked a tall grey hat off a gentleman hurrying past below the rail bed. She managed to catch the hat.

"I'm so sorry," she cried.

"Your pardon, mademoiselle," he said at the same time. "I didn't see —"

He broke off his sentence with a dazzling smile as he looked up into her face. "Madame Duval? What a pleasure to meet you!"

Jacqueline didn't recognize him and could not fathom how he would know her. She turned her head and mumbled, hoping to avoid conversation.

"From the Brussels Exposition last year?" he pursued. "Forgive me, we haven't met, but I found your presentation on the conservation of engine emissions fascinating."

Jacqueline looked again to assess his features. She was never good with names unless they came attached to commissions for her engineering designs, but she considered making an exception for this man. He was older than she, probably by at least ten years, and his wild, curly blond hair suggested he was of that fashion called "Romantic" by the effete. He stood tall and muscular, with a long, earnest face, clean-shaven, bright brown eyes, a Greek nose, and a bow to his upper lip that fascinated her as he smiled hopefully. Jacqueline curtsied with a slight nod, and she couldn't help returning his smile with equal warmth. "Please," she said, "just Duval."

"Alain de Guise," he returned. "I work with the railway. Your designs are quite revolutionary, if you don't mind my use of the word."

She smiled even wider, blushing. "At least two investors thought so as well."

"Ah, that explains why the prefect was so interested in you," he said. "I let him know his error. Imagine France's foremost engineering genius stealing some bauble from a Moroccan prince."

Jacqueline's breath caught. Angélique whined and circled. Embarrassed for her sister's sake, Jacqueline curtsied again and excused herself, but de Guise stayed where he was and extended his hand. "Please allow me."

Jacqueline gathered her skirt and petticoats and accepted de Guise's hand to guide her down the steps. He caught her as she jumped from the bottom step, holding onto her waist until she regained her balance.

Unaccustomed to such intimacy, Jacqueline pulled away. De Guise then offered his arm.

She considered it with a growing sense of discomfort. "Thank you, but I need —"

Angélique nosed between them and pushed Jacqueline forward. De Guise stared in astonishment as Jacqueline set her hand on the wolf's head instead of on his arm.

"Thank you again, Monsieur de Guise," she called as she took her leave of him.

Mud pulled at her short boots and spattered her stockings and hem as she hurried forward. De Guise followed, which made her worry she had offended him, for he had been nothing but charming for those brief moments. Surprisingly, she rather enjoyed his attentions. But for the nonce, she was more concerned with the annoyance of the delay.

"If I'm eating supper at midnight, I shall be very put out."

Angélique snorted an agreement.

Jacqueline's complaint was mollified somewhat when she came around the front of the great green locomotive and saw what had halted the train. The men who had gathered formed a wide circle beside the track, ignoring the engineer's admonitions to keep back. As she pushed her way forward, they parted to allow plenty of room for the she-wolf at her side. Jacqueline smirked, sensing their dilemma in deciding which was the more bizarre sight, the girl and her wolf or the metal form lying across the tracks, clanking almost as much as the locomotive. Its legs jerked and twitched as if an interior engine had caught somehow.

"A mechanical man?" she said, puzzled.

"Please, madame, return to your coach." The engineer turned to de Guise, "Just came barreling up the rails, sir. I couldn't avoid it. It fairly threw itself at the locomotive."

"That's all right, René. We're all safe. That's what matters."

At this exchange, Jacqueline took a second glance at de Guise, evidently someone of status in the railroad. She thought she knew everyone associated with the Paris-Orléans, from executives to designers to coal-stokers. Still, his name was not familiar, and surely if they had met, however briefly, she would have recalled that lovely smile.

The automaton hammered its fists into the rail, refocusing Jacqueline's attention. As the engineer continued conferring with de Guise, Jacqueline ventured closer to examine the clockwork mystery.

A suit of armor but cast in something far heavier. Not iron. Bronze perhaps? That would make for an incredibly heavy machine for any delicate clockwork drive, yet the form was too refined to contain a full set of mechanical engines. A full two and a half meters in length — or rather, height when it stood — with a barrel chest and well-defined limbs of burnished metal, the machine probably weighed a bit more than a hundred kilos.

Jacqueline knelt beside the figure to feel the armor.

"Careful, mademoiselle," a conductor warned, blocking her with his arm. "It's very hot. You'll burn yourself."

Jacqueline moved his arm aside. The calluses on her fingertips protected her from much of the heat, and her gloves, though trimmed in dainty lace, were thickly padded with insulation, a precaution she'd devised to protect herself from her own impulsive curiosity in cases such as this. Nevertheless, she tested warily. Bronze indeed, and extremely hot.

The arms and legs were cylindrical and articulated, attached to the metal torso in cogwork designed to regulate speed. The torso seemed surprisingly slender for so ambitious a machine. She could not figure out how any system of steam or coal fuel could be tucked away in so small a confinement. The head resembled a helmet similar in construction to a diver's casque, with a hinged faceplate riveted shut. Three dials notched by degrees sat positioned where the left ear would be, with two gauges in place of the right ear. The needle of the upper right gauge hammered emphatically into the red, while the lower gauge's needle sat idle at zero, but since they lacked marking, she had no idea what they indicated. To Jacqueline's shock, no vapors hissed from the rivets along the body's seams.

"The pressure is tremendous. No regulators? That's insane. But what powers the boiler?" she muttered. "I hear no pistons, no engine. It will explode at any moment without some system to…"

She tried to turn the form over, to the gasps and protests of the gathered crowd.

The engineer spluttered. "Mademoiselle, the danger! Come away now."

But Jacqueline remained intent on the automaton. "Help me, monsieur. It's far too heavy for me alone."

"Please, Madame Duval," de Guise argued. "Let us worry about this machine."

"But I'm not worried," she replied. "Won't someone help me?"

Three dashing fops came forward to help, one wrapping his hands with his cravat, the others using riding gloves. Over the engineer's protests, they rocked the massive body until it finally heaved to its back with a violent clatter. The fops backed off again, congratulating one another's masculine show even as they skittered away.

Jacqueline wiped the glass faceplate and tried to peer into the suit to find the secret of its workings. White vapors swirled about inside the casque, but just as the train's billowing smoke had obscured the countryside on her ride, the vapors confounded her view.

"There's nothing here. Nothing I can see. Perhaps lower? Behind the breastplate? If I could open..."

Her voice trailed off as the vapors suddenly coalesced to the image of a face, deathly grey sunken flesh, like one recently dead. The shifting vapors obscured any details of its features except its eyes, wild and terrified, pleading in an awful expression of agony and anguish. They met Jacqueline's gaze in wordless communion. As their awarenesses connected, the erratic clanking of the bronze suit eased. She caressed the glass, half in fear, half in consolation. The figure's taut lips moved, but Jacqueline couldn't make out the silent words.

"A pry bar," she cried. "Please, we must open this casque at once."

At the urgency in her voice, the crowd backed even further, fearing the machinery would indeed explode as she had said. The engineer folded his arms and shook his head.

De Guise came forward to stand behind Jacqueline. "A pry bar, please, René."

The engineer glared, but he stomped back to the locomotive and returned with the large tool, which he grudgingly handed to de Guise.

"Will this do?" de Guise asked, offering it to her. "Or shall I?"

Jacqueline grabbed the bar from him and placed its claws at the seam of the faceplate, catching a rivet. The figure within began to thrash, desperate to be freed from the confining helmet. The entire form rattled all the more.

Behind her, Angélique gave a low moan. Jacqueline ignored her sister's warning, intent on the eyes behind the glass. She tried leaning to the pry bar, but her corset, with its steel-and-bone stays, prevented her from bending enough to gain leverage.

"Such a stupid fashion," she grumbled.

She threw off her travel coat and reached around to untie the lacing knot, fumbling through the fabric of her skirt to undo it. The few women in the crowd cried out aghast and moved away from the scandalous scene, dragging their escorts with them. The younger men laughed, catcalling.

Again, de Guise came close and assisted her, unknotting the laces and loosening them. "I only wish to help," he reassured her. He even took up her coat to cover her again.

Jacqueline didn't answer, too engrossed with her goal to be embarrassed. She drew a deeper breath, braced her stance, and pressed to the pry bar once more. This time she succeeded. The rivet popped, and the faceplate flew open.

A high-pitched scream more ghastly than the locomotive's whistle burst from the bronze mechanical man. The compressed vapors billowed from the opened mask in an explosion of steam and sound. As the others fled with echoing cries, de Guise pulled her closer. Jacqueline covered her ears, keeping her eyes fixed on the surreal sight before her. The pressure gauge dropped to five hundred, two-fifty, and finally zero as the vapors within cleared, revealing nothing. Literally, nothing. No face, no form. No more than a shriek fading on the summer breeze.

Restrained by de Guise, Jacqueline leaned closer to peer inside the casque. From the depths, a skull peered back, gleaming white, polished, as it were, affixed atop a copper pipe that disappeared down into the cavern of the chest.

"Did you see that?" she cried. "Did anyone see that?"

She looked to de Guise, but he shook his head, confused.

The engineer stepped closer, his demeanor more respectful. "I saw you released the pressure, mademoiselle, preventing this machine from destroying the track and killing us." He gazed about as if expecting to spy the perpetrator of such ruination lurking at the edge of the field, behind the goats, atop the dike. "Canal drovers sabotaging the rail, most likely. Would have killed us all."

"Angélique?" With her keener senses, Jacqueline hoped her sister could confirm that something — *something* — had escaped the metal automaton.

Angélique howled, long and low, then glared. She huffed in disgust and slunk back to where Delacroix stood by the engine, swiftly sketching the tragic scene before him, likely through his Romantic lens:

portrait of the lady and her armored knight dying in her arms amid the billowing breath of a great green dragon. Angélique *whoof*ed at him to get his attention, wagging her tail and prancing in invitation. He grinned, following her away from the crowds and into the meadow.

Jacqueline watched them go with frustration. Of all times for her sister to play the bohemian grisette!

She smacked dust from her gloves. "I should like this machinery placed among my luggage in the guard's van. Are your bogies strong enough to bear it?"

Exasperated, the engineer yanked off his hat and wiped his brow with it. "Madame, have you not done enough to delay us?"

Jacqueline knew better than to lose her temper, though she, in fact, had resolved the delay, not caused it. She smiled sweetly, batting her lashes. "Please, monsieur. Surely someone will indulge me in this whim?"

"Herz, Hoog, help me with this thing," the engineer called to the stoker and the conductor, who had held back.

De Guise said, "Are you sure you are not making a mistake, madame? By rights, I should convey this to the offices at the Gare d'Orléans, but I recognize that you are foremost a clockwork engineer and more likely to figure out the nature and purpose of this machine."

"I am sure of nothing except what I saw."

She extracted herself from de Guise's grip and tried to re-tie her corset and adjust her skirts, bothered by her disarray now that she'd accomplished her goal.

De Guise laughed quietly. "You do manage to get your way, don't you?"

Jacqueline grinned. "I do. But I can't help it. A machine of such intricacy that I didn't make myself? A puzzle! I must know more about it."

And softer, to herself, she added, "And about the poor soul that roiled in its furnaces."

De Guise escorted her as she oversaw the transport of her newfound prize and helped her into the guard's van to watch over it. When the locomotive whistle blew to signal departure, he turned to her with regret in his gaze.

"You amaze me so," he confessed with a chuckle. "I hope we shall meet again soon. Then you must tell me what you learn about this automaton."

He took her hand, still gloved and now filthy from her work, and pressed it to his lips. At her quiet gasp, he said, "I have held you close twice today. You must allow me a kiss."

He moved off before she could find her voice to reply. Without a doubt, had she been fitted with gauges like the automaton, they'd also be hammering at the red zone.

Jacqueline looked around for her sister and caught sight of her at Delacroix's side, wandering back from the tall meadow grasses. Jacqueline shook her head. Despite the mystery and wonder of the clockwork man, her sister—as usual—pursued more carnal pleasures with real men. Jacqueline had hoped Angelique's latest escapade in Paris would have tempered her compulsive self-indulgence. But, no… 'I'm bored, grab a partner and hie off to the meadows.' Clearly Delacroix was amenable to the distraction. Given Angelique and Delacroix both frequented the bacchanalian revelries of Paris salons, the artist probably recognized Angelique's amber eyes. Perhaps even knew of her unique nature. Perhaps had even enjoyed her womanly favors before that day.

Angélique paused at the third-class car, sensing Jacqueline in the van behind it. She whined querulously at Jacqueline's choice of seating and continued to their first-class coach with Delacroix rather than join her sister.

2.

THEY REACHED THE TERMINUS NEAR ORLÉANS ALMOST TWO HOURS LATE. By the time they had loaded their diligence and secured a wagon to transport the mechanical man, it was past six o'clock. It took the conveyances yet another hour and a half to reach home. Angélique ran on ahead, eager to stretch her legs. When Jacqueline finally arrived at the gates of Forge-à-Bellesfées, the gas lamps along the drive were already lit, for the surrounding forest was too dense for the early-evening sun to adequately light the road that wound three kilometers through the ancient woods. Only when Jacqueline came through the gardens and the sun turned the turrets and friezes of the modest château a rose-tinged gold did she breathe easier and allow herself a smile.

Bellesfées and its forge had stood in one form or another since the thirteenth century, although the forge had shut down long before the Revolution. A citizen bought the land. He renovated the towers and turrets and repaired the keep with a mansard roof, only to forfeit it all to the state. Once the state realized it could no more afford the upkeep than the bankrupted citizen, they sold the little château to the highest bidder, Jacqueline's father, a beleaguered widower in need of an out-of-the-way nursery for his two unruly daughters while he was away on business, as he often was.

Michel Duval leased the southern-pitched fields to a nearby vigneron, keeping the forest parc and château as a playground for Jacqueline and Angélique. He hired a governess and two tutors, along with Marthe and Luc Benet, a local couple, as housekeepers who occupied the "cottage" — the original fortress tower a short way along the road to the forge. The girls tore through the poor governesses one a month, but the Benets kept them in line around the house, and the tutors were able to tame the intractable twins by discovering their nascent brilliance: the sciences for Jacqueline, and the arts for Angélique. Their father had the forge rebuilt and added another wing to the château as a private musical conservatory, with rooms above for the progression of instructors both girls would require.

Jaqueline could not help her prideful smile as they approached the front of the château. Thanks to her innovations, Château Bellesfées stood as the most modern estate in all of France. For her Polytechnique entrance project, thirteen-year-old Jacqueline redesigned the château's plumbing. Her design turned the two corner towers into water closets upstairs and down, with hot and cold running water. Likewise, she installed a mechanical pump for fresh water and a septic system to manage her innovation.

Her smile, of course, flattened with annoyance as the entrance came into view. Angélique waited in the open doorway, smoking a cigarette she hastily crushed as the diligence emerged from the forest. She had changed form and dressed in a light chemise à la reine, her tawny, black-tipped hair undone, lifted by the evening breeze. Her amber wolf-eyes, the most evident of lycanthropy's physical changes to her human body, gleamed with exhilaration from her run. As the diligence drew to a stop, Angélique stepped forward, along with Luc, his young son Jean-Paul, and a pair of clockwork vehicles Jacqueline had built to serve as luggage porters.

"You left me alone with Delacroix," Angélique scolded as she grabbed her own bag from the carriage and plopped it on the porter. "Hours of tedium. And now you smell like coal oil and smoke from sitting in the back of the train."

Jacqueline returned in kind. "You stole from a prince. And now I suppose I'll have to pay him off to keep you out of prison."

"He tried to make me his *seventeenth* wife."

"If you'd quit dallying—"

"You're such a prude."

"And you act like a selfish child."

Jacqueline finished unloading her bags and sent the porter on its way. She then turned to her sister and hugged her in silent apology. Angélique kissed Jacqueline's cheeks, then paid the coachman as Luc and Jean-Paul, accustomed to their mistress's predilection for heavy machinery, set up the tow-cart and winch to transfer the machine to the workshop attached to the forge. The self-driving porters followed the girls into the foyer. As Jacqueline closed the doors against the night, she felt like a clockwork spring too tightly wound had finally uncoiled within her.

She sighed deeply. "It's so good to be home. Now get me out of this crinoline and corset and into some trousers so I can work on that thing."

"*Ooh, là!* Would your new gentleman friend approve of trousers?" Angélique teased. "He looked like he enjoyed getting you out of that corset."

Jacqueline huffed. "I am not a strumpet like you. Honestly. Delacroix?"

Angélique bumped Jacqueline's shoulder. Jacqueline returned the playful blow with a pillow to the face. The two laughed.

"I fear, chère Jacky," Angélique said, "you will die a spinster. Old, wrinkly, single, and choking out your last breath under one of your machines. Do you think you can take the time for some supper before you head to the workshop? Marthe has strawberry soup and a plank of cold meats and fresh cheese."

"Which you'd better eat, or I shall beat you both, and you know I will," Marthe bawled from the kitchen. Jacqueline chuckled, picturing the plump woman's weathered, heart-shaped face growing ruddier as she brandished her rolling pin in the air in her usual empty threat.

"I'll take some with me, then," she called back. Then in a lower voice, "Mon Ange, did you—did you *see* it?"

Angélique nodded. "Saw it. Smelled it. Felt it. Yes." She took Jacqueline's arm and tugged her toward the stairs. "But it's gone now, so you won't have any way of knowing how it was done, no more now than by the light of day. Come upstairs and get comfortable. I've filled the bathtubs. We'll have some supper and discuss this rationally before you fire up the forge and wake the neighbors."

Jacqueline snorted. The closest neighbors lived in the village several kilometers away. But she took her sister's point and complied.

Worn marble steps wound up to a second storey, four suites, each one with a dressing room, a bedchamber, a water closet, and a bathtub. The windows were thrown open in anticipation of the sisters' return, and Angélique had already set out a chemise for Jacqueline beside the bath.

"The water's nice and cool," she said as she helped Jacqueline out of her clothing. "It'll do you good after so long a trip."

"No, no," Jacqueline protested. "Just a wash. If I step into that tub, I'll fall right to sleep, slip down, and drown."

"But you stink. I mean, you *really* stink. I'll bet you haven't bathed in the past four days."

"You mean these past four days when I've been hiding *you* from the police?" Jacqueline poked her sister in the chest to emphasize her words. "I'll bathe in the morning."

Angélique shook her head, but Jacqueline knew she wouldn't argue. She'd already won two points getting Jacqueline to change and dine; she wouldn't risk those triumphs fighting for a third.

Jacqueline used the ewer to fill the wash bowl with water from the scented bath and wiped the soot, cinders, and travel dust from her face, neck, and arms. Angélique found all the pins holding her honey-blonde hair in chignons and curls and combed them out with her unnaturally long fingers.

"Tresses?" Angélique asked.

"Not tonight."

Jacqueline twisted her hair into a knot that flopped loosely at the back of her neck. She donned the chemise, a light peignoir, and a pair of silk slippers and followed Angélique dutifully to the dining room. She had to admit she was hungry. Unlike a road coach, the train did not stop for meals, and she hadn't eaten since breakfast in Paris. When Marthe pressed a glass of rosé d'Anjou on her, she finally conceded the mystery could wait until after they dined.

The housekeeper kissed Jacqueline's cheek. "Glad you're home, my girl." She waggled her finger at Angélique. "And you, little one. Stay out of trouble! If your father only knew…" But she kissed Angélique as well. "Eat. Rest. I'll see you in the morning. Leave everything."

Jacqueline caught her hand and squeezed it. "I'll get it all away, Marthe. Thank you."

"You're a good girl," Marthe said. "Both good girls." She sniffed dismissively and went back to the kitchen.

Angélique stuck out her tongue. "Such a good girl."

Jacqueline took a petit pain and buttered it. "I'm not the one who stole Prince Abadi's ruby."

At nine-thirty, Luc lit the argand lamps in the salon for them before retiring. The sisters settled down to play cribbage as the night finally grew dark and cooler air breezed through the open windows and doors.

The frogs in the pond down the hill squawked and barked to one another comically, and the women couldn't help giggling.

Jacqueline set out her hand after play. "Fifteen-two, fifteen-four, and a double run. Hah!" As the clock struck eleven-thirty, she placed her peg into the winning hole of the cribbage board and stood, stretching her back. "Enough. I'm going to see to the machine before I retire."

Angélique arched a brow. "In your night clothes?"

"I want to at least detach the skull from the mechanism. Leaving it would be most unseemly and disrespectful. Downright blasphemous, I would say. I don't think I could sleep until I secure it more properly. Then I will go to bed. I promise," she said to Angélique's skeptical look. "Go on. I'll put out the lamps when I come up. I won't be long."

Angélique lit a candle to guide her way upstairs. "I only badger you to have some amusement for your sake, you know," she told her. "If not for me, you'd work yourself to death. You could enjoy so much more of life, Jacky. You know, 'Où sont les neiges d'antan?' Carpe diem and all that."

"Oh, yes? Well, I must carpe the day with only two hands, not four paws. Someone has to pay your way, my dearest prodigal."

Angélique's eyes twinkled mischievously. "You missed your chance to carpe today. I think that gorgeous gentleman hoped to charm you."

Jacqueline blinked in surprise. "Really? De Guise? I don't... What makes you... *Euh*..."

"Silly." Angélique patted Jacqueline's head as if she were a child. "That's what I mean, Jacky. You miss all the clues, so you miss all the fun."

"Fun?" Jacqueline waved her away. "One day, you'll realize a quick tryst in a field is not contentment."

"It's contentment enough for now."

Jacqueline refused to argue propriety with Angélique anymore. Her sister's former life as a piano prodigy had taken her to the heights of society, but her traumatic metamorphosis five years ago left her with a petty and somewhat vulgar taste for self-indulgence that disgusted Jacqueline: expensive dresses and jewelry, fine dining, and all-night bohemian revelries with unsavory sorts. But Jacqueline had long since left off lecturing Angélique on her profligacy. If only Angélique would likewise stop dragging her away from her work.

Jacqueline took up one of the argand lamps to guide her way and headed outside through the salon doors. As she strode down the hill toward the pond, the frogs silenced at her passing. They resumed their raucous chorus only after she cleared the hillside and neared her workshop a few hundred meters through the woods, attached to a former weapons forge built on the stream that fed the pond.

Luc and Jean-Paul had set the automaton on her workbench. The bronze now cool to the touch, Jacqueline opened the hinged glass plate and pondered the skull inside. It stared back at her without answers. She thumbed the flint switch of her lucifer lamp, bathing the workroom in a phosphorous light. The skull gleamed. It had not yellowed with age, nor did it show any signs of decay. Jacqueline shuddered at the thought of someone beheading a victim for the sake of... what? What possible purpose? Grisly ornamentation?

Gently, she explored the skull with one hand until she found the means to pry it from the copper stem and collar. She might have imagined a face, vapors clinging to the skull, the odd formation of white and gray about the eye sockets giving the impression of those wild, agonized eyes. But that Angélique, in her lupine form, had not only sensed the presence of something otherworldly but also marked the passing of that spirit as it was released from whatever devices had bound it—this more than anything convinced Jacqueline she had stumbled across too great a mystery to ignore.

Could someone harness a spirit? Could a spirit be pressed into service pumping the pistons of an engine? An engine, Jacqueline reminded herself, she had not yet discovered.

She carefully placed the skull on a clean utility rag and covered it as reverently as if it were the altar bread. Holding the lamp aloft, she ran her hand along the bronze form, probing each rivet along the ventral seam to find another access plate for the lower workings of the machine.

A dark movement in the window above the bench made her suddenly aware of the ominous silence of the night. The frogs had ceased their noise. Her hand slid from the bronze form to close on the claw hammer hanging within reach. Slowly, she set down the lamp and took the hammer into her right hand, hoping to hide her actions. As the frogs began barking again, she called out with forced casualness, "Jean-Paul, is that you? You should be a-bed!"

No response, no footsteps, no tell-tale sound.

The fatigue of the day, the eerie shriek of the escaping spirit, the skull gleaming in the light of the lamp... Could she have imagined the shadow? Returning the hammer to its hooks, she took up her argand, shaking her head. Perhaps she was too tired for work, just as Angélique had suggested. She closed the lucifer lamp, locked up the workshop, and headed back to the château.

Halfway up the hill above the pond, Jacqueline remembered the reason she had gone to her workshop in the first place. "The skull. *Zut!*"

She debated leaving it rather than trooping back to the workshop. Her slippers were already wet from the dewy grass. But having removed the remains from their casing, she felt she owed them a more proper resting place for the night than a rag, so she turned back.

As she neared the workshop, she halted and set the argand down. This time she knew she did not imagine it: a faint light shone through the dirty windows, casting a shadow of someone moving rather noisily within. Her heart pounded, more in anger than fear. *A trespasser! Who would dare!* With rising fury, she threw open the door to the workshop and stormed inside.

"Who in blazes are you to break into my shop at... at this hour?" she demanded, faltering upon finding no intruder.

Before she grasped her mistake, the door slammed, and rough hands seized her from behind. Jacqueline cried out and fought the intruder's grip, but he locked her arms behind her with one powerful arm, swiftly tying her wrists. Although she struggled, she could not wriggle around to see who held her.

"Who—are—you? Damn you!"

Her assailant reached both hands around her and snatched at the waistline of her chemise. Jacqueline barely gasped her horror when, in a quick movement, he stuffed the cotton gown into her mouth until the corner of her lip split. The mass of gauzy fabric choked her, causing her to gag and cough for lack of sufficient air. Panic evinced tears, which closed her sinuses. When dizziness threatened to overtake her, Jacqueline forced herself to focus, breathing slow to garner what air she could through the fabric.

The man dragged her back to the end of the workbench, straining her shoulders. Tears of pain joined those of fear as he pushed her into a chair. Infuriated, she lifted both feet off the ground to kick at her attacker. With raw strength, he turned her chair and slid her out of reach, her legs flailing helplessly.

"For the world, I wouldn't hurt you," he said, his French heavily accented with decidedly British overtones. "I came only for this machine."

He knelt to secure her ankles, his shoulder pressed to her calves to keep her from kicking, though still, she tried. Outraged, Jacqueline roared through the gag and fought his grip to no effect.

As soon as he finished binding her, he stood and stepped back, his features hidden in shadow. The rogue ducked his head as he turned away, denying her even a glimpse of his face. When he moved to the workbench, she thumped her chair around. The dim light of a candle he had waxed to her workbench shone on a mariner's dark coat and white trousers, and a black, red, and white tartan ribbon secured his long dark hair at the nape of his neck. She saw nothing else to identify him.

The intruder drew up a small gardening cart and began inching the mechanical man off the bench. Jacqueline glared at the audacity.

He would steal my cart as well? And why such a small cart? Does he really have no idea what he's doing?

She watched intently, looking for an opportunity to outmaneuver him, but her pulse hammered so loudly in her head that she couldn't think.

As he shifted to get under the helmet to pull it off, Jacqueline spied his reflection in the window. She sketched him mentally with the keen eye of a draughtsman. A powerful build, around eighty kilos. A rough beard, brow high and broad, a narrow face, high cheekbones. She would know him again if she saw him. Though he wore a dark coat, he sported white breeched pants and black boots. Not the typical habiliments of a vandal.

Concentration served to clear away her fear. He hadn't harmed her, only angered her. He claimed to have come for the mechanical man, but he obviously hadn't been aware of the exigencies of his task—the weight of the cast bronze, the contents of the helmet, the need for a sturdy cart. How did he plan to escape hauling such a heavy burden?

As he tugged first the feet, then an arm, then the head to little avail, Jacqueline realized he must have come at someone else's bidding. He didn't own the machine, nor had he had any part in its construction. He didn't know enough about engineering to recognize the system of winches above the bench, there to aid in the manipulation of such heavy machinery. He was a mercenary, sent on an errand to fetch back someone's objet d'art, an object she had technically appropriated from its owner, its inventor maybe, who had somehow lost track of its path. This man might be within his right to take the machine from her, presuming he had been hired by that inventor. But why the secrecy? Why not simply ask her? Honesty would have won her help, but this—!

The mechanical man teetered on the edge of the workbench, its leg catching the rag that contained the skull. With a final heave, the man pulled the automaton over. It landed on the cart, snapping one of the wheels, then tumbled to the floor with a resounding clang as the man danced out of the way of its fall. The skull spun out of the rag, dropped to the floor, and rolled to Jacqueline's feet, landing face down against her slipper.

"Ho-ho!"

The villain spun to follow the path of the skull. He appeared older than his reflection had let on, perhaps in his mid-thirties. His beard looked a scant week old, not so rough as his reflection had suggested, and his bright blue eyes contrasted sharply with his dark hair. He bent down to retrieve the skull and studied it with some keenness.

Jacqueline's eyes narrowed on the markings on the back of the skull: fine gold filigree etched in a circular design. There appeared to be letters. Not Greek or Arabic. It resembled Sanskrit but didn't seem to spell out any words she recognized.

Oddly, the rogue kissed its brow reverently before he slipped the skull into a satchel at his hip. He then met Jacqueline's gaze, his expression one of chagrin.

"I thought you had gone for the night," he said. "I thought you were your lad coming in, or I would never have—"

"Untie me, salaud!" she yelled, stamping her feet, but muffled by the gag, she didn't sound very threatening.

He bowed slightly, backing away. "I've behaved monstrously toward you, ma'm'selle, and that's not like me. I count it to my shame. My quarrel isn't with you, and perhaps I should have approached you openly rather than—"

The rattle of chains came too late for him. Before he could whirl about, a winch hook slammed down on his head, dropping him to the floor. Jacqueline thumped her chair around to find Angélique at the winch controls, wiping grease from her hands. With a mischievous grin, her sister shrugged.

3.

"Aïe!"

The chemise stuck to Jacqueline's split lip. Angélique gently tugged it free and daubed the blood away, then worked to untie her sister's knots, ankles first.

"How did you know?" Jacqueline asked.

"I smelled his nervousness, a little sour tang of deception, coming from the forest. I thought him a poacher I could chase off. I'd have been here sooner, but you stink so badly. I didn't sense your fear and anger until I was closer. Next time, take a bath when I say you are rank."

"Did you kill him?" Jacqueline's voice quavered as she tried to peer over her sister's head to see the intruder.

"No, I can hear his heartbeat," Angélique answered. "But if you want me to—"

"No, that's fine."

Angélique finished with Jacqueline's wrists and slowly guided her arms to avoid spraining the overly strained muscles. Jacqueline leaned her head to her sister's, welcoming her ministrations.

"I want to know who sent him and why he felt it necessary—"

"Did he violate you?" Angélique demanded. She stood and took up the claw hammer. "If he did, I *will* eat him."

"No, no. He didn't." Jacqueline pressed her legs even closer together. "He claimed to have come for the machine but seemed intent on just the skull. How would he have known about it? This is more than the mere theft of an artifact. There is some greater conspiracy."

"A *cons*-piracy of *cons*, perhaps."

Angélique pulled her to her feet, but Jacqueline knelt beside the unconscious man to examine his head. There was a gratifyingly large lump but no blood, thank heaven—Angélique had used one of the smaller winches.

"He'll have a concussion," she murmured, then said loudly, "Can you hear me, monsieur? Are you awake?"

The man groaned and gasped. "—I won't—count—" He lay still again. Jacqueline inspected his jacket, finding all his pockets empty. She took the leather satchel from him and put it on her workbench. It was heavily lined, and it held only the skull. This she removed. She showed her sister the gold lettering.

"Have you ever seen writing like this?"

"It's very pretty, but what is it?" Angélique sniffed at the skull as if it would reveal its secrets to her keen senses.

Jacqueline tasted blood on her lip again. She pressed her sleeve to the cut. "There's too much to do all at once," she said with a frustrated sigh. "I'm still shaking, this man needs attention, and—"

"This man we can ignore."

"No, we can't. I want answers. Wake Luc and Jean-Paul. Have them bring him to the house. We should—can you bind his hands and feet? He must not—*euh*—escape us."

She stared in confusion at the blood on her sleeve. She didn't remember cutting her lip.

Angélique took the skull from her and placed it back in the satchel. "M'amie, you're in shock. Sit."

Jacqueline obeyed and watched her sister secure the intruder. Angélique then wrapped her arm around her and led her away. Jacqueline snatched up the satchel again and clutched it tightly, lest she should lose her only clue to the mysterious mechanical man and the even more mysterious intruder.

They left by the drive so they could stop at the Benets' cottage a half-kilometer along. Luc answered their knock at the door in his nightshirt, but Marthe appeared right behind him, tying her peignoir closed.

"What are you two up to now?" Marthe asked, yawning. "Eh? What's this? Fighting again?" Marthe pushed her husband out of the way to examine Jacqueline with maternal concern, cupping her face and peering into her eyes. "What's happened? You look like a toddler hugging her teddy."

Angélique calmed her. "We're all right, but Jacky's a little shaken. An intruder broke into her workshop to steal her new toy. He treated her roughly, but we don't want to call the prefecture just yet. Luc, you'll find him tied up like the beast he is, and I may have cracked his skull. I doubt he'll regain consciousness for a while. Would you bring him up to the house on a porter? We're hoping to winkle some answers from him, should he wake up."

"I'll get bandages and send Jean-Paul to the ice cellar." Marthe shuffled off.

Luc, stolid and rarely talkative, gave the twins a reassuring nod. "Jean-Paul will escort you home," he said.

Angélique dismissed the suggestion. "We'll be safe," she said. "I smell no one else in the forest tonight."

Another nod. "As you wish, mesdemoiselles."

Jacqueline grimaced. Despite the twins' majority, he persisted in referring to them as girls.

Once inside, Angélique settled Jacqueline on a couch and put her feet up on a stool. She poured a brandy, pressed the snifter into her sister's hands, and then poured one for herself. "Let cooler heads prevail here, Jacky. I'll fetch a basin and a cloth. You lie back and collect your thoughts."

"I don't have enough thoughts to collect," Jacqueline retorted, a fact that gnawed at her. She was accustomed to analyzing information, not speculations.

"Come now. You're the genius, after all. Talk. You know I can hear you," Angélique said as she moved off.

Jacqueline savored the burn of the brandy, regaining some grounding as she leaned her head back on the couch, closing her eyes. "He didn't know much about the machine beforehand. He knows the skull is significant. He had no idea of the magnitude of his task trying to move that thing."

"He's a brigand," her sister called from the kitchen. "You should have let me eat him." She returned to the salon carrying a basin and cloths. "Accustomed to treating people brutally and taking whatever he fancies, and so much the worse if he was hired to do so."

Jacqueline sat up as her sister set the basin on the low table in front of her. "He did apologize prettily," Jacqueline reflected. "That speaks well of him."

"You speak well enough of him. He said 'count,' so perhaps that's who heads this great conspiracy you think you've uncovered."

"A person?" She sipped more brandy, igniting a new logic path. "I hadn't thought of that. I assumed he referred to numbers."

"As you are wont to do, little miss engineer. He bound you with a sailor's knots. I'll wager he's a pirate."

"I don't believe so. He seemed too stupid."

"Ah, you now insult him. Much better." Angélique soaked a cloth, wrung it out, and tossed it over Jacqueline's face. "We'll settle for a sailor then, hired to do a job beyond his abilities. Do you really think this mysterious Count didn't know how inept he was when he hired him?"

Jacqueline washed, then set the cool cloth to her forehead and lay back on the cushions. "If he did, then perhaps this was a test. All of it. This Count Quiconque, whoever, set the machine on the tracks for me to discover. He planned for me to bring the machine here and sent this intruder to see how far I had proceeded with it."

"That is a lot to presume." Angélique swirled her brandy. "Honestly, you could drown in a glass of water, the way you think. You believe this count knows you, knows your reputation, knows your abilities. Knows even that you were on that train."

Jacqueline gave a most unladylike snort. "*Bof!* What do you think? I spent three very successful and lucrative weeks in Paris with my new pressure gauges and recycle systems, and what greets us on our way home? A hermetic system begging release."

"Yes, I understood that." Angélique grinned. "You see? I was paying attention despite my amusements."

"I troubled the station master and the local carriages to bring it home. You didn't ride home with me; you ran ahead. So, if he had been waiting for me in the parc, you would have sensed him without my 'stink,' as you so politely put it. There was no horse. No carriage. He must have come in by the backwater at the edge of the estate. It's the far end, so beyond the reach of your nose."

"Ah," her sister commented. "Now that makes sense. Your scent covered his until he was much closer. There, you collect your thoughts rather well, after all. Let's see how much further we can test ourselves." Angélique wrung out the cloth and mopped up spilled drops. "Does Count Quiconque know you found that skull? Does he realize your interest is now focused beyond the pressure-release system? Does he know you have discovered him to be some sort of ghoul, this necromantic engineer? Does he know you won't rest until you have unmasked all the players and put the skull to a blessed rest?"

"Now you're mocking me."

"Well, if it's a conspiracy, you must think of all the wildest possibilities. If he dabbles in the arcane, he may have a crystal ball or a genie or something. Sacrebleu, if I can suddenly wake up as a shapeshifter, who knows what arcane forces plot the ruin of Mad Madame Duval?"

Jacqueline's brow furrowed as she focused on a hangnail on her right forefinger, annoyed by her sister's sarcasm in the face of the logic before her.

"Everyone gathered around the machine, including Delacroix and de Guise, knew I took possession of the automaton. People at the Orléans station observed me transporting it, but no one stopped me. No one came forward to claim ownership. We were home for hours. If someone were waiting here to steal it, he certainly had plenty of time. But our intruder came later, and I think he came by the river. His costume would suggest it. And it all suggests conspiracy. Something about the skull and the writing on it, because in the end, that's all he was interested in."

Angélique chuckled quietly. "Much better. All we can really deduce is that someone at the station could have passed along the details, and our intruder followed up on orders from an unknown count to retrieve the skull. Now, why a skull?"

"Ah, there's where we need to focus. You and I both know a spirit escaped from that automaton. There are no engines inside the casing, so I can only deduce the spirit was the soul of whoever's skull that is, and the soul powered the automaton."

Angélique heaved a sigh. "Poor little miss engineer. Once again, your ordered life of science and analytics and machinery is disrupted by the supernatural." She downed her brandy in a single gulp.

Jacqueline frowned, tapping her calloused fingertips against the snifter. "Trust me, it brings me no pleasure. Power. Fuel. The source. The secret is in that skull. I am certain of it."

"Then take it back to Paris, to your Université Polytechnique."

"No. The Collège." She recalled names of former professors. "I'll need to consult some antiquities scholars."

"But carefully. At the Collège, many students remain volatile. Beardless revolutionaries crawl the Boul'Mich like rats. Barricades are still too common down at—"

Angélique broke off her warning as Luc came through the salon doors, followed by a clockwork porter carrying their prisoner, still unconscious, his limbs bound securely. Marthe followed with an ice bag and bandages to administer medical aid. They got him to the divan, where Marthe wrapped his head and set the ice bag on the wound to prevent swelling. Throughout her efforts, the prisoner did not wake.

"I really don't know how you girls manage to get into such mischief," Marthe grumbled good-naturedly as she left. "Be careful."

"Mesdemoiselles?" Luc indicated the man, then glanced around the room and returned his gaze to Jacqueline with unspoken doubts.

Angélique said, "No, dear Luc, we are quite safe. There's nothing within reach for him to free himself. Even if he somehow manages to bite through his ropes without my knowing it, I can always rip his throat out."

Luc wagged his head and tossed his shoulders but didn't argue.

Jacqueline told him, "Thank you, Luc, for everything. I shall be taking the steam coach tonight. Would you load my travel case and stoke the boiler? I haven't unpacked yet, so my bags are still on the porter at the foot of the stairs."

Angélique chuckled as Luc rolled his eyes and left the salon. She turned her attention to the man on the divan. "Well, now. He's quite pretty and all wrapped up like a present," Angélique said. She leaned over his face and breathed in. "Mmm. His sweat may stink of lies, but his skin is... Sweet. Exquisite. If you don't want to be bothered with him, I could take some time."

Jacqueline pressed a hand to her aching head. "I'm sure you could. I don't know if I can trust you with him. Angélique, this is serious. For once, can you be the responsible one?"

Her sister laughed. "Let's sleep on it," she said.

"No! I want to get back to Paris right away, and if I can't leave him in your care, I'll need to consider other options." Jacqueline chewed her cheek. "I could take him with me, I suppose. Question him when he wakes up..."

"What? You truly are an idiot."

"And you truly are a spoiled brat," she retorted. "But this man is not some new toy you get to play with when I'm not looking."

"I know that." Angélique pouted. "I'm not stupid."

"But you are reckless, which is why we fled Paris today." Taking her sister's hands in hers, Jacqueline pleaded gently. "Listen. I don't think he saw who dropped the winch on his head. I don't know how much he knows about us, so it's possible he doesn't know of your other form."

Angélique flashed a wolfish grin. "I like the way you think, my dear genius sister. That's our solution. I'll go change into the wolf and guard him through the night. Tomorrow I'll keep watch. He may not realize he's giving away information in front of a wolf." She eyed the man again. "But I must rely on Luc and Marthe if I'm to remain wolf the whole while. How long will you be away?"

Jacqueline stood. "I'll return as soon as I can. Classes are still in session, so I should be able to find Professor Bernouf, the professor of Sanskrit, or Letronne in archaeology. One of them may be able to translate the writing. From there, I don't know, but at the very least, I'll return after three days to make certain you're still safe."

Angélique set her hand to the lump on the man's head. "I hope I didn't smash his brain. He might lose his memory. I've seen that happen in bar brawls." Shaking him by the shoulders, she called, "Monsieur Thief, wake up!"

When the man made no response, she lifted his left eyelid to peer deeply. "Hmm. A concussion this bad, a day abed, another day awake and disabled, and a third astir. I might be able to spare you four days, but no more. Anyway," she finished as she tested the knots she'd made, "I'll make certain he doesn't escape." At Jacqueline's doubtful glare, Angélique folded her arms. "I promise!" she said, then shoved her sister toward the stairs. "Go. And get that bath before you leave. Heaven knows you'll forget the social niceties once you reach the College."

Jacqueline chuckled. "Eating has never been a problem in Paris, mon Ange!"

"*Bathe!*" Angélique called after her. "I mean it, Jacky! I could smell you all the way from the workshop, remember."

"Of course you did. You can smell a boar from two kilometers."

"If you smelled as nice as a boar, I wouldn't be telling you to bathe!"

Jacqueline obeyed, knowing her sister wouldn't let her board the steam coach unless she had done so. She donned her preferred work clothes: trousers, shirt, waistcoat, and jacket. She found, as had the notorious Madame Sand of Nohant, that no one interrupted needful discussions to marvel at her knowledgeable conversation if they didn't immediately recognize her gender. She didn't mind being called "Monsieur Duval" if it meant she got the needed answers.

As Jacqueline boarded her custom coach, Luc filled the coal bin positioned atop the boiler at the front end. The odor of carbon always piqued a sense of new adventures in Jacqueline. She was never more at home than in an oily, smoky, greasy workshop; her steam coach provided the ambience she needed, yet with all the amenities of her own chambers at home.

"Marchand will reload when you arrive," Luc said as he closed the hopper. He cranked the engine to the conveyor that would distribute the coal apace with the speed of the self-contained locomotive.

"Thank you, Luc, for everything." She hesitated, then said, "You'll keep an eye out? You know how Angélique can be."

"I do. I will," he said. "Never had a goat get loose. Nor a pig. Don't think he'll go anywhere with his head bashed in." Tossing his shoulders in his usual phlegmatic way, he added, "Not with the way I tied him."

Jacqueline chuckled and gave him a farewell hug.

After setting her travel case and the satchel on the couch, she fired up the boiler, feeling that clockwork spring coiling up inside her once more. Thankfully, the comforts engineered into the coach's design, far more opulent and spacious than the Paris-Orléans first-class car she had occupied only this afternoon, would provide a few hours of decent rest. The soft hunter-green velvet of the couch and matching overstuffed chair, both anchored to the floor for safety, tempted her to settle in right away, as did her bed, tucked at the far end of the coach, forming a cozy nook. Instead, she lit the lanterns on her desk and side table, casting a candescent glow on the rosewood and polished brass surrounding her.

Once the boiler gauge indicated sufficient steam pressure, Jacqueline engaged the engines. The car trundled along the short private side-rail she had built the year before in anticipation of the railroad's completion. The few kilometers to the switchover past Ormes gave her just enough time to prepare the precious skull for a closer inspection. Jacqueline pulled a fresh sheet of paper from her desk, smoothed it out across her draughting table, and clamped it into place. With a tickle of excitement, she brought out the brand-new brass eidograph her father had sent from London. Opening the mahogany box engraved "Charles Baker of London," she gently ran her hand along the polished brass.

"Oh, Papa, you spoil me so."

Ignoring the directions tucked inside the lid of the box, she affixed the eidograph to her tabletop, then fastened a vise to the side of her table, the clamps of which were lined with heavy velour. She fetched the satchel and carefully removed the skull. The perfection of its integrity fascinated her, from the smooth neurocranium down to the health of the individual teeth. No evidence of trauma marred the features. Its texture, like polished marble, gleamed in the light.

"You and I should get to know one another, my friend," Jacqueline murmured. "Come, tell me your tale."

She secured the artifact face down in the vise, giving her a clear view of the gold script on the occipital bone. The switchover was just a few minutes away, so she made a cup of tea and curled into the overstuffed chair to wait, breathing in the tangy aromas of apricot and ginger. Once the coach shunted to the Paris-Orléans rail and settled into an easy rhythm, Jacqueline left her empty cup on the side table and took up the clock she had fashioned to mark specific times, setting an alarm for the switchover in Montrouge.

"Now, my friend," she said, taking her seat at the draughting table, "I don't want to tote you all about Paris, so I'll make a quick copy of your message before I catch a little bit of sleep."

The spacing of the script and the embellishments seemed to start at the top of the filigreed circle, so Jacqueline began her copy from there. Accustomed to working under locomotion, she'd trained her body to adopt a rolling movement to accommodate the sway of the car on the track, and the desk and chair were further stabilized, being gimbal-mounted. Still, the work was too delicate for her to hurry, lest she miss a crucial element of the script.

When the clock chimed, Jacqueline jumped, almost ruining the last arabesque she was tracing. Focused on the work, she'd lost all awareness of time. The Montrouge switch was two minutes away. Her shoulders ached from hunching over, more so because of the earlier restraints, *curse that brigand*. With difficulty, her stiff fingers released the stylus, but she reviewed her work with a sigh of dismay. Four hours of laborious effort yielded only the first five groupings of letters, along with the flourishes that defined the circle. Jacqueline pressed her fingers to her eyes and rubbed, then blinked to clear them, but the room remained a hazy blur. Swirls of mist had gathered around the base of her drafting table and chair, billowing out to fill the little salon, carrying with them the fragrant tang of apricot and ginger.

"The boiler!" Jacqueline half rose, then fell back again, stunned.

Someone sat in the overstuffed chair sipping a cup of tea, so obscured by the mists it took Jacqueline a moment to identify the figure as a woman, much older than she, with dusky skin and dark, deep-set eyes that fixed on hers. She wore a *bork* – a tall, red turban – a long, heavy, embroidered blue jacket over a quilted vest and loose layers of cotton, a dark blue sash that secured some sort of sword, and pants à la Turque. Jacqueline was fairly certain she *was* a Turque.

"Not the boiler," the woman said, her accent confirming Jacqueline's assumption. "It would be best to destroy that paper now."

Jacqueline backed against the worktable, protecting her work, outrage and indignation rising in her gorge. "Twice today, my privacy has been invaded. I don't know what – "

"You do not know what you have conjured," the Turque interrupted quietly. "Please, kizim, my child." The woman beamed at Jacqueline, crinkling her eyes, and spread her hands to indicate the rising vapors. "Let this soul be."

"Soul – " Jacqueline caught her breath. Looking about her then, she noticed the vapors spun from the skull in the vise, curling up in a thin wisp but building and flowing down to the floor of the salon toward the stranger.

The Turque set down her cup of tea and stood. She loomed several centimeters taller than Jacqueline, broad in the shoulders. Despite her gentle smile, her stance possessed a subtle menace made more immediate by the curved kilij tucked through her sash, the scimitar's blade slender but as long as Jacqueline's arm.

"Come now, güzel-kizim," the Turque gently coaxed. "This is not your calling. It's not your war. Let it go."

Güzel-kizim – beloved daughter – rather presumptuous of one both a stranger and an intruder.

Jacqueline's eyes hardened. "It may not be mine, but I've earned an explanation, at least, and if this helps me get one, damn it, I'm not giving it up."

She quickly unscrewed the eidograph, tore the paper from the drafting table, and jammed her work into her trouser pocket. "And who are you to tell me – "

The coach jostled and lurched on the switchover to the Montrouge rail. Jacqueline caught her balance on the table. When she looked up again, the Turque was gone. Jacqueline spun about. The door to the coach shut quietly. Turning back, she discovered the skull missing from the vise.

The car jolted again, dumping her into the chair. Triggered by the switchover, the engine shut down. The furnace drafts closed, and the boiler vented its pressure with a loud hiss. The car slowed. By the time Jacqueline regained her feet, she had to abandon the chase and head to the front of the car to maneuver into her berth at the station. She made it just in time to pull the handbrake gently enough not to squeal and wake the town. Over the last half-kilometer, the car barely crawled to a terminus, where it rocked back as if surprised before halting. Jacqueline jumped down from the car, secured the hitch, and then climbed back up to monitor the panels until the engine quieted and the boiler cooled.

Her knees threatened to buckle. Jacqueline stumbled back to the salon and threw herself onto the couch. Exhausted from lack of sleep, too much painstaking work, and an overwhelming sense of vulnerability after two intruders, she could only curl to her side and hold her dizzied head.

The mysterious vapors had vanished along with their source. At least she had retained her paper copy of the enigmatic script. Someone at the Collège should be able to identify it with what she had so far.

And what did she have? Some sort of spell? Well... part of one, anyway. But how could the mere tracing of filigree summon a soul, as the Turque suggested?

"This makes no sense," Jacqueline muttered with a weary edge to her voice. She sat up and rubbed her head to ease the ache in her temples. "I must get to the Collège. Surely Letronne will know something."

4.

THE FIACRES FOR HIRE AND PUBLIC OMNIBUSES WOULD NOT GATHER AT THE station for at least another hour. Jacqueline couldn't wait that long. She wanted to be in Paris by five-thirty to have a café-au-lait and croissant chocolat, then get to the Collège before classes began. Gathering her satchel and overnight case, she locked the coach and set out.

At the far end of the trainyard stood a series of sheds, one of which stored her MacMillan velocipede, yet another whimsical gift from her father. The childish thing, with its horse-head frame and rickety wooden wheels, nevertheless featured a comfortable, efficient design of pedal cranks. The conveyance would get her and her luggage to Faubourg Saint-Germain in twenty minutes, whereas walking the six kilometers encumbered would take more than two hours. As she secured her bag behind the saddle, she realized with dismay there were no supports for the rough seat.

"First thing I do when I get to the school will be to install a set of springs," she grumbled. "Provided I survive this bone-shaker."

At least this was a pedaled mechanism, unlike the bone-shaker she rode as a child, which was no better than walking.

Jacqueline secured the leather safety spectacles she had invented to protect her eyes and wheeled the MacMillan to a flat place away from the rails to give herself a smooth start. She heartily approved of Mr. MacMillan's ingenious modifications of downward-forward pedal strokes. She had no problems along the dirt roads into Paris, but once through the Barrière d'Enfer, the cobblestones made it nearly impossible to stay on the street. Instead, she rode the pavements until she got to where the cobblestones had been torn up by political unrest in previous years. Not that the streets were any safer nowadays, but in the predawn hours filled with the aromas of baking breads and brewing coffees, there was not much in the way of unrest to fear, as even the most severe ideologues were having a Paris petit déjeuner. After that, it was a quick jaunt to her house on Rue Cler, where she and Angélique had spent the past month. Her housekeeper Agnès raised a brow at Jacqueline's unexpected reappearance, but merely shook her head.

"I know, I know," Jacqueline said. "Just a few days more."

She unfolded her clothes and got them hung up or put away and washed the dust of the ride off her face and arms. By the time she got back onto the street, shops had begun to open. She had her usual breakfast as the sun rose, then headed to the Collège's antiquities building. There she found her former archaeology teacher Professor Letronne in a classroom preparing for his morning lecture.

"Duval! What are you doing back here?"

She smiled. "I have a question I think only you can answer."

The stout little professor waved his hand to dismiss her. "Witch. Full of mischief, as usual." A smile tugged at the corner of his mouth; flattery was never wasted on a French professor.

The paper she pulled from her pocket crinkled as she smoothed it out across his lectern. He glanced over as he fussed with his notes. Then he paused and perused the script a little more closely. Jacqueline waited, still smiling. Letronne tossed his notes aside and pressed out the paper, poring over the script as if tracing it with his nose.

"This is impossible," he declared. "Where did you get hold of this?"

"Of what?" she asked. "You recognize it?"

Letronne fixed his lorgnon to his right eye and peered even closer. "If I'm not mistaken—and I am *never* mistaken—the language is demotic Egyptian but calligraphed in a Persian hand." He put his lorgnon away again. "That is to say, the text is borrowed from ancient Egyptian and transliterated into Sanskrit."

"Borrowed from what?"

He tossed his shoulders. "I cannot read it. I merely recognize the syllables from my work with Champollion and the Rosetta Stone. I could translate it for you if I had the time, but I do not. I have a lecture to attend to."

As groups of young men entered the room from the student corridors, Letronne began to fold the paper, but Jacqueline took it from him.

"That's all right, professor. Another time, perhaps. When you aren't so busy."

He reached after it, surprised at her abruptness. "By this afternoon then?" he offered. "I'm sure I can—"

"Thank you, no." She tucked the paper back into her pocket and turned to leave.

Letronne caught her by the shoulder. "One hour, Duval. Come back in one hour, and we will look at it together."

She glanced back at him and grinned. "One hour."

As she left, she heard him announce, "Today will be a short talk on the Mongol presence in Serbia." His announcement elicited indignant protests from his students.

Jacqueline used the hour to take her MacMillan to the Université Polytechnique to find someone to install coils to absorb some of the shocks to the saddle. A group of fawning young polytechs willingly agreed to have it finished for her by the evening. She returned to the Collège as Letronne finished his lecture. He ushered her into his office and began pulling down stacks of books and bound volumes and loading them onto his desk.

"You may assist me," he allowed, like a king bestowing grace upon a peasant. Jacqueline didn't mind. Anything to discover the root of all the intrigue that had plagued the past twenty-four hours.

"You still haven't told me where you found this script," he said pointedly.

"Professor, I don't think you would accept any explanation I could offer," she replied. "I'll tell you it was inscribed upon a skull, though."

He nodded thoughtfully. "That's helpful." He set aside two stacks of texts and pulled a third stack closer. "These are the funeral texts." He cut the stack as a gambler would cut a deck of cards and pushed half toward her. "Bring out that paper again."

She obliged, and he took a moment to identify the script he needed. "There." He pointed, then traced a section of the script with a nicotine-stained finger. "Find these three Brahmi figures together. They translate as 'death,' or 'dying.'"

Jacqueline took up a piece of firm stock and pulled a razor pen from the utility pocket of her jacket, her private version of a chatelaine. She cut a square just large enough to frame the three letters he had indicated. Then she sat across from him at his desk, and the two began poring through the volumes of Egyptology. Letronne smoked cigarettes one after another as he worked. Jacqueline wrinkled her nose at the acrid aroma and waved the smoke away from her as she slid her frame along each line as a scope. Letronne chuckled.

"Always the polytech, aren't you, Duval? What a waste of your talents."

She shrugged and kept working.

At the end of two hours, she'd found twelve references and Letronne twenty-two. "I think from here, I can manage," he said. "Go fetch us some luncheon, and by the time you return, I should have something for you."

"Fruit, cheese, bread, beer. Or would you prefer wine?"

"Beer. And a pâté, if you don't mind."

Jacqueline stood and rolled her neck and shoulders. She hated close bookwork, and she felt the weight of over twenty-four hours without sleep. Fresh air and the bustle of the streets revived her. Just beyond the Collège was a market square. Jacqueline gathered a nice collection for lunch and was paying the beer merchant when she spotted a familiar tall grey hat above the market crowd. Alain de Guise hurried along the square with a determined gait.

"De Guise?" she called.

He spun about, startled, and glowered at her. His body coiled like a serpent ready to strike. Jacqueline realized he didn't recognize the "young man" who had called to him, so she shifted her packages and lifted her leather cap to let loose a cascade of hair.

His face broke into a confused smile, and he straightened. "Madame Duval? What's this masquerade?"

Jacqueline struck a pose to show off her lab coat, shirt sleeves, and trousers like a window display. "If I cannot be fashionable while I work, at least I'm comfortable."

She waggled the modified safety spectacles in her vest pocket with a coquette smile. "No corsets to untie, I'm afraid."

His quiet laugh endeared her. "What are those spectacles? Did you fashion them yourself?"

"I did, after the third time I singed my eyebrows while welding." Jacqueline demonstrated her invention. "Glass protects my eyes, and these added loupes are for close work. The leather strap keeps them secure and doesn't allow —"

She halted, embarrassed, staring at de Guise's magnified face gaping at her. "Forgive me. I don't mean to boast. I must look goggle-eyed." She yanked the spectacles off, heat flaming in her cheeks.

He beamed. "Indeed, I am agog at the sight of you."

She gave a rueful chuckle. "I should call them 'gogglers,' non?"

But his smile continued to warm her. "I'm delighted to see you again. And in Paris! So soon?"

Of course. How could she justify her presence in Paris at this hour? No coach would have brought her so quickly, and the Paris-Orléans wouldn't be back until evening. She certainly couldn't tell a railroad agent about her private rail. Her face grew hot as he neared.

"Business," Jacqueline said vaguely, "never ends." She matched his beaming smile. "What brings you to the student quarter?"

"You're hurt," he said, deflecting her question. "May I?" He reached to gently examine her cut lip.

"It's—nothing." A frisson of fear made her flinch. "Just—" She shivered as his thumb brushed across her lower lip, sending a thrill throughout her body.

"Let me help you." He took a few of the bundles from her. "May I walk you home?"

"Home? Oh! No, I'm having lunch with one of the professors." Too late, she realized the bluntness of her response. Embarrassed, she hastily added, "But you're very kind."

"Then I shall accompany you." He tucked her packages under one arm and crooked his other with hers, steering her back up the avenue. "Tell me, madame, what urgent matter brings you back to school? Did you forget to turn in your assignments?"

She giggled nervously. His blithe manner begged her confidence. She wanted to tell him, *No, I was assaulted last night, I have a prisoner in my salon, a janissary mystic stole away a ghostly artifact, and I feel quite alone in all this and would love your company.* But the details were nearly too much for her to accept; she doubted anyone else would believe them. She fanned herself lightly and answered, "My old professor. We're working—on a project."

"Anything to do with yesterday's excitement?" he teased, his warm brown eyes dancing. "How did you manage with your mechanical friend?"

"He's quite secure now," she replied, "but I had no time to have a closer look."

"No, of course not. You had to get back to Paris."

Jacqueline didn't dare look at him. "Another project," she said. She hated lying to him, especially when he proved so helpful and kind, and his pretty bow lips produced such an alluring smile. "It is very nice to see you again, de Guise."

She meant it, she realized with a growing sense of surprise and wonder. Jacqueline rarely appreciated the presence of men, as they usually had little regard for her as a proper match: forceful, determined, intelligent but unladylike, and more often than not preoccupied with endless ideas for designs dancing around her thoughts. Who had time for silly distractions like men? Her confusion only compounded as his scent of sweet soaps, brushed worsted wool, and shaving salve filled her senses. Her cheeks warmed as she felt herself blush once more.

"Please. Call me Alain," he told her, bowing slightly. "Seeing you again is reason enough to give me the courage to ask if I might call upon you this evening?"

Her heart raced and she caught her breath on the impulse to grant his request. Then she remembered Letronne and their translation efforts. She had no idea whether she would even be free to receive callers that evening, and — *Dieu!* — she had no idea *how* to receive a gentleman caller. And what of the mystery of the Turque and the agent lying unconscious in Angélique's care? Her situation remained altogether too uncertain to indulge in a social visit.

"I—I don't think so." Jacqueline gave a hesitant shake of her head and chuckled, relenting at his exaggerated pout. "Perhaps tomorrow. I am uncertain of my schedule as yet, but breakfast chez Rugère, where Cujas meets the Boul'Mich, half past six?"

"Breakfast then. Now, where are we going?"

They had arrived at the antiquities building, but he didn't seem ready to relinquish her packages or arm, and she didn't know how to disengage herself from him without offering insult.

"Professor Letronne. Second floor."

"Oriental antiquities," de Guise observed, nodding his approval. "But I would have thought you a polytech."

"And so I am. But Papa made us study languages and culture as well for his travels, and to be honest, so many of our maths and sciences originate from Persia and India, it's a convenience, even an advantage to be able to read the primary texts."

He gazed at her with a new appreciation. Again, she felt warm all over, a sensation she could neither analyze nor excuse within the time it took to climb a mere the two flights of steps.

"I'm very grateful, de Guise," she said as she took back the items for her luncheon.

"Alain," he corrected her. He tucked a finger under her chin and leaned closer. "Please call me Alain."

Jacqueline stiffened, her eyes going wide as his lips neared hers. With a nervous laugh, she edged back, awkwardly fumbling to shake his hand as she glanced toward the professor's office. "I look forward to—"

She stopped in horror. The door to Letronne's office stood open, and a trail of papers littered the hall. Thrusting her packages back into de Guise's arms, she hurried to the open doorway, discovering a bedlam of scattered books and unbound sheaves. The professor's shelves had been emptied onto the floor, his desk swept clear. Jacqueline's heart pounded with dread.

"Professor?" she cried.

De Guise pressed close behind her, holding her by the shoulders before she could plunge into the room. "Be careful."

She shook him off and skidded over the piles of papers and books, coughing on the dust still hanging in the air. Her nostrils flared with the smell of bitter smoke from Letronne's cigarette mingled with burnt paper. The attack must have been recent.

"Professor Letronne? Are you here?"

A faint moan answered her from behind the desk. She waded through the chaos and found the scholar under a pile of the heaviest tomes. "Help me, de Guise!"

The railway agent stepped cautiously and made his way to her. Together they moved the mountain of books and uncovered Letronne, his face pale, clammy, and splotched, his lips blue.

"It looks like his heart," she said. "Sit him up just a little and fan him."

De Guise removed his coat and rolled it up as a pillow under Letronne's shoulders and head, while Jacqueline removed his collar and loosened his shirt. De Guise found a book cover torn from its source and used it to fan the scholar.

"I don't suppose medicine is one of your masteries as well?" de Guise asked, his face taut with concern.

"Alas, no. Can you stay with him while I fetch a doctor?"

Letronne coughed and caught Jacqueline's sleeve in a desperate grip.

She bent closer. "It's all right. Just rest," she insisted.

He struggled to speak, but she hushed him, not just to calm him but to keep him from saying anything of the translation in front of de Guise.

"He wants me to stay. Can you—?"

"I'll be back as quickly as I can," de Guise replied. He stood and worked his way across the room to the door, pausing to turn and incline his head, while offering an encouraging smile.

Jacqueline nodded. When he was gone, she bent back to Letronne. "Professor, who did this? Was it a Turkish woman? Does she have the paper? And did you—could you translate it?"

He shook his head, struggling to answer, his face contorting with the effort.

"No, not the Turque, or no, you couldn't translate it?" She patted his hand anxiously. "Oh, I'm sorry. I never thought there would be any danger." Tears welled in her eyes. "I'm so sorry, professor."

He tugged her sleeve, again shaking his head. He raised a hand to point toward the door. "Th—that—"

"No, no. Quiet. De Guise will get a doctor, and quickly, I'm sure of it." She resumed fanning him. "Don't try to talk. Rest."

Letronne lay back, and slowly his grip eased. He closed his eyes and sighed. Jacqueline made certain he still breathed and checked his pulse, finding it thready. She hoped de Guise returned soon.

At a loss, Jacqueline looked over the professor's office, wincing at the sight of the destroyed texts. Without a doubt, the scoundrel had made off with her only clue to the mystery, the inscription she'd worked so hard to trace. She got up and searched the professor's desk for any notes or bookmarks tucked into the volumes he'd consulted but found the mess overwhelming. Jacqueline couldn't even locate the books she'd been studying.

The violence of the room upset her. It suggested she had been followed once again and another intruder had visited harm. Had the professor resisted, or been taken unaware? Jacqueline much rather thought the former and almost smiled, picturing Letronne, the pillar of academe, assuming the bare-knuckle stance of Jack Broughton. She glanced back at him, then startled so suddenly she slipped on a pile of books and tumbled to the floor.

The Turque crouched beside Letronne, her right hand pressed to his chest. She gazed steadily at Jacqueline. The corner of her mouth curled in a wry smile. "He will live. His heart is strong. This was not your fault, güzel-kizim."

Jacqueline tried to rise but couldn't steady herself on the shifting books. She glared at the Turque. "Was it *your* fault?"

The woman's smile faded, and she shook her head. "If you pursue this any further, many more will be hurt."

Jacqueline's glare turned fierce. "How dare you threaten me!"

With the briefest of bows, the Turque stood and whirled in a single fluid motion, seemingly vanishing in the swirl of her wrap.

"Wait! Tell me —"

Frustration compounded Jacqueline's anger when she couldn't get to her feet fast enough. Slipping and slewing, she made it to the window but saw no sign of the Turque in the street below.

"*Zut!* How does she do that?"

5.

ANGÉLIQUE AWAKENED AND ROSE AT THE SOUND OF A GROAN. THE EARLY morning sun bathed the couch and the pale face of the man lying there. She arched her spine and yawned before straightening and padding over to where her prisoner stirred. She sat. When he didn't move again, she yawned and panted, anxious to know the extent of his injuries or, more accurately, the extent of his capabilities. She had promised the prisoner would not escape, after all.

He groaned again and winced but didn't open his eyes. "S-so. Sorry. Ma'm'selle," he murmured in English. His arm jerked as if he tried to reach out, but the bonds held tight.

Jacky was right; he did apologize prettily.

After pacing the length of the couch a few times, awaiting any further disclosure, she sniffed around his head again. The stress of his pain still tainted his scent with a faint urine-like odor, but the sour acid of deceptive intent had faded completely. Her prisoner turned his head away and grunted, then fell silent.

Marthe came in with fresh ice compresses and a glass of water. She lifted the man's head and checked the wound.

"No bleeding," she declared. "Swelling is down a little." She trickled water into his mouth. "He's getting better, I think. Swallowing now." Marthe set him down again and unwound the bandages holding the cool compress to his head. "Should wake up by evening." She proceeded to tend to the man's injury. "There's breakfast in the kitchen. I'll watch this one awhile if you want to get yourself decent."

By "decent," Marthe meant human. Angélique huffed, but the housekeeper merely grunted and waved her off. "Go. Eat."

Angélique had to admit she was hungry, but as she feared, Marthe had again left "decent" food: a petit pain with butter and preserves, cold meats, peach slices, and some cheese. While decent fare, none of it satisfied a wolf. She sniffed at the plate and snorted her frustration.

She hated being treated like she was still seventeen, still the pampered artist, the toast of Europe. That spoiled naïve young fool had died. The Angélique that lived and breathed today was no longer Sigismond Thalberg's favored protégée touring the royal courts and the salons of many nobles across Europe to perform. Since St. Petersburg and her unexplained metamorphosis, she no longer had a taste for lush banquets or polite society.

Marthe seemed incapable of accepting that truth, as if serving raw meat or a butchered bone slighted her culinary prowess. The hounds at Cheverny ate better than Angélique did as a wolf.

Huffing her displeasure, she licked at the cooked meats and swept them into her mouth along with the peach slices, leaving the rest. She'd finally overcome the urge to eat dairy as a wolf after several unfortunate gastric crises, but Marthe persisted in serving it. The simple breakfast barely touched her hunger, leaving more than a bad taste in her mouth.

Angélique returned to the salon to find Marthe crocheting calmly in a chair near the divan, her rolling pin in her lap, while Luc trimmed the roses around the courtyard outside the open summer doors. Marthe frowned at her for having disobeyed the order to change form. Ignoring the silent reprimand, Angélique padded out to lie in the sun, eyes closed, her ears flicking attentively. Beneath the *snick* of the shears, the steady, low pulse and the slight catch of the prisoner's breath continued to assure her the captive was not feigning debilitation. Sifting through the scents from the forest, alert to any other intruders lying in wait, she caught the meaty tang of wild pigs close by. Hunger stirred her to sit, and she panted, drooling at the thought of a sweet little shoat.

Luc gave an amused grunt. "He's not going anywhere, and neither am I," he said. "Have a quick run."

With a grateful *whoof*, she sprang down the hill, pausing to relieve herself beside the pond before diving into the woods to bring down a real breakfast, which she quickly dispatched.

Once she had cleaned her maw, she sniffed around Jacky's workshop to see if there were newer scents, but there was only the mechanical man and the intruder. The man's scent led her to the backwater of the Loire that bordered the woods. But he had to have walked *from* somewhere, so she followed the trail deeper as it wended toward the Loire.

Hauled on the bank, secured beneath a strong maple, Angélique found his fûtreau, its mast folded down. She hopped aboard the little boat and nosed around the stern until she found the source of his scent—a slightly mildewed duffel bag. Dragging it out, she pawed at the closure, but the intricate knot was beyond her current ability to undo. She took up the bag in her jaws and headed back to Bellesfées.

By then, the sun sat high overhead, the bag felt heavy, and the pond invited her to indulge. Making sure Luc still stood sentry trimming the garden, she set the bag on the bank and plunged into the cool waters, drinking deeply. Then she shook herself out, sated and restored, before reclaiming her find and trotting up the hill to check in on the prisoner. Satisfied he still posed no danger, she lounged in the sun, once again tuning her senses to the man's condition and the sanctity of the forest. Smug satisfaction warmed her, and she pawed idly at the mildewed duffle bag. Jacky would be proud of her.

Luc set aside the shears and stooped to examine the bag. "Sailor knot," he said. "Sailor pants." He met her questioning eyes. "White wool pants, ten buttons. Officer."

Luc's service in the last year of the Napoleonic Wars gave him a perspective she lacked, so she nosed the bag toward him. He undid the knot and spilled the contents: extra shirts, a canteen, and an oiled leather wallet. This last item Luc explored, but it held only travel papers.

"'Brigadier Gryffin Llewellyn, late of her majesty Queen Victoria's especial service as an emissary to Wallachia.'" he read. "Brigadier means Royal Marines." He tucked everything away again and tied up the bag. "Don't know how you girls manage to get into so much trouble. I'll deliver this to your room."

Angélique followed him inside, pausing to reassess all the scents emanating from Brigadier Gryffin Llewellyn. The bitter, peppery tang of stress from his pain now dominated even the sweet spice of his flesh. She whined and licked his ear.

"You might think twice before trying to kill a man next time," Marthe said, setting aside her craftwork. "Otherwise, keep your whining to yourself. I'm going to prepare supper. He's not going anywhere soon."

Grumbling, Angélique slumped to the floor, maw to paws, ears alert.

The captive's quiet, steady heartbeat marked the passing of the sun from midday to early afternoon, then suddenly thumped, and the tempo increased. Angélique sat up and panted as a sigh escaped the man's lips. She licked her chops, anticipating the gratifying look of terror on his face when greeted by a pair of fangs that could tear his face off.

His eyes fluttered open and he glanced about, then tried to turn his head. When he met Angélique's narrowed eyes he froze. "Down," he said in English, his voice hoarse and his tone somewhat less than assertive.

Angélique waited, amused.

"Ah. Well, good dog, then."

The man wriggled to sit up, keeping both eyes on Angélique, chary of provoking her. When she didn't react, he attempted in vain to stand, ending up face down on the floor.

"Most embarrassing," he declared, his voice gaining a bit of tenor as he rolled to his side. "It would seem I need to find a chamber pot, but I first need to find my feet. And I hope the latter comes before the former is no longer needed." He sighed. "I don't suppose you fetch, do you, puppy?"

At this affront, Angélique snarled. The man curled up defensively. The two locked eyes; then the man slowly averted his gaze, impressing Angélique with his knowledge of canid behaviors.

In a moment, Marthe appeared, her countenance as severe as Angélique's warning. "When Angélique snarls like that, she's not happy with you. You've insulted her." Marthe hauled him up and shoved him back on the couch. "I suppose you were looking for the chamber pot beneath the couch. Behave yourself, and I'll get it."

She got down on her hands and knees and retrieved the porcelain bowl. She plopped it in his lap. He grunted in alarm, which amused Angélique.

"Now," Marthe said, standing arms akimbo above him, a formidable glare on her face, "I'll treat your wounds, but I'm not untying you. Madame Duval will have questions once you're able, so you're going to remain here. The mistress says you assaulted her, which makes you a villain, in my opinion, but I'm to understand you're an officer, so I expect you to act like one. Unlike you, we are not barbarians. You'll be fed and tended. In return, you will behave like a gentleman, or as much a gentleman as you are able, or I assure you Angélique will tear your throat open and likely devour half your sorry frame before I can stop her."

Angélique seconded the threat with another snarl.

"Do you need help?" Marthe asked.

He shook his head quickly, too quickly. His eyes rolled back, and he groaned. "Yes," he admitted. "I am so sorry."

"That you truly are."

Angélique agreed. She lay down and rested her chin on her paws, watching as Marthe helped the man to sit and unbutton his pants. A salty tang of musk mingled with his earthy scent, arousing Angélique's interest. She stood and hunched, ready to pounce and bring him down should he attempt to escape. To her further amusement, his fear heightened his intriguing smell.

Marthe pulled him to his feet, and he slumped to her. His face colored, and Angélique wished her lupine vision could see just how red his cheeks were by the time he'd finished. Marthe let him fall to the couch again as she removed the bowl.

"I'll get a fresh ice compress for that thick head of yours," she told him on her way out.

Angélique stood, not trusting him to stay until Marthe returned now that he had tasted a soupçon of freedom. She needn't have worried. He remained on his side, his pants still undone. He had passed out again.

Marthe returned as promised and replaced the bowl beneath the couch. In her other hand, she held a basin of cold water and a bladder of ice. She set about changing his bandages, but her patient never budged.

"I don't think we have much to fear for a while," Marthe declared. "What do you think?"

Angélique wasn't ready to pronounce a verdict. His manner confused her. He had treated Jacky abominably, then apologized for his behavior. He could have clubbed Marthe and tried to fight off what he thought was a dog, but instead, he meekly submitted and surrendered himself to sleep again. Was he truly the inept fool he seemed? She nosed his shoulder; he didn't even flinch.

"Luc will watch," Marthe said. "Go get ready for supper."

Confident that their prisoner posed no immediate threat to Marthe, who could wrestle large farm animals out of the slough, Angelique trotted up the stairs to transform and dress.

"Brigadier Gryffin Llewellyn." She savored the feel of the name in her mouth. "Royal Marine and emissary to Wallachia."

Angélique chuckled. Though Victoria had newly ascended to the throne, certainly someone should have advised her not to send inept fools into the powder keg that was the Ottoman Empire. Although, come to think of it, the man seemed a little young to be a brigadier. Perhaps he wasn't as inept as he appeared if he'd advanced so far in the British services. What was he doing in Wallachia that would get him caught up with automatons and eastern European counts, bringing him to France?

The Ottoman Empire was a political mess, with open rebellions in Wallachia and various petty nobles and boyars jockeying to be the next Alexander the Great. Angélique recalled the bureaucratic nightmare of booking concerts and performances throughout the Caucasus in 1838. All she had wanted to do was play piano, eat, and flirt; all Thalberg had wanted to do was focus on his performances; all either of them could do was wrestle with border passes and turnpike guards.

Then came St. Petersburg, when everything fell apart.

Angélique took the servants' staircase downstairs and slipped along the back corridor to the kitchen to track down more peach slices, bread, and carrots, along with some cheese, now that she was human. She strolled the château, enjoying the cool of the marble floors under her bare feet. The sensation, along with her kindled memories of Thalberg, turned her thoughts to music. She headed to her concert hall in the music conservatory wing.

Jacky had furnished the concert hall with a single gasolier beneath the acoustic dome, but daylight streamed through six wide balcony doors, three to each side of the hall. Angélique found the natural lighting more conducive to her mood. She played through some of the newly published pieces she'd picked up in Paris—a Czerny, a Mendelssohn, and some Chopin études. One advantage of her lycanthropy: her fingers had grown long enough to handle any composition Liszt or Chopin could devise. Though she much preferred her lupine form, she could never lose herself in her music the way she could as a woman, even though, ironically, this euphoria of sound and sensuality strongly tempted her to change, a fact that had kept her from the stage since St. Petersburg. She might have surpassed both masters one day, as well as Thalberg, if only...

Angélique shook off the thought and warmed up with scales flowing into her favorite Chopin once she was ready, an impromptu fantaisie she had learned by ear after attending a few of his performances in Custine's Paris salons. Note by note, chord by chord, she poured the stress of the day into the agitato.

Rippling arpeggios flowed like soothing waters, and Angélique felt all the tension in her limbs and spine easing as she reached the largo. Let the pedants have their Mozart; only Chopin seemed to find the mystical connection between science and beauty, between form and fantasy. He had taken the thumb melodies of Thalberg to new levels of complexity. Tension and resolution evoked a sense of yearning in her for something she could not name. She savored the exquisite ache of longing as she thumbed the final capitulation of the melody against the right-hand arpeggios fluttering like a butterfly, now hovering, now soaring, now drifting dreamily to the final chords that rolled up the keyboard of her Érard grand.

Her toes released the sustain pedal. The last reverberations whirled about the dome of the concert hall, settled on the marble floor, and slipped out the open balconies on the night breeze. The profound silence gently folded around her. She strolled onto the balcony to survey the grounds and sniff the air.

The waxing moon fell away in the western sky, its light bright enough to illuminate the gardens and parc and the deer who had ventured out to graze while the cows slept. Wrapped in the serenity of the Chopin, Angélique suddenly ached with a familiar longing for the life she'd been denied. Perturbed, she turned to retreat from the balcony, quit the conservatory and her useless nostalgia, when an odd vibration on the night breeze caught her back.

She tensed. Her eyes swept the line of the forest, hoping something would show itself. She strained to hear any new noises and leaned over the balcony railing, searching for a scent, something she could track. Clouds crossed the moon, enshrouding the vale. Beyond that, nothing untoward.

Angélique reluctantly withdrew, her unease tickling at the nape of her neck where hackles would rise were she wolf. She hastened to her room to hang up her nightclothes and resume her wolf form to keep watch for the night. She descended to the salon.

Llewellyn slept fitfully, murmuring unintelligibly between pained grunts. Angélique padded to the summer doors, her ears pricked and flicking to find the source of her unease.

"You missed supper. I left some on the table for you." Marthe gathered up her yarn and hooks. "Luc and I are staying in the servants' wing tonight with the others," she said. She closed and locked the salon doors. "Holler if you need us."

Angélique whined. She missed Jacky already. The initial spark of adventure had become the annoying prickle of responsibility. That was Jacky's forte, not Angélique's. She wanted her evening brandy and games and lively conversation. Her dull vigil bored her.

Llewellyn lay recumbent, eyes closed, his brow knit. Angélique sniffed along his body, then stood to nose around his face. In repose, he didn't strike her as an enemy; more like an adversary, and adversaries could be persuaded. Perhaps it was that longing aroused by the Chopin that softened her regard, but Angélique could only see the similarities between them, lost in a confusion not of their own making.

Llewellyn awoke close to midnight. He sat up with less difficulty. Angélique sat up as well and watched him balefully.

"A little better," he said. "I suppose I have you to thank, Ma'm'selle Angélique?" He met her gaze, although not as menacingly, and his eyes crinkled when he chuckled. "I'm in your debt. And most grateful I'm still alive. Your mistress certainly made a fool of me. How the devil did she drop that winch with her hands tied, and I can't even stand up?"

Angélique's ears flicked, measuring the easy amusement in the man's voice with suspicion.

He winced again, closed his eyes, and sighed. "I suppose you're here to keep me from leaving. I'm in no hurry to do that. I should explain myself to your mistress. So, I am your prisoner, Ma'm'selle Ci Da."

He smiled at her, then looked closer. "Why, you're not a dog at all. No wonder you resented my asking you to fetch. Well, then, I won't pat your head and call you 'good dog' anymore. Rather, Bleiddast Da, good wolf. Wouldn't have you snarling at me again or waking your bully of a staff sergeant."

Then he spied the plate of bread and cheeses and the bowl of soup Marthe had prepared for him on the table by the couch, evidently intending to feed him by hand. His smile faded. "I shame myself at every turn."

Llewellyn leaned over the bowl, carefully tipping it as he consumed the clear broth. When he finished, he sighed. He tried to peck at a slice of cheese, but his strength gave out, and he leaned back on the couch again, his eyes rolling about unfocused.

"I failed to recover the skull, and now I've lost all notion of time. The Count's death-eater will have tracked his creation by now, but there's nothing I can do in my current state."

Hackles rose on Angélique's neck at the implicit threat in his statement, if not his tone.

He flopped over to his side. "I can only hope we both remain safe, Ma'm'selle Bleiddast Da. A day. Perhaps—" He fell silent. In a moment, he snored a quiet buzzing.

What did he mean by 'death-eater'? What made the skull so important? The gold script? Perhaps Jacky had been right all along about a necromancer fashioning the ghost-powered automaton. Angélique sniffed for tell-tale odors that would suggest any dealings with corpses, but there was only Llewellyn's sweet flesh scent, his sweat tinged with the stress of his concussion, and a scintilla of shaving cologne. It filled her head and made her a little deaf with delight. She poked about his head and shoulder, licking lightly at his throat.

Llewellyn didn't open his eyes, but to her surprise, he did nuzzle her ears. A thrill shook her, sensual pleasure with an edge of threat —That was Angélique's forte. And he had such a nice touch just— behind—her left ear—*ahh!*—that tempted her to sleep wrapped in his exotic aromas, pungent with salt and intoxicating musk.

She whined and edged back, not trusting the rogue's intentions. Had he planned to seduce her into dropping her guard that he might attempt escape? She lay down, panting, smug to have come away both safe and satisfied from her encounter. She rested her snout on the floor.

Llewellyn's snores eased to the steady breathing of sleep.

Angélique awoke she didn't know how much later, her ears thrumming with vibrations stronger, deeper, than what she had sensed before. The air rippled in a silent wake. Angélique whined and pawed at Llewellyn's chest. He stirred.

"Bleiddast Da," he murmured.

When she nipped his ear, he jerked and fell off the couch. He pushed himself to his knees, grunting with the pain of effort. "What is it?"

A growl rose in her throat. Men. Many men and the stench of rotting bodies, but she couldn't pinpoint the source of the scents. "Death-eater," echoed in her thoughts. She looked back at Llewellyn with suspicion, but he didn't seem to understand her concern.

Damn, it's too soon! Jacky isn't here. I can't leave Llewellyn unguarded, not with servants in the house. But what's out there making that noise, that smell? What do I do?

In such circumstances, she normally ran away rather than having to make any responsible decisions. Jacky might have identified the vibrations, but Angélique could not, and she feared them far more than she feared Llewellyn.

The vibration of the air now carried a quiet sound like gusts of thunder in short bursts. The stench of rot and death swept through the open windows. Angélique gagged and licked her lips. The stink of man-sweat grew stronger, too, along with the smell of bitter tobacco smoke stinging her nostrils. Her stomach twisted. Shoulders and haunches twitched, aching to pounce on something, someone. Her ears flattened. She yipped, then gave a quick bark to rouse Llewellyn again.

This time he sat up, and although he hissed against the pain, he took more careful notice of her anxiety. He cocked his head to listen, and his brow knit. She *whoof*ed and growled her urgency. Llewellyn shook his head.

"It's all right. Let me go. They're here for me and the machine. And they have no reason to hurt you."

But his scent soured, belying his calming words. She backed away and alarm-barked, three short gruffs followed by a howl. Her ears caught the sound of Marthe and Luc stirring in the servants' wing. Even as Luc called her, the salon doors exploded open. Four swarthy men rushed in.

Snarling, Angélique leapt at the first man to cross the threshold, locking her teeth around his throat. Blood, salty and sweet, filled her mouth as she thrashed her head, ripping out his throat. More blood spewed, spattering both her and the room as he dropped to the floor, choking. Her ears closed in delight with the taste of his death. Teeth bared in a wolfish grin, she wheeled to confront a second man. He swung his truncheon wildly, cursing. Dodging the blow, she darted close, clamping down on his wrist. Another thrash. The club clattered to the floor. Angélique released him and turned. The third man whaled the side of her head. Stunned, she fell atop the dead man, blood streaming down her snout and dripping onto the corpse. The intruder moved to strike again.

"No!" Llewellyn cried. "Let her — let her be. Let's just go. Now!"

Her attacker spun about. "Son of a bitch, lounging like a lord," he said.

In a blur, Angélique saw him take a knife from his belt and cut Llewellyn's bonds, then grab Llewellyn's arm and jerked him to his feet. She rose unsteadily while they escaped to the lawn, and she tripped after them

"The machine is in the workshop," Llewellyn shouted, "but it's too heavy to get it up to the ship. We'll have to leave it for now."

"But the Count—" one argued.

"The Count wants the skull. It's not there. Leave the machine!" Llewellyn said. "Go."

Between the blood trail and the yelling, she followed them with ease. She soon spotted Llewellyn, his pace more staggered than the others'. Her loping stride gained on him swiftly, but he faltered as she rounded the west turret. A yelp escaped her at the sight of a massive airship looming over the chateau. Skittering to a stop, she howled. In warning or challenge, she couldn't say. A loud bang answered her cry.

Something slammed into Angélique, her right flank exploding in pain. Yelping, she stumbled, tumbling down the hill.

Llewellyn cursed and halted, then lumbered back toward Angélique.

Shouts came from above, but Angélique could not make them out. Pain crushed her to the earth until she could not find her legs to make a stand. Llewellyn knelt beside her and pressed his hand to the wound in her flank.

"I'm so sorry. So sorry, Angélique."

She tried to snap at him but couldn't lift her head. Her vision swam. The smell of her blood mingled with the stink of rotting flesh made her retch as Llewellyn lifted her into his arms. Everything became fuzzy except the thought that he hadn't escaped her. Not entirely.

The man who had freed Llewellyn joined him. "Are you mad?"

"Take her. Move it."

Every instinct screamed resist. Angélique pictured herself snapping and thrashing, sinking teeth into flesh, but she only managed to twitch and jerk, too weak to struggle. She whined and snarled as the man jogged, jostling her with every step. Then the wrack of his footfalls ceased, and she floated, rising weightless. Smells assaulted her nose: machine oil, fuel smoke, tarry sisal and creosote, the urine stink of men's filthy bodies, and over all the rancid odor of putrefaction. When she caught the bittersweet bite of cherried tobacco, her skin rippled and twitched as anxiety built within her, triggering a visceral fear she couldn't name. She kicked, loosing a howling cry as pain speared her hindquarters. Gags and moans wracked her, nausea flooding her mouth with bile. The instincts to both fight and flee battled within her to control a body unable to do either.

The floating sensation ceased. A stranger's arms removed her from whatever cradled her and shifted her to Llewellyn's arms. She whined in relief as his familiar sweet, spicy scent enveloped her, but her instincts screamed danger.

"What is this?" a deep voice bellowed.

Angélique yiped, her eyes rolling and going wide as she scrabbled against Llewellyn's grip despite her pain.

She now recognized that burnt odor, just as she knew that voice. The horror they invoked bubbled from her memory. The horror of St. Petersburg.

Then she knew no more.

6.

Jacqueline absently stirred her café-au-lait, staring bleary-eyed into the swirl. She'd spent the remains of the day before and all of the night at the hospital, napping fitfully at Letronne's bedside in case he woke again, but he did not. She'd returned to the office in the predawn hours for a deeper search and finally discovered his notes. Her original drawing, however, had vanished, like the Turque — or along with the Turque? At least the notes would give her something to work on once the coffee wove its magic. She felt utterly drained, her limbs leaden, her eyelids like sandpaper; yet, she dared not close her eyes for fear slumber would take her, a luxury she could ill afford with so much more to do.

Gulping down the coffee, she raised her cup to call for another. As she waited, she pulled the sheaves of Letronne's notes from her inside pocket and smoothed them out to read as the patron brought another café-au-lait and croissant chocolat. She found the hasty scribbles sporadically legible, but only short phrases. *Twice dead... poor vessel... spirit wonder... eternity bound by essence? Essence = blood? Rule... command... govern.* No thought complete, although she began to formulate a vague theory of how in combination they once applied to the mechanical man on her workbench at Bellesfées.

"*Let this soul be,*" the Turque had said. "*It's not your war.*"

The theory Jacqueline considered felt too horrible to put into words, but the more she looked at the notes, her certainty in her hypothesis grew. With a cry of disgust, she shoved the papers back into her pocket. Dipping her pastry into her cup, she sighed as the blend of coffee and chocolate soothed her.

"Alas, if only that sigh were for me."

Startled, she looked up to find de Guise standing across from her, hat in hand. He smiled hopefully — *Oh, that lovely smile of his!* — and she remembered she'd agreed to meet him for breakfast. She gasped, and heat rose to her cheeks.

"Oh! de Guise, I'm so sorry." In an effort to stand and curtsy at the same time, she sent coffee sloshing across the table. Snatching a napkin, she swiped at the mess. "I was waiting for news of the professor, and I completely forgot after all that's happened since. Oh!" Jacqueline flopped back in her chair and waved him toward the other.

His smile broadened, and he took the proffered seat. "I am glad to hear you say that," he said, nodding a more formal greeting. "I feared you had changed your mind about seeing me. But hoping otherwise, I searched about the Rue de Santé until, well, here we are. What news of Letronne's health, then?"

She shook her head and signaled for the patron to wait on de Guise and bring yet more coffee. "When I left him, he slept. The doctors felt it best that he rested, so they gave him belladonna."

De Guise nodded. "Well, here is some news, anyway." He passed her an envelope. "This is from Rugère. I told him I was to meet you at his café, so when he saw me leaving, he asked me to pass it along."

"How curious." A faint frown ruffled her brow as she accepted the plain envelope with her name on it and nothing else. When she opened it, however, she smiled. "A Chappe telegraphic. From home."

"You have a Chappe system at Bellesfées?" De Guise chuckled. "Naturally. I should have expected."

Jacqueline pulled out the short strip to read.

A GONE STOP M TOO STOP LEFT CORPSE STOP ADVISE SVP

Abruptly, she shot to her feet, her hands trembling.

Angélique gone? Gone where? M — M? Monsieur? The captive? Corpse! What corpse?

"*Mon Dieu*, what is it?" De Guise rose and came to her side. "Patron, quickly! Some water!"

She crushed the slip in her fist before he could read it. "I — I need to go." Her eyes darted around rather than meet his concerned gaze. "My velocipede — oh, no!" She leaned to the table. "Still at the Université."

The world seemed to spin. *Angélique! Not again!* She couldn't bear it if she lost her only sister for good. The barman and de Guise each caught an arm. De Guise pressed a glass of water to her lips and set his hand gently to her back.

"What's happened? Madame Duval. Tell me."

Jacqueline's heart raced. Had the mysterious count made his move so swiftly to recover his player? Whose body was left behind?

She pushed the glass away. "No, thank you. I cannot stay. I must return home immediately. I need to get to the train station before—"

De Guise took her firmly by the shoulders, then tilted her face up to meet his gaze. "You look faint. I beg you, allow me to help." He flashed his dazzling smile. "I do have some pull with the railroad, after all. And the train doesn't depart for at least another hour and a half."

His smile… the warmth of his hands… both tempted her to accept his offer. But no. Jacqueline forced herself to wriggle free.

"De Guise—"

"Alain."

"Monsieur!"

She fished in her upper pocket for some sous to pay the patron. De Guise's gallantry began to vex her. If he didn't allow her to leave immediately, she wouldn't be able to outrun the Paris-Orléans train in her own coach.

"I promise I am not someone who swoons. I've received terrible news. I was startled. I do not wish to make you angry, but I must go. Now."

"But—"

Jacqueline rushed away without looking back. He called after her. She ignored him as she ran to the line of fiacres in front of the hospital and hopped into the closest one.

"Montrouge depot, and quickly, please."

The driver obliged.

Jacqueline got onto the main tracks before half past eight and set her alarm for the switchover to Bellesfées. Her thoughts tumbled over each other. *Who stormed the château? A small army? Who is dead? Did they take the mechanical man? The Benets!*

Surely, they must be safe; the telegraphic had Marthe's voice.

But Jacqueline kept coming back to the realization she never should have left her sister alone with that villain. It was the only thought for which she had words: *Never should have left her. Never should have left her. Never should have left her.* They came so easily she whispered them, and the words beat a steady rhythm with the rails until Jacqueline fell into slumber.

She dreamed she danced with de Guise in a gaslit corridor deep underground. They waltzed along earthen walls lined with thousands upon thousands of skulls amidst shiny knob-ends of long bones.

"Do you know the Count?" de Guise asked.

"Millions," she answered. "Too many to number."

The skulls whispered without unison. Their susurration rose from the depths along with fine wisps of vapor that smelled of bones and metal and blood.

The Turque perched on the sculpted bowl of a dry fountain. She grinned and winked conspiratorially. "Güzel-kizim, don't stay in your dream," she sang. Then she leapt down, swinging her kilij. The walls of bones trembled. A skull dropped and rolled to Jacqueline's feet. Then another, and another. Jacqueline tried to run. De Guise trapped her in his arms as the walls crumbled into an avalanche of skulls and long bones. The skulls rolled up in billows. They called her name, shrieked her name, screamed and howled her name. The howls were answered by Angélique.

"Güzel-kizim, don't stay in your dream."

The Turque beckoned from a darkened egress. Jacqueline fought to catch her hand. The bones rose up and walled her in.

"This is *your* war! *This* is your war!"

The skulls cackled. Jacqueline thrust out her arms and tried to climb the mounting pile of femurs and humeri. The skulls mocked her as they pressed in. The Turque vanished, still singing.

"Güzel-kizim, don't stay in your dream."

Jacqueline sat up, instantly alert. The cacophony faded like a long-distant echo. The coach remained silent but for the hiss of the boiler and the rhythmic clatter of iron on the tracks. She glanced at the clock. Two minutes to the alarm for the shunt. She blinked and stared again. Beside her alarm clock sat a cup of steaming tea. Apricot and ginger spiced the air.

When Jacqueline reached for the cup, her hand shook, sloshing tea over the rim. She sipped from the saucer and then took a long draught from the cup. Only after she drank did it occur to her to question the presence of the beverage, which she decidedly had not prepared herself. Setting down the cup, she reached in her pocket and encountered the crinkle of paper. Her breath fluttered in a relieved sigh. Letronne's notes. Though fear and exhaustion and dread warred within her, she felt perhaps she had made a new ally in the Turque.

"Are you here?"

No answer. Jacqueline looked around the coach but saw nothing. No surprise. She closed her eyes and counted silently to ten. When she opened her eyes, the Turque sat in the chair where Jacqueline had first seen her, with a steaming cup of tea in her hands. She grinned, her dark face crinkling almost merrily as her eyes twinkled. She lifted her cup in a salute.

"It would seem, hanim, my war is now yours as well."

First güzel-kizim, now hanim—a Turkish honorific. Jacqueline drew a long breath to calm herself. "What is happening? Who are you? Why have you been hunting me? What did you do to Letronne?"

The Turque finished her tea and set the cup on the side table. She doffed her oversized bork to reveal long grizzled black hair that, in all irony, made her face softer, more youthful. She also threw back her cloak and removed her kilij, setting the scimitar across her lap. Then she reached around and pulled a bullwhip from behind her and set that on her lap as well. She met Jacqueline's accusing glare with a soft smile.

"Bismillahi, I swear by the One God, I have not come hunting you, nor to bring harm to anyone. My tale is long, rooted in blood and battle and exile. But that much you needn't hear. I will tell you of the ghastly deeds of your enemies and the enemies of your dear sister. Their story is rooted in the fall of my people, the Janissaries."

Jacqueline frowned. "The elite Ottoman guards? What could that possibly have to do with Angélique?"

Before the Turque could answer, the alarm sounded for the switchover. Jacqueline jumped up and headed to the controls. "Go on. I'm listening. What's your name?"

The Turque smiled, relieved. "I am Pasha Elif Effendi."

"Pasha *and* effendi, two titles of rank," Jacqueline noted.

Elif acknowledged Jacqueline's understanding of Turkish culture. "I was commander of the guard in Bucharest when the Unfortunate Incident banished me."

"You mean the Auspicious Incident? Mahmud's slaughter of the Janissaries?" Jacqueline asked as she arranged for the tracks to shift.

Elif sniffed. "We would not call it so."

"No, I'm sorry. I suppose you would not."

"However, I escaped. I disguised myself as a servant in the household of a boyar in Moldovarabia, and when his son was born, I became the boy's caregiver. He was sickly from birth, his blood like water, his limbs no stronger than twigs. I was his constant companion, and I used my wisdom to strengthen him. He grew in grace, by the grace of the One God. But he seemed destined for a short life. So, the boyar sent for Mirrikh" — she spat the name — "a Persian büyücü — What is the word? a sorcerer — to discover the cause of the boy's illness and heal him."

With a jolt and a shrill squeal, the coach took the switchover, lurching sharply to the right before resuming its rhythm. When the track reset behind them, Jacqueline came back to sit with Elif.

"You mean a magician? Real magic?" she asked. "I don't believe in magic." Elif raised a brow, and Jacqueline squirmed. "Well, at least, I never have before. Surely the physical world has laws we have not yet discovered, but —"

"Your sister is a creature of science, then?"

Jacqueline opened her mouth to protest but closed it quickly and pouted. "Touché. Go on." Then she held up her hand. "Wait. You know about Angélique? Do you know *why* she is what she is?"

Elif grinned. "Just listen to my tale. Mirrikh had no real powers to save the boy, but I am of the Order of Bektaşi. I am master of mystical powers Mirrikh could never own, for I draw power from the Light. It was my powers that kept the boy safe, my prayers that the One God honored. But Mirrikh learned of my abilities."

Her dark eyes deepened beneath her knit brow. "And I learned Mirrikh was ruh çaðýran falcý! A student of the dark magic of death. Necromancy. Filth. He stole away many of my powers. But he did not understand them by the Light of the One God. He corrupted them into his own base spells."

Elif pointed to Jacqueline. "You have seen the result of his necromancy, here in this carriage. How that skull can be used to summon otherworldly forces. You have seen what destruction the translation of mere phrases loosed upon your friend, the professor."

Jacqueline gasped, guilt evincing hot tears.

"And your sister —" Elif's lips pressed tightly together to hold in her anger. "She too bears the curse of Mirrikh's blasphemy."

Jacqueline sat up. "How is Angélique connected to any of this?"

The janissary sighed heavily. "The boy would not survive long with his diseased blood. Mirrikh sought to provide him with stronger blood, other blood. He took lifeforce from an animal, a wolf, and wove his dark blood magic around the boy."

Jacqueline's eyes widened. "And made him a werewolf, like Angélique."

Elif nodded. "Of a kind. A shapeshifter. As you have seen, they are not mindless beasts tied to the moon. Nor can they create others like themselves with a mere bite. After Mirrikh changed him, there was no turning my boy to the Light. He became a wild thing, dangerous, not only as a wolf but as a young man. Profligate. A denier of the Day of Reckoning." Tears filled her eyes. "I couldn't stay to watch his debauchery. So young. Bismillahi, I swore I would try to defend others from Mirrikh's dark magic."

Elif fell silent, her head bowed. Jacqueline had so many questions, but she waited. She rose to make more tea for them both. When she had refilled the cups, Elif's black mood had passed.

"And how does all this bring me to you, you wonder," Elif continued. "It is this: Now Mirrikh wields his powers to bring his master, this same boyar, Draganov Dragul, to greater power in Moldovarabia."

"Draganov." Jacqueline tugged at her lower lip. "I sold my power-recycling system designs to a Vasile Draganov last week."

"The same. The people see Draganov as a great leader who will not retreat before the Turks or the Russians or the Serbs. He and his son Toma were at the center of eastern European society a few years ago, when who should come to Budapest but the enchanting Angélique Laforge. That was the name she adopted for concert performances, yes?"

A chill seized Jacqueline. *"Mon Dieu!"*

"Indeed, Alhamdulillâh. Toma met her; he courted her; he desired her. He followed her to St. Petersburg. Like a spoiled brat, he insisted he would have her for himself. But your sister, like you—" Elif again saluted her with her cup. "Was not a woman to be 'had' by anyone. She refused him, but Toma would not be put aside."

Jacqueline trembled. Her cup slipped from her hands to the carpet. "No. No, no, no. You can't mean..."

Jacqueline dropped through time.

1838. Her sixteenth spring. Home from her first exposition with seven commissions. A glorious start to May. The workshop air sweet with the fragrance of meadow flowers, blooming lindens, and quickening vines. Life had never felt so rich.

The courier, the wheels of his trap crunching on the macadamized paving. "Chappe telegraphic from Orléans," he said, handing her the envelope. He tipped his cap but hurried off too quickly. Jacqueline's scalp tingled as panic took hold. Her heart slammed against her ribs. Time froze.

"No!" Jacqueline leapt up and paced the coach, which for the first time felt too small. "They told me a bear. They said… They told me no one should have survived the wounds she had suffered. They told me she was dead!"

"So she was."

Jacqueline clutched at her hair. Her eyes welled, and she choked. "It took a week for word to reach me she had died. My only sister, my twin, gone!"

Papa clinging to her, his sobs tearing at her. Marthe weeping into Luc as he held her tight, silent as ever.

The empty ache gnawing endlessly as she stared unseeing out carriage windows. Weeks on the filthy roads, her back aching, her limbs numb, her heart in agony.

"I never got the second message saying she lived. By the time I arrived in St. Petersburg, I had nearly perished from grief."

"But she did live," Elif said.

"Yes!" Jacqueline nodded, the memory fresh. "And I was overjoyed to see her and hold her again. But—but—" Tears burned down her cheeks. "She had no memory of the assault. She was lost! A lost soul! Thalberg had left her behind, thinking her dead. Baron Spransky was kind enough to allow her to stay until I could fetch her home. The Spranskys had thought it a miracle she had survived. They said—"

The baron's description of Angélique's ravaged body had sickened Jacqueline. She had given it no more thought since the moment she discovered Angélique alive and whole, but now she recalled with outrage the grisly details she was told of shredded flesh, savage bites, her torn-out throat. She had thought them exaggerated, given Angélique's utter lack of scars or pain, only her eyes deformed.

"They said they had no idea how she survived."

"She would not have," Elif said, "if a mere wolf attacked her. I do not know how it came about, and such a thing should not be possible, but I believe Mirrikh's blood spell took hold of her through Toma's vicious assault."

"But why would he attack her like that? You're saying she turned down his advances, and he simply tore her to pieces?"

The Turque answered with a shake of her head. "I know no details of what transpired. Only that Toma had become vicious and intemperate, that he followed her to Russia, and that she is now as he is. I can think of no other explanation."

"Look at me!" Angélique wailed. "Look at these eyes! How can I appear in public? I can never take the stage again! They'll put me in a menagerie. I'm an animal. I'm – what am I?"

Jacqueline wept, pressing her twin to her bosom. "You're not an animal, mon Ange. Something mauled you horribly, maimed your eyes. You can wear Ayscough or Lavoisier glasses. I'll modify them. No one will know. I'll keep you safe," she murmured. "I'll protect you."

"You don't understand. You don't – " Angélique shoved away. She yanked her chemise over her head to sit naked on the bed. "Look at me!"

Her face shifted. Her nose jutted forward, and her ears elongated. Fur sprang through her skin. Jacqueline backed off the bed, not daring to breathe, terror stopping her heart. Angélique curled over in a spasm and vanished beneath a rush of heavy pelage, thick, tawny, black-tipped. She emerged, a wolf, to stand defiant before Jacqueline.

Jacqueline stared wide-eyed into her sister's sweet amber wolf-eyes and slowly slipped to her knees, trembling. She waited for the wolf to step closer before cautiously wrapping her arms around her sister's neck and drawing her close. A taut moment passed before her sister lay down in her lap. Releasing a soft sigh, she stroked Angélique's head and shoulders, then gently rubbed her velvety ears.

"I'll protect you," Jacqueline vowed.

And she had ever since.

"And you say your sister has no recollection of what happened?"

Elif's question drew Jacqueline back from the rush of memories, so vividly colored by her new awareness of the events that had transformed her sister into an angry, aloof, self-destructive dissolute.

The coach jerked with the catch of the track. They had reached the forest of Bellesfées. *Home.* Jacqueline wiped tears from her face and rubbed her eyes. She gave the Turque a long assessing look, then said, "Don't disappear. I want you to come with me to see to this mess."

Elif nodded. "It is why I have come to you now, for you would not cease your pursuit of the spell. Your curiosity has brought Draganov

Dragul and Mirrikh closer to your sister, whose blood will draw the sorcerer's attention."

"Yes, well, there is much more for you to explain to me," Jacqueline grumbled as she turned to the control panel and began the shutdown. "Like this brigand who attacked me, and why the automaton stopped the train, and—" She turned back again, arms akimbo. "By what power do you manage to disappear and reappear?"

Elif shrugged her wrap back on and reset her huge turban. She grinned back at Jacqueline. "Laws you have not yet discovered," she said.

7.

April of 1838 was the wettest month on record in St. Petersburg. Rain drenched the entire week of travel before Sigismond Thalberg and his protégée Angélique reached the villa Derzhavin, along with his entourage of fellow musical artists, but on the day they arrived, the sun made the bright yellow façade all but blinding. Two inches of water flooded the courtyard surrounded on three sides by the villa and its wings, fronting the Fontanka River, which had not borne the heavy downpours well. The carriages drew up to the steps of the entry, whereupon the footman descended to assist the passengers to disembark. Angélique, in Thalberg's carriage, deferred to allow him to exit first and behind him, his valet. She followed after, accepting the footman's hand to help her step down onto the huge staircase. Standing in the waterlogged courtyard, achy and dusty with travel, she took in the scope of the mansion with an appreciative eye. After the painfully long trip, she looked forward to availing herself of the amenities enjoyed by the Russian elite.

Her chaperone, a large fräu named Spreicher whom Thalberg's valet had secured for her, took her arm brusquely and marched her up the steps to the doors, which opened upon their arrival, revealing Baronin Spransky, their hostess, a petite young blonde with her hair piled high upon her head in a mass of curls, wearing an ornate coffee-colored day gown, with a tucker along the V-neck bodice. The Russian noble gripped Thalberg's hand far more tightly than he liked, Angélique noted with a smirk. The woman babbled effusive greetings and flatteries in that squeaky falsetto so de rigeur among the spouses of men of significance at courts. Thalberg responded with his quiet, self-effacing modesty that had women across Europe swooning. The poor baronin caught her breath and seemed unable to release it. Thalberg took the opportunity to slip from her grasp, turning to introduce Angélique, who received the barest nod of acknowledgment from the dazzled woman. With an impatient huff, Spreicher took up her march, her bulk forcing them all through the doors and into the front hall. Here a small army of servants took over, leading the party up a wide marble stair and along the corridor to their suites. The servants deposited their trunks and boxes near the wardrobes and vanities, bowed impersonally, and vanished.

Spreicher opened the door between her chambers and Angélique's.

"Geh schlafen!" she commanded. Or at least it felt like a command. Perhaps it was simply that everything in German sounded like an order. It never sat well with Angélique. To spite the woman, she replied in French.

"No, I will not go to sleep. I'm restless. I've been sitting for the past five days. I need to get out of these travel clothes, find something comfortable to wear, and walk. Exercise."

Spreicher looked like she'd shoot steam out her ears, but Angélique waved her hand. "You needn't worry. I'll not leave the grounds of the estate. I'll be perfectly safe."

The woman glared but relented, returning to her chambers and slamming the door behind her. Angélique was quite certain Spreicher didn't realize Angélique understood what "Schlampe" meant.

Stripping off her dusty traveling clothes, Angélique washed, then changed to a day gown and slippers. She brushed her hair and ribboned it up at the back of her head in a careless fashion. Wrapping herself in a heavy shawl, she sallied out to explore the villa.

The upper floors were mostly guest rooms, which held no interest for her, although she appreciated the splendor and luxury of their appointments. She caught the strains of a violin from one of the rooms, a cello in another, and somewhere along yet another corridor, the sound of a low brass horn. A thrill surged through her. She loved the electricity in the air before a grand recital in these noble houses. People of rank and title and money bowing to her and asking her opinions over caviar and cake. Gentlemen of a certain age begging to sit by her. She had no fear of jealous rivals, for the young women would be fawning over Thalberg. Angélique sometimes wondered if he had brought her along, seventeen and wide-eyed, expressly so he would not have to face the wrath of spurned husbands or beaux. Angélique's dance card was never empty. And all she had to do was play the piano.

It was like her friend Charles used to say in Paris: "Go get drunk! On wine, on poetry, on virtue, whatever! And if they ask you what time it is, tell them it's time to get drunk."

Of course, Charles preferred to get drunk on wine and opium and hashish, but she would be drunk on music, especially music on the world stages of these grand European estates.

Downstairs she immersed herself in the clatter of the servants bustling this way and that, some to ready the little theater, some to set up the ballroom, still others to place chairs about the salon for recitals. Further on, a crew of kitchen workers prepared the banquet hall for the midnight repast. Angélique scurried among them and found her way to the garden doors.

To her delight, the gardens were not the stiff formal gardens of a French château but an expanse of green with occasional beds dotted here and there with a folly. One gazebo looked like a Persian bedroom; another fashioned like a Greek temple. Impressive busts stared imposingly while various stone nymphs simply posed. Belvederes rose to either side of the huge lawn, one featuring a medicinal garden and the other an orangérie. After making free with a few lavender stems, she crossed the lawn and climbed the steps to the orangérie at the far end of the belvedere.

Moisture from the previous rains steamed off the windows and roof beneath the steady warmth of the sunlight. As she closed the door behind her, Angélique breathed deeply. The humidity and warmth soothed her nose and throat. She draped her shawl over a chair and again breathed in, this time to enjoy the fragrance of citrus blossoms, tea roses, and lilac. She strolled, savoring each breath. Dust from the journey had burned and choked her for weeks from Paris to Prague to Vienna to Budapest, and then the long trek to St. Petersburg. She was not the only one of Thalberg's entourage to fall sick along the way, forcing delays, making the journey that much longer. Every new city meant parties, concerts, salons, and balls, as well as many charming nobles to keep her thoughts occupied. Once back on the road, however, homesickness set in. She missed her own orangérie, as well as her sister and her father and her own piano in her own hall.

"I sensed you would be here, dearest Mademoiselle Laforge," came a voice from the doorway.

She spun about in surprise. A young man stood holding her shawl to his face, inhaling her scent like a cur on the street sniffing at skirts.

Angélique looked around for company but found no one else. She came forward carefully until she recognized him: Toma Draganovich, an annoying young nobleman she had met briefly in Budapest. His father was by title just a boyar, though he had introduced himself as "Count Vasile Draganov of the Dragul, the equivalent of a prince in Transylvania. She had gleaned from conversations he was setting himself up to be closer to the center of the political maelstrom of Moldovarabia, gathering monetary support from eastern Europe's wealthiest families while amassing forces from the splintered Turkish mess. Angélique had listened politely to the man's professions of wealth and strength and leadership, but it was evident he lacked the armies he so desperately desired. He wasn't the first petty noble to try to seduce her with claims of glory to come, nor would he be the last, but he was at least handsome, deferential, and hospitable, even if he did smoke a disgusting leaf in an ugly Czech bulldog pipe. He had invited her to his villa in Chisinău, boasting of the dignitaries he could introduce to her and her art.

The boyar's son Toma had just as smoothly insinuated himself into her circle and at first introduction had taken her arm and steered her away from others to corner her for himself. She allowed him his opening salvo but soon grew tired of him. On the edge of manhood, but not quite there, Toma was not unpleasant to look at: tall, solidly built, with prepossessing features and a mass of black curls, shaven but for his adolescent fringe beard. However, he studied the world through brown-tinted, octagonal Ayscough sun-glasses that made his smile somehow sinister. His speech demonstrated an arrogant overuse of "I" and "me" and not enough attempts at flattery or solicitude for someone who saw himself as a ladies' man.

Angélique dipped her chin rather than give him a full curtsy. "Master Draganovich, is it not?"

She held out her hand for her shawl, but instead, he claimed the appendage as well, kissing it. She snatched her hand away.

"You make too bold!" She grabbed her shawl and wrapped it about herself so she might grip it and not leave her hands exposed to another affront. "Besides, it is poor manners to seize an artist's hand. The slightest twist and I should lose my career."

Draganovich reddened. "My sincere apologies, mademoiselle. I simply could not resist."

"Then you must learn restraint," she scolded, then teased, "I can tutor you."

He grinned. "I'm certain you can. Will you walk with me?"

"I must return to the villa. You may accompany me if you behave yourself. Otherwise, I shall—"

He cut her off. "Angelique Laforge, I have followed you across Europe. I have scaled the Carpathians and braved the vampires of Transylvania, from my home near the Black Sea here to the Baltic Sea. For you, for your beauty, your music, the—the beauty of your music..."

His declamation faltered.

Angélique forced a smile. "How commendable of you."

He cleared his throat and offered his arm. She ignored it, as there were no chaperones. He frowned—more a pout, actually—and took up beside her.

"I was truly moved by what I heard, Angélique. It was beautiful. I can't recall anyone else who has performed so—beautifully. It seemed to me I heard the beauty of heaven."

She rolled her eyes at his clumsy words. And honestly, addressing her by her name! Always "I, me." So young and already a boor.

They left the orangérie and descended the belvedere steps. She turned toward the villa, but he stepped in front of her.

"Please, a short promenade," he demanded.

She frowned. "Completely improper, Master Draganovich. You may escort me to the villa or not at all." She tried to brush past him, but again he blocked her.

"You don't understand," he said. "I didn't come all this way for a mere concert." He wrapped both arms around her and pulled her close to him, despite her struggle. "I came for you," he whispered. He held her more tightly, crushing her against him. "You have charmed me utterly. I must have you for my own!"

He pressed his mouth to hers, stifling her protests and ignoring her efforts to free herself. Furious, she bit his lip until she tasted a coppery liquid burst. He pushed her away, holding his lip as blood streamed down his chin.

She slapped him, sending his glasses flying.

"Monsieur, you offend me!" She spat at his feet. "How dare you violate me in this manner!"

He glared at his red-stained hand, then turned his beetle-browed eyes to her. "You should not have done that."

She laughed. "I? *I* should not?"

He seized her arm, twisting it in his grasp. "You should not have done that!" he shouted.

Angélique stared back at him, her eyes widening with growing horror as his face somehow changed. Darker, wider. Shifting. His eyes were all wrong—light brown animal eyes slanted back. His fingers dug into her bare arms like claws.

She jammed her knee upward between his legs. He fell with a yipe and covered his bruised member.

"Never—*never!*—touch me again, Toma Draganovich!"

She spun on her heel, but he snatched her ankle. She broke her fall with her hands and cried out as her right thumb snapped. Draganovich rolled on top of her. He shoved her face into the grass and ripped her dress from her shoulders.

"You should not have done that!" he roared.

He kept roaring until his voice rose to a deafening howl. Claws raked down her back over and over, shredding her dress, shredding her flesh. Pain seared her neck. An icy emptiness overwhelmed her. She struggled to breathe, but the grass was a warm bog. She gasped for air. Blood filled her mouth. An animal snarled in her ear. Piercing blades tore into her, ripping at her arms, her breasts, her hips. Pressure and a sharp pain *inside her! Mon Dieu!* Blackness—*was this death?*—closed over her. At the edge of her consciousness, she heard another voice, enraged, bellowing.

"What is this!"

Angélique had not dreamed in the five years since St. Petersburg. She either slept or not, even when human. At times, she missed the coziness of that half-awake state when the last of a dream tempted her back to sleep or the sun in the open windows called her to a glorious day. When she could lie abed, eyes closed, and slowly and sensuously stretch her body as she debated her choices.

She no longer had choices. Her eyes flew open. Stench and pain immediately overtook her in the darkness. She moaned, cut short when someone smacked her head. Yipping, she curled herself away from the smell of men and terror, pressing against a wall in quiet whines.

"Keep your damned mutt quiet," someone said, one of the men from the assault on Bellesfées.

Llewellyn neared. He sat, then stretched out beside her, spooning her close, his hands tender as he pressed his fingers into her ruff and traced gentle circles against her skin.

"Shh. Stay with me, Angélique. Good girl. Dda bleiddast. Shh."

With a whimper, she leaned into him, then groaned in pain. Her whole right side burned, and her left eye had swollen shut. She lay on a pallet in close quarters with at least two other men besides Llewellyn, and their odors filled her with horror, shaking her to her soul. Thank the stars she hadn't changed while unconscious. Her wounds would heal faster in her wolf form. Even now, she felt her flesh healing, twisting about the bullet, forcing it to the surface in a slow, inexorable healing as painful as the wound itself.

Something gnawed at her thoughts, though. Something she needed to focus on, prepare herself for. If only the hammering in her head would stop long enough for her to remember what that was. She tried to relax into Llewellyn's massaging fingers. He seemed to sense her need and moved his hands closer to the nerve clusters behind her ears. His ministrations sent waves of cool comfort through her body. The painful pulse in her head eased. She panted lightly, thirsty for fresh, clean air.

"Fetch me some water," Llewellyn ordered one of the men. "Something for bandages too."

"For a dog?" the other said, sneering. "Bitch killed Szolt. Tried to take my arm off." He held up his bandaged limb.

"For *my* dog. Do it."

Angélique was glad Llewellyn had some authority here. But where was "here"? An airship, she remembered. A huge vessel, no mere gondola, sustained by a monstrous bladder that had blacked out the sky.

The one left. The other came closer. "The Count's not happy with you."

Angélique froze. The Count! That was the terror pounding in her mind: the strange burnt-cherry odor of his awful pipe and the bellowing voice of Vasile Draganov Dragul. *"What is this?"*

"Shh," Llewellyn whispered again as she struggled in panic.

He couldn't know, could he? He couldn't know that by trying to save her life, he had drawn her deeper into danger, plunging her into a horror she had utterly buried.

How could she have blocked all of it so completely for so long?

She and Jacky had racked their brains to learn how her change had come upon her so inexplicably after the attack. A bear had mauled her, Baron Spransky had claimed. And so she had believed these past five years. How could she have forgotten? Draganov's son tearing off her clothing, digging into her flesh, shoving her face into the ground while he—

Dieu!

And the Count had stood by and seen it all. He had discovered them, and he had abandoned her there, dying in a pool of her own blood.

Llewellyn tried to lull her as she writhed, reliving the nightmare. Why was he here, with that self-styled Count? Yes, Draganov had made a place for himself in the high society of the Ottoman world, but why would an agent of the British empire be in his company? Angélique couldn't reconcile such a betrayal with the pleasure she felt at his touch. Why couldn't he be a mean son-of-a-bitch that she could hate without reserve, for Jacky's sake?

The one returned. Llewellyn sat up, and Angélique lifted her head groggily to examine their surroundings. By the shape of the outer wall, the tiny cabin rested amidships, with a drop-chain pallet berth, two drop-chain shelves, a chair, and a lantern. The one who had fetched the basin and rags stood by the open door letting down a shelf to set the water on. The other man sat with the chair tipped back, his arms folded, glaring at her and Llewellyn. She lowered her head again as Llewellyn took a rag and drenched it to wipe her haunch.

She tried to keep her whining soft and high, but the pain moved through her in waves. Her flesh pushed at the bullet as Llewellyn flushed the wound. *Oh, to change form and down some brandy!*

Llewellyn stroked her head gently, then settled in to slowly trace circles behind her ear. Angélique closed her eyes and let him care for her. The man knew a thing or two about canids, and despite all, she surrendered to his ministrations.

"Count says you're to see him straight away." This from the one holding the rags.

"I will when I've finished here."

The cold water relieved some of her pain. Her whines softened to sighs.

"Yorg, fetch the rum from my trunk there," Llewellyn said. "Put a little in my mug. It'll numb her up some."

Oh, you wonderful man! Now she truly wanted to change form so she could kiss him.

The man on the chair complied, but he wasn't happy about it. "I'm not your varlet," he grumbled. "Waste of good rum."

"Depends on your definition of waste," Llewellyn returned. "Or varlet."

He gave her water first, and she licked his chin lightly. He then held his mug of rum to her maw. He didn't have to coax her to drink. She settled back again, the rum warming her stomach and easing the ache in her skull.

He wrung out the rag and bandaged the wound, wrapping strips around her waist. "This should help until I can find a surgeon," he murmured in her ear. "Dda bleiddast." He rose. "All right, men. Everyone out. I'll lock her in."

Yorg began to protest, but Llewellyn pushed him out of the little cabin. "I don't want anyone near her. You saw what she can do."

"Yah, she ought to see what I can do."

"She already knows what you and your musketoon can do. That's what I've been patching up for the last half hour."

So Yorg was the musketeer? She would not forget.

Though the door closed, and she heard the lock turn, she waited until their heavy tread climbed the ladder and their voices faded before sitting up enough to seize the rum bottle by the neck and thump the base against the hull until the cork rose. She tugged the cork out and took a few more hefty swigs, then lay down again to let her wolf blood finish her healing. She trusted Llewellyn to safeguard her sleep.

Angélique jerked awake at the sound of the key in the lock. Llewellyn entered and locked the door behind him. She lifted her head and shifted slightly. The rum bottle clunked on the floor.

"What the devil?"

He picked up the bottle before it completely emptied and glared at it as if the object would render up the story of its uncorking. Angélique hiccupped and put her head down again. Llewellyn found the cork near her front paws and replaced it. "The devil indeed you are, fy merch euraidd, my golden girl."

He sat across from her and stroked her side. "You followed us out into the night. I can't imagine why. I thought at first you were merely attacking those who invaded your home, but no, I think you were defending me. Or were you pursuing me? I was your captive, and you were obligated to keep me so, eh?"

The gentle stroke of his hand soothed away the burning in her side. When he leaned his brow to hers, she nuzzled his ear. Though he had shown no weakness before the two minions, his whole body trembled as the tumult of the past hours took its toll on his concussed senses. Still, he continued to lull her.

"Fy merch euraidd, fy nghariad, my deary."

Her pain subsided. She tried moving her legs. Her flank still hurt, but she sensed the ball was almost clear of the wound. Another short rest would seal the wound completely.

Then she would deal with Draganov.

8.

"*MERDE! SAX.*"

Marthe looked to Luc. Luc shrugged. He stood, arms folded, keeping an impassive watch.

Marthe shook her head. "Was that his name? How do you know that?"

Jacqueline knelt over the bloody mass on the carpet of the salon. She had rifled the intruder's pockets, finding nothing, and was now examining his face.

"No. Adolphe Sax owns a foundry," she answered, distracted. "I was supposed to pick up tubing from his factory the other day, but I forgot all about him. It seems I get delayed at every stage. It's… f—"

Marthe swatted Jacqueline with a dish towel. "Language, ma fille. You may work in a forge, but that is no excuse."

"And no one heard any horses? Carriages?"

"Just the howling and that shriek."

"It's all my fault. I forced her into this. I told her to keep watch. Dared her to take responsibility." Jacqueline grimaced. It would do no good to anyone to call in the prefecture to make an investigation; she didn't know how she would explain the man's wounds.

"Luc." She hated to ask, but it had to be done. "Use a porter. Take him to the woods. Let the scavengers have him. Marthe, send in a scrubber to get the blood cleaned out of here."

The man reluctantly left the room, and his wife followed, nattering grumpily.

Elif stood in the open doorway. She pointed to the dead man and remarked, "I know him, one of the Count's men, Szoltan. He is not one of the elite guard, but a—what is the word? Uşak? Hunch man? Hunched-back?"

Jacqueline chuckled. "Henchman."

"They attacked quickly and were away again, counting on surprise and stealth."

She studied the ground and followed a trail Jacqueline couldn't see down the hill to where it stopped.

"What is it?"

Elif stopped and cast about. "Airship."

Jacqueline snorted. "That's not possible. A charliere isn't dirigible. I know because I've been working with a friend who will probably build the first one if he accepts my idea for the propellers rather than a system of paddles. We just need to figure a better way to power them without the use of flame. I'm thinking of an injector system, steam, and I'm close to a design. But Henri wants to—"

"You only know the laws of this world." Elif stared out over the rolling hills to the north. "Mirrikh makes use of those laws you haven't discovered yet."

"You think it can be steered by magic?"

"I think there are ways of learning that do not involve books."

Jacqueline blew an exasperated breath. "Effendi, to carry away a captive man and wolf, and we don't know how many others—"

"Four. At least. Four other tracks, one dead in your salon, plus one to shoot from above."

"Shoot? What do you mean?"

Elif pointed to various places, but Jacqueline couldn't see what she indicated. "And, of course, those aboard to operate the ship. Unless he uses revenants to do that."

"Revenants? You mean—"

"I do. Men once dead, now not."

"But the gondola for such a vessel would be huge. The envelope would fill the sky. How would that go unnoticed?"

"The trails all end hereabout," Elif answered. "How else would they vanish from the earth if not taken up into the heavens?"

Jacqueline conceded. "And someone was shot, you say?"

"Yes." Elif hesitated, then admitted, "Your sister. But remember, she will heal!" She hurried to assuage Jacqueline's fear. "They took her with them. That is a good sign. And, of course, she is still alive. Her blood will heal her." She shook her head. "Her kind cannot be killed by a mere bullet. Beheading, perhaps. Her heart cut out, perhaps."

"Shot? Angélique was shot?" Jacqueline quaked with rage. "How do we find them? They can't just hide a gargantuan dirigible, but in which direction? How far could they be by now?"

Elif laughed. "Güzel-kizim, trust me now, as I trust the One God. Let me seek our path by those means only I know, that we may go more swiftly to find them out."

"No, you don't understand. My sister — No one else can — She needs — "

"Yes. She needs *us* to find her. Please let me do this."

"But I have to do *something!*" she protested.

Elif folded her arms. "What? What would you do but seek out someone who knows where she is? I *am* that someone. You found me. Now let me work."

The Turque turned Jacqueline by the shoulders and gave a gentle push toward the château. Surrendering to the janissary's wishes, Jacqueline trudged back up to the salon, where Marthe prepared the clockwork scrubber.

"Marthe, leave this to me. Would you get a guest room ready and prepare dinner for us?"

"With *this* in the house?" the woman demanded, almost apoplectic as she pointed to the grisly scene.

"Marthe, please. I haven't eaten a complete meal in two days, and I need something to keep me going if I'm to find Angélique."

The housekeeper threw her hands in the air and stormed back to the kitchen.

Angélique shot. And kidnapped as well. How could she rescue her sister this time when she had no clue to her whereabouts?

And to learn the truth of St. Petersburg after all this time. Rape, savagery, cruelty, and sorcery. She had no idea Angélique carried such horror. How was it she showed no scar? It was too terrible to hold on to. No wonder Angélique had repressed the memories.

Jacqueline went to her room to wash and change the clothes she'd been wearing the past two days. For a moment, she could almost hear Angélique admonishing her to bathe. With a frown, she shooed the thought away before she lost herself in grief. Pausing by a window overlooking the hillside, she spied Elif kneeling, wrapped in a black drapery. As she watched, the Turque rose and shrugged off the drape.

She was dressed in white, with a billowed blouse and a long multi-pleated skirt. Jacqueline wondered where she'd gotten the change of dress. Elif clasped her hands on opposite shoulders and bowed. As she straightened, her right arm extended outward, her hand raised. Her left arm also reached out, but her left hand turned down. The janissary tipped her head as if studying it. Slowly, Elif began to twirl. Her long skirt flared and rippled as she moved, not only spinning but tracing a large circle about the field as she moved.

Jacqueline had heard of the Sufi dervishes, but she had never witnessed the ritual. She and Angélique used to spin themselves around in the garden, but it only made them dizzy until they fell. Just watching now made her queasy, and she wondered how such behavior would help Elif figure out their next move.

A shriek interrupted Jacqueline's musings. She hurried downstairs to the salon where a strange tableau awaited her. Luc and Jean-Paul pressed back against the mantle, their faces pale and their eyes wide, the clockwork porter and scrubber puffing steam as if impatient, Marthe standing atop the divan, arms crossed, her expression a mingling of outrage and fear. When she saw Jacqueline, she merely pointed to the bloodied body on the floor. The one Angélique had clearly killed.

Jacqueline blinked rapidly as the corpse's right hand slowly crept toward his throat.

She would not have survived if a mere wolf had attacked her.

Jacqueline stared, frozen, dizzy as Elif's words echoed through her thoughts.

Her kind cannot be killed.

His body had been cold. He had been dead, she'd made certain.

Her blood will heal her.

"*Mon Dieu.*"

Had Angélique also been dead before turning? Her body so torn and ravaged—She must have been. Jacqueline quaked, and she felt ill.

"He was dead," Marthe said, more in confusion than fear. "I know he was dead."

"Yes, Marthe," Jacqueline said with a groan.

Marthe heaved a long-suffering sigh. "What have you been up to this time? I've gotten used to your machines running around on their own, but not dead bodies."

"I'll take care of it," Jacqueline snapped, more sharply than she had intended.

But how? What had Elif said? Beheading, perhaps? Cut out his heart, perhaps?

Jacqueline shook her head. "Forgive me. I *will* take care of it. You may go. All of you."

The housekeepers looked to one another. Jean-Paul needed no further encouragement. He fled, and his parents followed reluctantly.

Elif appeared at the doorway, kilij in hand. When she saw the twitching body on the floor, she grimaced. "It remains a mystery to me. I have seen Toma attack others, even slay them, but Angélique is the only victim to take on the power of the wolf. Now it seems she too has the power to transform others."

She approached the man and knelt beside him. She set the kilij on the floor in front of her and folded her hands before her face. "Inna lillahi wa inna ilayhi raji'un. We belong to the One God, and to the One God we return." She picked up the kilij in two hands and bowed her head to the blade. "Astaghfiru lillah." Elif smiled sadly. "A prayer. For forgiveness."

The man groaned a hoarse gurgle. He looked up at them in panic and confusion as blood bubbled from his throat. Elif stood and set her feet in a solid, wide stance. With a swift slash of her blade, she severed his head from his body. She then used the hem of her robe to wipe the blood from her kilij and slid the blade into place at her waist.

Jacqueline's knees trembled and a gasp caught in her throat. She stumbled back into a chair, her eyes never leaving the rolling head.

Elif gently cleared her throat and stepped between Jacqueline and the bloody sight. Jacqueline's eyes widened and snapped upward, locking on the janissary's face.

"It was necessary," Elif said softly.

Jacqueline nodded. Her heart raced, and she couldn't find air enough to answer. Elif flipped the bloodied carpet to cover the grisly sight, bundling the head tightly with the body. She then hoisted the revenant, as easily as one might lift a child, onto the porter, and the automaton chugged away out the salon doors and off to the woods. Once it was gone, she turned to Jacqueline.

"When you are ready, I have learned what we need to know."

Angélique awoke hungry. She shifted, sat up, and stretched. The lead ball slipped from her bandages and clacked on the floor, waking Llewellyn. He righted his chair and slowly bent over to collect the ball. He studied it, then pulled away Angélique's wrappings to see her haunch had completely healed. She answered his gaze evenly. He wagged his head.

"First, it's revenants. Now magic healing. Up in the air, I am quite at sea here."

Revenants? Of course. That was the disgusting stench in her nose. Dead bodies, sour and earthy and sickly sweet.

Angélique leaned closer and licked his face. He caught her snout playfully and growled. "I suppose a little secret magic on my side can't hurt." He kissed her brow. "You are a beauty, though."

She snuffled and gave a quiet whine. He seemed to read her mind. "Hungry? So am I. Nothing aboard, though, so we'll have to wait until we land. Shouldn't be long now."

Even as he said it, the ship shuddered and tipped. Llewellyn grinned as it began its descent. "What did I tell you?"

He continued to stroke her head, but his mood darkened. "You've crossed over into a very dangerous game, Angélique, siding with me. Far more than Her Majesty could possibly have guessed." He pushed his face into her ruff and hugged her. "God help us both."

Angélique grunted reassuringly. *Her Majesty.* So, he had not been dismissed. He was, she supposed, a clandestine agent of the young Victoria. *And what is he doing in France with Draganov?* she wondered. At least she could deduce he didn't seem to be "siding" with that *salaud.*

He stood and made room for her to slide down from the bed. He looked at her thoughtfully, tugging at his slight beard. "Hmm. No good letting them know. Let me get that bandage back on you."

Angélique approved of his wisdom and let him wrap her again. She even feigned a limp as they left his cabin and climbed the ladder.

The airship's envelope hung monstrous above her, blocking out most of the sky. Angélique paused in wonder at the sheer size of the aerostat, the conceit of a naval vessel retained by its prow shape and elevated decks fore and aft. She recoiled. Along the main deck, shambling corpses chained to the bars operated four large capstans, two to each side. As they turned the axle, cables worked outcropped, wing-like rotary paddles to drive the airship forward.

Angélique shied from the revenants, grey monstrosities with sunken faces, barefoot and still clothed in ragged funeral attire. Soulless white eyes stared without seeing. Mouths hung agape as though they sang in chorus a silent dirge for their lot. What would possess a man to dig up

corpses rather than conscript able-bodied men? Perhaps none of the Count's "loyal" citizens were enthused about serving his ambitious ends. More likely, these would make for fewer witnesses to his abominable means. Angélique's eyes narrowed at the obscenity of the rotting bodies pressed into such degradation. A growl rose in her throat, and Llewellyn stroked her head quickly to quiet her.

Two dark-cloaked figures, one wearing a black dastaar—a Sikh turban—stood on the forecastle, the upper deck at the bow, silhouetted against the morning sky. As Angélique and Llewellyn mounted the ladder, one of them half turned, and Angélique knew him, not so much by his current appearance but by the Czech bulldog pipe he clenched in his teeth and the indifferent frown he gave Llewellyn. The same frown he wore upon discovering her, despoiled and dying at his son's hands. A rush of memory swept over her: despair, anger, desperation, surrender. She snarled.

Draganov pulled the pipe from his mouth and waved it toward Angélique. "This is the wolf that killed my man?" he asked, his tone dispassionate, disinterested.

Llewellyn and Angélique joined them on the upper deck. He knelt to scratch her ears, his arm draped over her protectively. "She's not a wolf, Excellency. This is my dog, and she merely defended me. She's a Jenkins hound, my family's own breed, only a quarter wolf but bred for appearances and their aggressive skills. I am quite certain I told you I'd be bringing her along. I could never have found the machine if not for her." He kissed her snout. "She knew I was hurt, and the way your men rushed the doors, she assumed they were attacking. My Anyel."

Anyel. Angélique didn't speak Welsh, but she had a pretty good idea that was her name.

"What do you say, Mirrikh?" Draganov asked his companion.

The man in the dastaar turned to look at Angélique, his keen gaze narrowing as a sly smile teased the edges of his mouth.

Her ears flickered, and a high whine escaped her. He *saw* her.

Mirrikh nodded and grinned, revealing a mouthful of stained teeth. "Very nice," he said. When he bobbed his head, his heavy jowls shook.

Angélique turned her head away, panting. The man stank of blood and sulfur, peaty loam, and decaying sedges. She shook off Llewellyn and glared at him. He gave a last reassuring scritch behind her ears before taking his place beside the Count and Mirrikh.

The gondola settled rockily, then stilled. Yorg appeared from below along with his partner and the two that had invaded Bellesfées. They gathered the chains from the capstan bars and pulled the revenants away from their posts. The pitiable creatures staggered or shuffled purposelessly in aimless circles until Yorg corralled them and led them below. Anchors were cast and secured somewhere on the ground. Yorg and his partner returned, and from under the gunwale, they unbattened a fretted gang board, one end of which they pitched over the side, then hooked the near end to the gunwale. They set a short step at the deck and stood to either side to await the Count and his two advisers.

Angélique followed Llewellyn down the gangplank. She glanced overhead, expecting the envelope to deflate upon them at any moment. To her wonder, she saw it had somehow changed color, now almost matching the bright blue of the mid-morning sky. She hadn't the knowledge to understand how it acquired its chameleonic properties, but Jacky would have been fascinated.

Angélique disembarked and limped along behind the men as they crossed the courtyard of a medieval château, glad to discover they had not left France. She paused by a fountain in the courtyard to relieve herself. A small village huddled below the keep's walls, and the parc beyond seemed endless in all directions, like the parc at Chenonceaux or Versailles. Easy to hide an airship in such a wilderness, especially one that could be made invisible against the sky. Angélique wanted to run the parc and catch a good meal, but she didn't want to leave Llewellyn in the company of these two men.

And why was that? Angélique still wasn't sure what had driven her to attack the intruders at the château or pursue Llewellyn even when it was obvious he chose to go with them. He had told her plainly they wouldn't hurt her if she just let him go. She had promised only that she would keep watch until Jacky returned. But then he had hastened to her rescue at the sound of her cries. He had bully-ragged the minions to help him tend her wounds. And he trusted her; he had made her his confidante, albeit without knowing she understood every word he said.

Or was it just that he smelled so wonderful and his low voice in her ear made her whole body melt?

Angélique had never melted for any man. Not since her turning. She sized men up, sniffed out their foibles, bent them to her will, and once she got bored, discarded them, unless they proved useful in other ways. Life had abused her no less dispassionately, and she felt no shame returning in kind.

No other man had treated Angélique so attentively as a woman, but Llewellyn wasn't aware of her womanhood. He lavished his care on a wolf, and as a wolf, she responded instinctively with trust.

For the first time, she wondered if her instincts had led her astray.

Despite its medieval structure, the château was well appointed with tapestries, heavy wooden furniture, and massive portraits along the walls. Draganov led them through the entrance hall into a sitting room. Immediately, a door in the back wall opened, and servants came through with trays of food. They deposited these and took Draganov's and the other man's heavy cloaks and coats. The acrid reek of their sweat overpowered the aromas of food.

Angélique recoiled. She nudged Llewellyn toward the table. As he took up a plate, he looked over the board of cooked or dried meats, cheeses, and vegetables, a faint frown furrowing his brow. Turning, he caught one of the servants leaving.

"Do you have any raw meats? A rabbit? Bird? My dog can't eat most of this, and she needs food and water."

The servant nodded a slight bow, leaving the way they came in. Angélique looked up to Llewellyn gratefully. The three men began filling plates, and Llewellyn tossed her some sliced beef to tide her over, but the servant returned within two minutes with a bowl of water and a copper charger holding a brace of skinned rabbits. In the instant, Angélique forgot the men and their odors and their talk as hunger filled her senses with a cotton fuzziness. For the next half hour, she engaged in the pure delight of raw meat, soft bones, and cool, fresh water.

Once the rabbits were gone and she had cleaned most of their remains from her maw and forepaws, her ears gradually began to twitch, and she became aware of the arguments going on. Mirrikh spoke a language she didn't recognize. She regretted she had never learned the varied modern languages as she'd toured Europe. Everyone she ever needed to know spoke French. She curled up at Llewellyn's feet and pretended to sleep.

"At most, nine hundred thousand," Draganov was saying, "but they are much occupied elsewhere and will not be looking to defend themselves against such a force as ours. That would be our foothold."

"But Russia's growing more powerful, and expanding, while the Ottomans lose more and more of their holdings with each treaty," Llewellyn argued. "Their armies are in chaos over the reforms Abdülmecid is bringing in. It's the better bet. Why else do you think Wallachia is already up in arms?"

"Ahriman," the Persian muttered.

"Say rather 'shaitan,' not Satan," Llewellyn retorted, "as my advice is sound, just not what you want to hear."

So, not only was the rogue not stupid, but he also knew a thing or two about the cultures of the Orient. Angélique snorted her amusement as the Persian resumed his muttering.

"Let Wallachia go after the droppings," Draganov continued. "Russia is the empire to conquer in this new era of modernization. Russia now owns my country. I will have it back. I have word that two hundred thousand casings await installation. All they lack is Duval's engineering. And, of course, imbued skulls."

Angélique's ears perked up at the mention of Jacky.

"When I secured the contract, I had her designs sent to the foundry in Trnava, with a copy for Brodeur to work on a new prototype in Paris." Draganov rose and headed back to the table to refill his wine. "My agent in Paris assures me Brodeur has almost completed that task."

Angélique held her breath. *That was all? Nothing more about Jacky?* Draganov referred to "Duval" as if he was not aware his men had stormed her home, refuting Jacky's theory of a conspiracy against her, personally.

The Persian made an angry comment, which Draganov answered with equal vehemence. He drained his glass and set it down.

"I will retire now. You, brigadier, you must rest, for I will have need of you in the coming days. I will send you my physician this evening. I am certain that blow to your head troubles you." He strode to the door, then paused. "Notwithstanding all that has gone wrong in our designs, we are still on schedule. But it will be for naught if we do not recover that skull."

Llewellyn met his eyes. "We will."

The skull, the skull, the skull. Why that *skull?* Angélique whined in frustration. What made it so special, other than the gold writing? Why had Llewellyn tried to secure it for Draganov if he was working against him? She could make no sense of his actions.

Draganov left. Angélique sat up, panting lightly, glaring at the Persian, who returned her gaze. She didn't like the way he grinned at her so hungrily. She growled and whined. Llewellyn was quick to respond, scratching her ears and pulling her into his arms. The Persian chuckled mirthlessly. He stood, bowed low to Llewellyn, gave Angélique a parting grin, and left. Angélique followed as far as the doorway and squatted there to leave a puddle.

Llewellyn laughed, then held his head with a grunt. "*Ych.* Come on, my little angel, let's go outside."

She eyed him as a mother might a recalcitrant child, then barked sharply. She trotted out of the dining room to draw Llewellyn to his chambers. Draganov was right; the brigadier needed rest more than she needed exercise right now, so she waited where she was until he gave in, leading her down a corridor and up a back stairway to the third storey, which was the tower room. As he closed and locked the door, he leaned into the door and sighed. The tension of the last twelve hours fell away from him.

Angélique assessed the room's privacy: locked door, two high narrow windows, heavy drapes that could be drawn. If Draganov sent a physician, he would have to knock and wait. She stood on her hind legs and pulled away the tiebacks on the window facing the courtyard. Llewellyn took the hint and pulled the other set of drapes closed. Then he dropped prostrate on the bed without bothering to pull off his boots.

Angélique paced the room and made certain they were truly alone and secure before jumping onto the bed and taking her place beside him, pressing against his side and laying her head on his neck to feel his heartbeat slow. When his breathing was low and even, she nudged him to make certain he was asleep. She wrapped one forepaw over his shoulder; the other cradled his head.

Then she changed.

9.

JACQUELINE HAULED ANGÉLIQUE'S TUB, ON CASTERS, INTO HER BATHING room and connected its screw-tap to her water supply so she and Elif could soak side by side and lay plans before supper for the upcoming hours. Water poured in, already steaming, and Elif gazed in wonder.

"Truly, you are a magician," she declared, climbing into the filling tub. "You not only own a bathtub but two of them! And piping hot water."

Jacqueline shook her head. "My father brought home the idea from England. They're still a long way from a patent. Luckily, I have my own forge, gravity-fed pipes, and the Loire."

"And an ingenious mind."

Jacqueline smiled weakly. "So, tell me where they've gone. I would have sworn that man would not be able to move before tomorrow, yet you tell me he carried off Angélique as if she were a puppy."

"No, I believe his strength was born of panic. It speaks well of him that he tended Angélique rather than leave her wounded."

Jacqueline smiled again, hearing the echo of Angélique's earlier words, *"You speak well enough of him."*

"They are outside Paris, to the south and east. All forests and hillsides. Very well hidden."

"But you found them." Jacqueline sounded doubtful.

"I *can* find them," Elif corrected. "My question to you, kizim, is this: Do you really want to go with me into the den of this serpent who is now your enemy? Angélique is safe."

"But you said they shot her!"

"And she has already healed. You have seen for yourself the power of this magic. A simple bit of shot will not kill her. If I go myself, alone, I can find her, speak with her, and know her mind, all unseen. And I might also learn what Draganov plans with his machines and Mirrikh's spells. I have a deeper experience."

Jacqueline shook her head. "I need to go. I have to know for myself my sister is safe. Papa would be devastated if I let anything happen to her. Again! No, I must be there with her. She's — she's my sister. I promised I would keep her safe. She needs me."

Elif nodded in sympathy. "This I understand. But it means we must travel slowly and cautiously."

"I have a carriage and a stable of horses," Jacqueline said with a frown. "But I don't have gaited horses for any great distance. It's over one hundred kilometers to Paris. Four days — far too long. We might take my coach to Paris, arrive before morning, and travel from there. Then…"

"Yes, then?" Elif screwed the tap closed and sank under the water.

With her silence, Jacqueline succumbed to the exhaustion that should have overtaken her long before. Easing back and closing her eyes, she relaxed to the sound of water splashing in Elif's tub. From outside, the frogs' unique chorus of quacks and squawks began, for the sun had left the hillside. The sweet aromas of roasting garlic, basil, and thyme permeated the room, rising from Marthe's kitchen.

Elif hummed, a melody that wound itself around the modal scale Jacqueline had heard in the Islamic calls to prayer from minarets in Algeria and Spain.

Jacqueline and Angélique had been eight then, playing cache-cache among the market stalls, hiding in baskets, driving their umpteenth governess to a nervous collapse. With her ear for music, Angélique could mimic those muezzins exactly and repeat the melodies on the piano in her compositions well enough to impress her music master. And the dancing! Even as a little girl, she had grace and beauty to her form. The muezzins would call out over the city, and Angélique would strike a pose and begin an impromptu ballet. The Musselmen scolded them, and thinking of it now, Jacqueline suddenly understood the blasphemy they had committed. But the memory was no less beguiling, Angélique dancing and Jacqueline trying to imitate her, the two of them falling together giggling.

She was surprised to realize tears streamed down her cheeks, and she straightened up as if awakening from a faraway dream. She poured water over her face to clear her vision and found the bath water tepid.

Elif was gone, and either she hadn't even left footprints, or Jacqueline had daydreamed long enough that they had dried.

"Zut alors! How does she do that?"

There was a tap at the door. "Your visitor has arrived, Jacqueline," Marthe said. "A gentleman. Alain de Guise, his card says."

De Guise! The man was persistent. At that moment, Jacqueline didn't know whether she should be annoyed or flattered, but his visit was untimely. Still, a thrill ran through her when she heard his name.

"I believe he has stolen your velocipede," Marthe continued. "I would send for the prefecture, but the salon is still not fit for viewing."

Jacqueline chuckled. "No, no. He's an acquaintance. Show him to the study. Have him stay for dinner and prepare a room."

"Yes, yes. You don't have to ask twice," the woman grumbled as she went away again, muttering complaints about keeping track of the comings and goings.

Jacqueline looked around again for Elif, but the woman had disappeared along with her clothing. Jacqueline had no way of knowing whether the janissary would return.

She finished her bath and dressed for dinner in a lilac gown that made her grey eyes appear somewhat less dull. Without Angélique's assistance with her thick, unruly hair, she made two simple braids to loop below her ears and weave together into a chignon atop her head. Certainly not enough curls for the demand of the occasion, but Jacqueline was never one to worry too much about fashions or styles. If simplicity was good enough for the young Victoria of England, who was she to challenge royalty? A fresh spray of tea roses and a gold ribbon finished the coiffure.

She studied her presentation in a full mirror and frowned. Tuckered or décolleté? Angélique would have insisted on décolleté, but she was not Angélique. Still, the off-the-shoulder fashion and short, tight sleeves made her muscular arms look too manly and exaggerated her large, callused hands. She decided a light silk shawl and matching gloves would cover the multitude of flaws she viewed in the mirror.

The dinner bell rang as she descended the stairs, and de Guise emerged from the study, the golden curls along his brow still damp from washing road dust from his face. His eyes lit up in wonder when he saw her, and his smile widened. She probably would have laughed if she had been in a better mood. Jacqueline couldn't deny a twinge of delight at his greeting after worrying about her appearance.

He extended his hand. "Madame Duval."

"Monsieur de Guise," she answered with a more graceful curtsy than her last and allowed him to kiss her hand.

"Alain," he reminded her.

She took his arm, wagging her head. "How do you come to be here this evening?"

"I've come to return your velocipede." He pointed to the entrance hall, where her MacMillan leaned against the half-table for receiving. "You said you had left it at the Polytechnique, so I fetched it. I hope you don't mind I rode it in from Orléans. I owe those polytechs of yours a debt of gratitude for their masterful installation of coils on a base below the saddle. What a brilliant piece of engineering. Will you patent it?"

"I don't think so. France hasn't yet accepted the velocipede as something a Frenchman should deign to use."

"Well, I believe you should. This Frenchman would be more than happy to finance it."

She smiled distantly. "I have too much else to occupy my thoughts, monsieur. By any chance, do you bring news of Letronne?"

"There's no change, I'm afraid, but he is well looked after," he replied. "What were you working on with him?"

She shrugged. "It's not important anymore. Come, our dinner awaits."

Jacqueline led de Guise into the family dining room, a less formal setting than the grand banquet hall her father had insisted on keeping despite the fact they hadn't used it since the girls' début ball the season they turned fifteen. The modest table was set and laden with appropriately light summer fare of roast poulet à l'ail, pommes dauphines, roasted tomatoes, haricots verts, and a bowl of sliced fruits. Jacqueline took her place at the head of the table with de Guise to her left. He glanced at the seat of honor to her right, which Marthe had set out in the event Angélique returned, but he took his assigned place graciously. As she discreetly removed her gloves and set them and her hands in her lap, he spooned modest helpings onto her plate before serving himself.

Marthe swept in and deposited a pitcher of clear water between them and two unlabeled bottles of wine in the center of the table. "The '36," she said, and as quickly as that was gone again.

"Ooh!" Jacqueline reached for a bottle, then, thinking better of it, handed it to de Guise to pour. "One of our better recent vintages," she told him.

"Chenin?" He poured a small measure of the amber wine, swirled it, and tasted. He blinked in surprise. "A blend?"

"No, a varietal. Our very own. It also makes a light méthode champenoise. Perhaps if you are very good, I'll tell you."

He filled their glasses, nodding his approval of the wine. "I shall endeavor to earn your trust. But I would believe it was created by the lovely fairies for whom this château is named and who seem to run the machinery around here. Is this a family home?"

"My father was awarded the Legion of Honor for his work, which is why we have so ungainly a full name, but no, we are bourgeois here."

"The true glory of our king is that he recognizes the bourgeoisie as worthy of honor. I have no doubt you will earn such an award yourself one day. Dame Jacqueline, Chevalière de la Forge-à-Bellesfées."

"Goûtons voir si le vin est bon!" she sang, the rest of the line of a drinking song. She laughed.

He didn't. He raised his glass to her, and she blushed with a sudden rush of warmth.

"I wonder, if I may ask, have you had any progress with that mechanical beast you recovered the other day?"

Jacqueline bit her lip. How much to tell him? The automaton would lead to the intruder, and to the skull, and then Elif, and then Count Draganov Dragul. It was all connected, and she couldn't see involving an outsider, particularly with Angélique missing.

"A little," she said. "I was distracted by my unfinished business in Paris. And my sister's unexpected absence." She indicated the empty place setting.

"You have a sister? The telegraphic. Is that what upset you so?"

Jacqueline caught herself again. Already she had told him something he hadn't known. "Angélique. She was due home a few days ago. She hasn't arrived. We have no word." She forced a smile. "So, if I seem less than —"

"Jacqueline." He closed his hand over hers and looked into her eyes. "You are never less than."

Her cheeks blazed at his flagrant attempt to charm her, but at that moment, she needed that much comfort. She patted his hand gratefully but quickly withdrew her rough hands to her lap again.

De Guise took over the task of entertaining, regaling her with stories of his time as an agent along the developing railroad lines and the more outrageous behaviors he had seen along his journeys, keeping her laughing between bites. He likewise kept her wine glass full until the bottles were empty and then made sure water cut the wine to the brim of her glass with each sip she took. Thus, the evening wound down slowly, and Jacqueline barely reckoned the passing time.

"Mademoiselle?" Luc's paternal voice broke in.

She startled. The housekeeper stood in the doorway. The lamps were all lit, and the table had been cleared without her noticing any of it being done.

"Oh, my. We haven't even had our brandies. I am so sorry."

"Marthe has prepared rooms for the gentleman," Luc informed her, hinting more than stating it was past time to retire.

"Of course," she responded, rising, and de Guise rose with her. "Luc will show you to your chambers and take your clothes to be cleaned."

De Guise sized up the stalwart housekeeper and demurred. "I wouldn't want to put anyone to extra—"

"This way, monsieur, if you will follow me." Luc's deep voice carried the weight of insistence.

De Guise took Jacqueline's hand in both of his and kissed each of her fingertips. "Until the morning, then."

Perhaps it was the wine, but the gesture took her breath away. Not for the first time that evening, she regretted her harsh calluses. She swallowed, pulling herself together.

"No, I'll come with you," she said, snatching his hand and pulling him along behind her. "You may need instruction on using my water closet."

He stopped short, and she rebounded into his arms. Solemnly, he looked deep into her eyes and said, "I assure you I've known how to use a W.C. since I was very young."

A sudden image of a four-year-old Alain de Guise using a typical W.C. struck her as hilarious. She tittered, then giggled. Laughter brought with it a release of all the tension of the day. Delight rose to her head in effervescent bubbles. When he joined in, his laugh deep and resonant, she nestled against him happily, savoring the heat of his hands on her back easing away the knots in her spine. A sensation new and intriguing dizzied her thoughts. Her father often hugged her this way, as did Luc, wrapping her in their arms, gently embracing her, comforting her. Why did de Guise's arms feel so much more secure, so much more healing? Was it the pounding of his heart beneath her cheek? The scent of his soap and cologne mingled with the savory smell of… Jacqueline blushed but clung to him. What she wouldn't give to be able to unburden all she carried in her heart to him, even the growing attraction she felt, an emotion she could not explain or justify to herself, a fact that evaded analysis. She patted his chest with both hands and reluctantly pushed herself away. His hands lingered on her shoulders.

"Jacqueline?"

"De Guise—"

"Alain."

She nodded. "Alain."

"Until morning."

He followed Luc up the stairs while she watched him go with regret. Another time, another day—any day that didn't involve ensorcelled skulls and aeronautic pirates and clockwork behemoths and so much blood on the salon floor—that day she would gladly give him.

"Sleep now, kizim," Elif said, appearing at her side from the darkness. She wrapped her arm around Jacqueline's waist.

"But I—don't—I have to—"

Her protest faltered when she realized how exhausted she truly was. Leaden limbs failed her, so Elif guided her up the stairs and played lady's maid, helping her out of her clothes and into bed.

"I could sleep for a year and a day," she said with a yawn, still grinning.

Elif closed the lantern on her bedside table and leaned over to kiss her brow. "Sleep then."

"Oui, Maman." Jacqueline giggled again, then sighed, then slept.

After a heavy, dreamless sleep, Jacqueline woke to the dawn chorus of birdsong burbling up from the forest: shrills of sparrowhawks, piccolo trills of finches and tits, peeps and chirrups of nuthatches and pipits, accompanied by the drilling of spotted woodpeckers. Closer to her window, a white wagtail nattered cheerily like a gossiping villager. With a wide yawn, Jacqueline stretched luxuriantly in the warmth of the rising sun.

It took a second yawn to remind her of all she had to weigh this morning. She jumped from her bed to see to her toilette. Scenes of wonder and delight from the night before played over in her mind as she washed, but the unprepossessing face in the mirror of her vanity reawakened her doubts. "Vanity" — the perfect word for women who saw anything better in the glass than what they truly were.

Perhaps Angélique's assessment carried more weight than she had granted: She must have misread the signs. De Guise... so attentive, so flattering, so intoxicating. Why would any man be taken with that face?

Still, one must entertain one's guests. Tossing aside her usual work clothes, she headed to her wardrobe to decide on a color of day dress.

A carriage crunched along the macadamized drive away from the château. Jacqueline poked her head out the window in time to see her cabriolet disappear into the woods.

"De Guise?"

The face in the mirror decided for her. Throwing on a set of coveralls, she trudged downstairs to the kitchen, where Marthe set a plate of brioches and a bowl of coffee at a corner seat.

"I see that long face." The housekeeper pinched her chin. "Can't say I blame you. I don't trust that one. Prowling the grounds in his nightshirt at dawn? After that new machine of yours, maybe, like the other one? What have you girls gotten yourselves into this time?"

Prowling the grounds? Jacqueline glumly smeared a huge dollop of red currant jam on the pastry, unable to make any comment that wouldn't earn a towel snapped at her mouth. Hope rekindled when she wandered out to the foyer and saw an envelope addressed to her in a tight script. Her breath hitched as she tore the letter out and read:

> *Dearest Jacqueline,*
>
> *Forgive my early departure, but I must be in Orléans to attend to some business before taking the return train to Paris once more. I hope you do not mind that I have pressed your young Jean-Paul into driving me to the city. I fervently hope to see you again soon, as my affairs allow. Meanwhile, the next time you find yourself in Paris, do not hesitate to call upon me. I can be reached at my office in the Gare d'Orléans, across from the Pont d'Austerlitz, if I am not en route.*
>
> *Cordially,*
> *Alain*
>
> *P.S. You might have warned me about your roving automatons. One made off with my boots and I had the devil of a time hunting them down.*
>
> *P.P.S I should have taken your advice about the W.C.*

The relief his note elicited ameliorated the ache of disappointment she felt at his leaving. At least, she consoled herself, he was not "prowling," as Marthe had put it, but tracking down the automated boot-black. On the other hand, what if that was merely an excuse to spy out her workshop to gain what that other fellow could not? *"Fervently hope to see you again."* Yet, he had scampered without even saying goodbye.

So her thoughts vacillated, like a schoolgirl plucking a daisy, *he loves me, he loves me not,* except Jacqueline's petal-plucking tried to determine whether *he's polite* or *he's a scoundrel.* At the end of an hour, she had yet to know the answer. Piqued at being abandoned, she went in search of Elif but found no sign of her on the grounds. Had she also gone on to Paris without her? Jacqueline slapped her work gloves against her thigh in frustration and headed to the only place she knew to find peace.

Luc and Jean-Paul had returned the bronze man to the workbench. Removing the helmet and slipping her hand inside, she explored the piping that had held the skull. To her frustration, she found nothing within her reach but had no way of getting deeper into the belly of the thing unless she opened the torso to see what sorts of engines those gauges on the helmet monitored. She gave the body a good thump. It rang with a hollow, metallic *bong!* She assembled the fusion welder and set to work melting the rivets.

Once the torso finally cracked open enough to slip her arm inside, her hand met only the single pipe on which the skull had rested. She winced with the effort to push farther down, to no avail. Despite twisting her arm this way and that, all she found was the pipe.

"I don't understand," she muttered. "The engineer said the thing ran. The gauges were tipped to red. The heat—"

"No. The power." Elif was at her side, peering over her shoulder.

Jacqueline jumped, then yelped, her arm now caught at an uncomfortable angle. Elif gripped the breastplate and easily lifted it enough for Jacqueline to retrieve her arm. Rubbing the pinches and creases, she scowled.

"What power?"

"The power of a soul. Summoned. Captive. *Controlled!*" Elif reached into the top of the automaton and, with a quick motion, retrieved the curious shaft of piping.

Jacqueline examined the pipe. "It's split. From the inside."

"Yes." Elif handed it to her.

The tear was uneven as if the length of metal had exploded. She glanced up and met the pasha's eyes. "The spirit of the person whose skull—"

"Yes."

Jacqueline blew out a breath. For the first time, she felt hope spark her thoughts. "Contained in too small a vessel to hold it."

"*Enslaved.*"

"Yes. Commanded to operate this machine, I know. That's what led me to believe Count Draganov deliberately sent this machine to cross my path." She waved the split pipe wildly. "But if that spirit had been enslaved in a cylinder too small to contain its power, and it burst its containment, wouldn't the spell be broken? Could this automaton have escaped from the Count rather than being sent by him to seek me out?"

"Indeed, if the spirit was freed from the skull, it would be free from the spell's hold upon it."

"So, this *was* all a coincidence. The Count may not know of my involvement with his machine at all, or even that this thing found its way to Angélique or to me, and that we are connected."

"Blood calls to blood." Elif tapped Jacqueline's brow. "Mirrikh worked blood magic into that skull. That blood sought his blood magic in your sister. The lackey you stopped tried to retrieve the machine without recognizing the power behind the spirit that drove it. He could not know whether the spirit would be loosed or the skull removed. He could not know you would abscond with the skull."

Jacqueline pushed her hand away. "*Bof!* Then *you* absconded with it!" She studied the pipe again. "He needed a system to contain the power. A closed system, but one that would allow the power to cycle. Re-cycle." She tried to peer into the torso. "What does it attach to? What does the power *drive* in there? There are gauges. What do they gauge?"

"Laws you have not yet discovered."

"But you have to understand, Elif. My designs. My systems. They're the perfect means to the Count's ends if he wishes to contain and reuse a source to power this automaton, a source that can't ebb. And that source—"

"Kizim! Stop for once thinking of these pipes and these machines and think instead of what they are designed to do."

Jacqueline blinked at her, confused. Then she shook her head. "I like to know how, not why. It's easier for me."

"It is safer."

"What do you mean?" Jacqueline bristled, drawing herself up. "I'm not frightened if that's what you mean."

"Good." Elif crossed her arms. "Because there will be much to frighten you."

Jacqueline blew a petulant noise. "More ghosts? More revenants? More werewolves? You must know I'm accustomed to all that by now."

"Very good!" Elif grinned. "Now ponder, güzel-kizim, why. Why make this device? Why should a lowly boyar require any such infernal machine? What can it do for him?"

That was a question she could tackle. This bronze behemoth, an iron maiden designed to torture a soul, what other use might it have? She spun about to look at the thing again.

"You said this count wants to become a European power. Clearly, he'll go to unreasonable lengths to accomplish his aim. What if this is the foundation of his army? An army of metal that can't be killed because they're already dead."

Cradling the helmet, Jacqueline recalled the terror and desperation in the eyes of the haunt she had released. Then she traced the line of the helm and along the shoulder. "Huge. Larger than any man, any soldier it would come against." Once again, she thumped the resonant chest plate. "Strong enough to resist—who knows? A cannonball?"

She bent down to study the mechanics of the legs. "See? Ball bearings. No cogs or sprockets. They run smoothly, gliding instead of ratcheting. That's how this thing came running so quickly up the track, as the engineer said. An indomitable army of metal, invulnerable and relentless, charging over the Carpathians. And the foot, broad, flared about the sides with slightly convex soles for easier running. Unless he's thinking of Russia? It's a bit of a mess these days, and the Count can't be happy the Ottomans sold Moldovarabia to them. Or Odessa! Seize the port and from there control the whole Black Sea? No. No, he's going to challenge the Tanzimat. Every other fringe group is trying to overthrow those reforms, so if he gets there first and with an army like this, he could seize the throne of Constantinople. But then—"

Plots and more plots whirled in her imagination as she grabbed the metal hand of the left arm and probed the articulated digits and wrist. "These aren't designed for operating guns. More for crushing or seizing, perhaps. There are subtle grating catches on the fingers. Climbing features. They can scale walls, so that presumes they're designed to hoist their own weight." She flexed the elbow and shoulder joints and nodded. "These are formidable soldiers, both offensive and defensive capabilities. I doubt any army could stand against them once the Count achieves his purpose. Of course, we still don't know what that purpose is. And where would he find so many skulls for an army of such numbers?"

When she turned to Elif for answers, the janissary was gone.

"Zut!"

10.

ANGÉLIQUE AWOKE AT THE SOUND OF FOOTSTEPS ON THE STAIRS. Llewellyn didn't stir. She breathed in his scent one last time.

"I hope I reached you," she murmured. "I need you to be mine."

She kissed his neck before sliding off the bed and removing herself to the privy corner behind the screen. Crouching to the floor, she breathed deeply, and as she exhaled, she dismissed her human form with a thought. A quiet groan escaped her at the sensation of hair follicles widening to accommodate her pelage. The shifting of her musculature and skeleton felt pleasurable, a slipping, gliding feeling, like sledding down the back lawn of Bellesfées as a child or skiing the slope of Mont d'Or last winter with — well, she couldn't remember who it was, lovers came and went so quickly. Her bones and tissue slid along themselves until they found the shape she loved — the wolf. The silk of her hair slid over her bare skin as it thickened and grew out into a rough mane and soft tufts. Her tail emerged from her spine and sprouted its luxuriant fur. With a final hum of delight, she arched her back.

Her metamorphosis complete, Angélique trotted to the door just as the visitor knocked quietly. She barked, waking Llewellyn. Still groggy, he called, "Come!"

The doorknob rattled, and the knock repeated, eliciting a grunt from Llewellyn. Angélique shook her head, laughing inwardly as he rose unsteadily and lumbered to the door to unlock it, then flopped on the bed without bothering to welcome his visitor.

A middle-aged man wearing glasses poked his head hesitantly in the doorway. Angélique growled a warning as he cautiously entered.

"Dr. Fleury," he announced himself, "to see to your injury?"

Llewellyn waved to dismiss him. "It's a concussion, nothing more. It hurts. I'm tired. I need rest and water."

Angélique padded over to the bed and sat beside it, panting in amusement at Fleury's timorous approach.

"Any dizziness? Vision problems?"

"No."

"Nausea or vomiting?"

"God, no."

"Hallucinations?"

Llewellyn didn't answer, but a smile spread across his face. "Just some very strange but inappropriate dreams." Then he frowned, troubled, and reached down to stroke Angélique's scruff. "Hmm. A little too pleasant."

Llewellyn's scent took on a slight bitter taint of anger. Angélique got up to sit in the corner, panting.

Fleury pulled a chair over and seated himself, and for each movement, he seemed to ask Angélique's permission. He put his hand on Llewellyn's brow to check for fever, then moved to the top of his head. "Mon Dieu, what hit you?"

"A winch." Then Llewellyn grinned and said in English, "A wench with a winch." He chuckled at the wordplay. When Fleury looked at him quizzically, he answered, "Chain, hook, heavy."

"Ah. Sit up."

Llewellyn obliged. The doctor proceeded to check his reflexes and eye movement. "And this dream?"

"Nothing. If you've quite finished?"

Fleury nodded. "As you say, you need rest and water. I'll inform the Count you shouldn't be roused for the next twenty-four hours. I'll call again."

"I'd rather you didn't."

The doctor stood, and so did Angélique, glaring at the man until he backed out the door. When she swung her head to Llewellyn, he was frowning again, studying her. Angélique trotted to him and sat, then put a paw to his knee.

He leaned over and gripped her ruff. "How did we end up together, Anyel? Did I choose you, or did you choose me?"

Reflexively, she pulled back, but he held her and drew close, so they were nose to nose.

"And how much wine did I have to give me such shameful dreams, eh? Not that much, I think, O Ma'm'selle Heals-Her-Wounds-So-Swiftly. I don't know what you did or how, but don't ever do it again."

Angélique stiffened, licking her lips in panic. She dropped her gaze and pinned back her ears. When his grip tightened, pulling her fur and jowls, she stood her ground silently.

She didn't understand him. He was angry? Because she wanted him to feel loved? No one had ever rejected her. And so defiantly! Had she whispered the wrong words? Perhaps his French was not sophisticated enough to understand what she'd said to him as he slept. Or perhaps these Welshmen had different preferences. Maybe if she had spoken in English... She wasn't sure she even knew all the right words in English. Perhaps his tastes ran to men instead of women?

"I have tried to deal kindly with you," Llewellyn said, his voice stern, like Papa scolding her when she was a child. "I didn't strike you. I've nursed you, made certain you were well treated, got food for you. Why would you turn your magic on me like that? That was most improper, Anyel. I felt—I feel violated."

Angélique whined a protest and pulled away. She slunk over to the far side of the room and lay down with a *harrumph!*

"If my assumption is wrong, I'm sorry," he continued as he followed her across the room. "Perhaps my concussion caused these unseemly images, but I doubt it." He squatted beside her and stroked her flank until she sighed and eased to her side.

"You are a magnificent creature," he said, "and I don't want to lose your favor. But let us be companions, eh?"

He massaged her ear, and she couldn't help a quiet moan of delight. Annoyed at her own easy response, she stood and shook Llewellyn off, and she walked in circles, feeling the confinement of the small room. She was accustomed to taking men as she wanted, will-he nill-he, for her own purposes, not theirs. Some, like Delacroix a few days earlier, reveled in her delights. Others became disoriented and surrendered to her. Never had anyone pushed her away.

And Llewellyn—who had bound and gagged her sister, she reminded herself—how did he dare claim the higher moral ground?

But the words he'd chosen—*improper, violated*—yes, she had used those exact words in St. Petersburg. Shame rose up in her gorge, and she barked in frustration.

Llewellyn stood and sighed. "Come on. I'll take you out to the parc."

She growled. She didn't want to be with him in any way just now. He no sooner opened the door when she launched down the stairs, racing through the château halls until she reached the courtyard.

Llewellyn called to her, but she ignored him, intent on escaping into the night. Just out, where she would not smell his sweet-salty body. Nor the Count's tobacco smoke, nor Mirrikh's obsession with blood, nor the minions' urine smell, nor the putrid stench of revenants. Just the forest, sweet rye grass, piney duff, and the alluring scents of rabbit, fox, deer, and boar. Summer.

She ran until she came to a stream. She drank long and deep, the water cold on her throat and in her belly. She stood in the flow until she had cooled herself completely, then made her way back at a leisurely pace, pausing to sniff the air and to make her presence known. As she drew closer to the château, the stench of the revenants roiled her stomach.

This madness had all begun with a tormented spirit, and now shambolic corpses surrounded her. No doubt that Persian Mirrikh was behind both phenomena. An ugly man with a blighted aura and a foul stink about him. Mirrikh behind the filthy magic, and Draganov behind Mirrikh. Draganov, father of Draganovich.

How impossible that Draganov, Llewellyn, and she and Jacky could be so entangled in such intrigue. But this could make for an opportunity she had long desired: revenge for the loss of her career. Her life, as she had known it. She had raged impotently at the world for five years. Finally, she had a goal. Tear Draganov's throat away and eat his entrails. Dare she hope his damned spawn was here in France with him? If so, what a delight to dispatch him as well.

Angélique jerked to a halt and dropped to the ground, tense, ears twitching to catch the source of her sudden wariness. These were not her own thoughts, more as if someone whispered them on the breeze and into her ear.

This *wasn't* mere happenstance. Reunited with her enemy by chance? No, there was more. A deeper connection. Mirrikh, Draganov, Draganovich. They—herself included—were all bound somehow at a visceral level.

Panting failed to cool the sudden fire in her, and her heart hammered against her ribs.

What other explanation could there be for her unique ability? A werewolf, loup-garou, a tormented being tied to the full moon, a feral life, and a bestial existence—this was not Angélique. Woman and wolf, fully aware of who and what she was, fully conscious of her actions in all phases of the moon. Lycanthrope. A metamorphosis that began after

Draganovich raped her and tore her to pieces, the long-lost clue to her condition.

She gruffed and whined as anger arose again, recalling the moment she had awakened after the attack.

The maid screamed in Russian when the dead girl opened her mutilated amber eyes and weakly asked for water. The rush of servants gawked and crossed themselves in her presence. Baronin Spransky squealed in feigned delight, trying to hide her absolute terror. "My dearest Mademoiselle Laforge, we thought you were dead! You seem — much improved."

Angélique spent those first hours in a daze. Agonizing pain dulled her senses and thoughts. No recollection of where she was or had been, nor with whom she might have been. No flashes of memory beyond her visit to the lavender patch in the medicinal garden. *"Perhaps you ingested one of our nightshades?"* No, she wouldn't have done. Another day, another two days and her flesh was somehow made whole again. Not a single mottling or scar remained.

Weeks haunting the halls of Derzhavin, no one speaking to her, servants crossing themselves as they scuttled away the other direction. Baron Spransky told her a gardener had found her after a bear attack. He apologized so profusely and wept his shame so elegantly that she forgave him at once, for fate had determined she would not die, and the baron had clearly saved her life. Yet he and the baronin kept their distance as if her survival and recovery had affronted them. Forbidden to roam the grounds, her only companion, a terrified lady's maid, since Spreicher had returned to Germany upon news of Angélique's death.

Then came word Jacky would soon arrive at Derzhavin, and in her elation, Angélique had changed.

The transformation took her alone in bed, the servant having left after delivering the Chappe telegraphic. A heady rush overwhelmed Angélique's thoughts. The room tilted as though she were dropping into herself and her skin opening up to receive her, enfold her, reshape her. Angélique had moaned in wonder and delight as if coming home after an arduous journey. Whatever preternatural or supernatural power had transmuted her shattered form into this glorious shape was beyond her comprehension. Still, it had felt so right and so wonderful that her only response was to embrace it, rolling about the bed, knotting herself up in her chemise and bedclothes, which set her to giggling, whereupon she changed back. Then she laughed even more.

But how could she tell anyone what had transpired? The servants already believed her some undead creature, while the nobles bore the onus of the death of a guest, never mind she had recovered. How would she tell Jacky? Ah, that would likely be the least of her concerns. But how would she ever tour Europe again if at any moment she might transform into a beast? How would the nobles of Vienna or Venice receive her if she could not control this change? Her eyes! What had happened to them? She was lusus naturae, a deviant of nature. Perhaps a spot at the Grand Guignol would suit her better, or Mr. Barnum's sideshow of grotesques—freaks, he called them. A *freak* of nature. She could never tell Papa. He would be so ashamed of her.

Angélique grew angry then that her career was likely at an end, angry that whatever had taken place in the villa's gardens would now reign over her existence. She wore veils to hide her deformity and remained bitterly committed to mastering her emotions to better sense when the change might occur. She spent days in her room trying to force the metamorphosis, learning how it felt, how it filled her, and how she could move within it and make it part of her.

It had never occurred to her that someone had *done* this to her. That she—Angélique Laforge—had been a *victim*.

Now, at last, the concatenation of figures became clear. Draganovich, the son of Draganov, in the company of Mirrikh, a necromancer. Draganovich, who had stalked her to the orangérie and who had demanded she be his. Who had—*ah, Dieu!*

So, she had not imagined the bestial turn the boy's features had taken nor the ferocity of claws and fangs that had obscured all memory of his savagery from her mind. Mirrikh had created Draganovich the creature, and the creature had somehow created her.

Yes, the breeze whispered.

The realization both calmed her and presented a new fear.

If Mirrikh was indeed the mystical force behind her lycanthropy, and if Mirrikh had summoned the spirit of the dead to quicken the mechanical man, her sister was in grave danger by tinkering with his infernal devices.

But should Angélique try to find Jacky in Paris or return to Bellesfées? Or stay with Llewellyn where she could keep an eye on Mirrikh and perhaps learn what devilry he was up to?

Angélique barked and gave a short moan. Horrible decisions! She rose and circled, unable to settle, huffing in frustration. There was no one she could bite to resolve her dilemma.

Except Llewellyn. He had begun this entire misadventure. Breaking into the forge. Attacking Jacky. Stealing that automaton. Absconding with her in the night! Why? She could have been safely tucked at home had he not carried her off!

Angélique dropped to the ground again to still her wild thoughts. No, not Llewellyn. He wasn't one of them. The other minions disdained him, though he had some authority over them. He had brought her with him because he feared she would die without care.

And he cared.

She trusted him. It wasn't human to trust him, but she wasn't human just now. It wasn't his scent alone that enraptured her. The way he caught her ear, the way he scritched at her ruff and shoulders. He didn't just know canids; he knew tenderness and caring and openness. And he was decent, proper, like Jacky.

How had he come to be in the company of those disgusting bastards?

The papers from Victoria put him in the service of England. Perhaps he was sent to explore the political terrain but found Draganov too dangerous to proceed unmonitored? "Especial service." As good a term for espionage as any. British spies, Ottoman magicians, Russian boyars. Angélique whined. What could one woman do in such an imbroglio, much less one wolf?

Jacky. Jacky would know what to do. But Jacky was in Paris. Or perhaps returning to Bellesfées? Angélique had no way of knowing where, or whether, or which way.

"Anyel!"

Llewellyn's voice, through the woods, sounded ghostly thin. Stupid man. He'd followed her out here despite the doctor's admonitions to rest, despite the deepening night. Angélique sniffed the air; he was not alone. *Mirrikh!* She rose and stealthily moved Llewellyn's way until she saw him on the path. Then she crouched in the brush.

"It is a mystery how she runs this far with a lead ball in her." There was a smug undertone in Mirrikh's voice that grated on Angélique's nerves and worried at the edges of her thoughts.

"It's the Jenkins breed," Llewellyn said, his voice even. "A Jenkins is headstrong and hardy. They will ignore all pain in service to their duty." She could tell by the way he bit off his words he fought to control his anger. He called her again.

"She is not well commanded, this *dog*," the sorcerer commented. "Not submissive."

"I wouldn't have her so," Llewellyn replied as he scanned the woods. "I have no use for more servants."

"But an obedient servant—"

"No dog is a servant. A Jenkins has no master, only a trusted ally. And Anyel is more than a mere dog, sir." His eyes, searching, found hers at last, and he grinned. "She is a boon companion and stalwart defender. I trust her with my life."

Angélique emerged from the brush, remembering to limp for Mirrikh's sake, but she refused to come closer while that death-monger stood beside Llewellyn, hands behind his fat little body and a self-satisfied pout to his fat face. Llewellyn approached and knelt, pressing his face to hers. She licked his ear and pawed his shoulder.

"And she knows she can trust me. With anything."

Angélique gazed coldly at Mirrikh. The blackness in his eyes wanted to swallow her. She fought her instinct to look away or huff, returning his sardonic smile with steely eyes.

Her mind made up, she fell in at Llewellyn's side.

Doctor Fleury stood in the courtyard, his twitchiness making his anger somewhat comical. Angélique growled quietly just to rattle him further.

"Rest, I said. Twenty-four hours, I said." He *tsk*ed like a chittering squirrel. "Do you suppose you haven't aggravated your condition enough? Stop!"

He put up his hand, trying to look authoritative before Llewellyn, who stood almost twice his size. "Twenty-four hours. You may not leave your bed until tomorrow night. I will make sure of it."

Llewellyn swept past him, but the doctor caught his arm. "Wait. At least—" He pressed a packet into Llewellyn's hand. "Take this.

It will help with the pain and let you sleep more deeply. No more dreams."

Llewellyn eyed the packet warily. He glanced at Mirrikh. The sorcerer spied the packet and gave a slight sneer. Llewellyn closed his hand around the medicine and nodded to the doctor. Angélique panted in amusement.

He loathes Mirrikh as much as I do.

Back in his room, Angélique was delighted to see he had provided a bowl of water for her along with some scraps to snack on. She wasn't hungry, but she was grateful. If she was to be locked in with him for a whole night and day, she'd be wanting something. She watched him undress and put himself to bed more securely. He poured a glass of water from the ewer and mixed in the powder Fleury had prescribed. As she lifted her head, she caught the floral fragrance of belladonna.

He set the glass down again and met her gaze as he had before. This time she returned it evenly.

"If I was too harsh with you, I apologize, Ma'm'selle Bleiddast. I am in your keeping now, as I was not so long ago. I swear I will keep you safe and return you to your mistress's hearth." He sighed heavily and lay down. "As soon as I figure out how."

She rose and climbed up on the bed to curl on his feet. He chuckled and sighed again. "My guardian anyel. Nos da, fy nghalon. Good night, my sweet Anyel."

In the early morning, a servant crept in quietly to leave a bowl of hot milk and breakfast on the bed table. Angélique took advantage of the open door to head down to the courtyard to relieve herself and visit the fountain for a drink. When she returned, the door was closed against her. Whining and scratching the wood to no avail, she lay down, chin on forepaws, listening to the voices of the château, measuring the new arrivals and new scents.

After a while, footsteps alerted her, and she sat up. Draganov rounded the corner and climbed the stairs. Pausing, he smiled, then approached with his hand extended. A low growl welled up in her throat, but she restrained herself and let him near. He clumsily ran his hand along the top of her head. His stained fingers stank of the bitter tobacco he smoked.

"Pretty dog."

Imbécile.

He continued to stroke her roughly. Annoyed, she shook him off and pawed at the door until he opened it and entered ahead of her.

Llewellyn lay as she had left him, and his breakfast remained untouched. She went directly to his bed and hopped up, standing over him defensively. Draganov grinned at her. He placed the Czech bulldog between his teeth and lit it, stinking up the air. Then he surveyed the room, strolling with his hands behind his back like a general inspecting his troops. He paused over the chest containing Llewellyn's clothes and possessions, then abruptly lifted the lid. Angélique snarled a warning.

"Liniște!"

Angélique grumbled, indignant. She couldn't speak the language, but she had no doubt he told her to hush.

After rooting about for a minute, he quietly closed the chest again and rose, dusting off his knees. "Hmph. Damnable thing." Without another glance at her or Llewellyn, Draganov left the room.

All this fuss and intrigue over a skull.

But now that she knew Draganov would come and go as he pleased into his guests' bedchambers, she realized she could never change again while in this château. Glumly, she lay down and licked at her pads.

11.

Jacqueline pulled off her heavy leather gloves and lifted her welding goggles up to her brow. The automaton's gauges slowly rose to a moderate level. She checked the stability of the new buttons she had added to its chest, then pressed her ear to its abdomen to hear the steady *ronronne-ronronne* of the engine she had installed.

"Eh bien, mon bonhomme," she muttered. "Allons-y."

She pressed the lowest button, and the machine sat up with no effort. A tiny puff of steam pooted out the top of its head. Another button commanded it to turn where it sat, its legs dangling over the edge of the table. With a third, it stood. Again, a small puff.

"So far, so good." She pulled down one of the levers on its side, and the mechanical man lowered its head.

Elif suddenly appeared next to her. "What are you doing with that abomination?" she cried.

Jacqueline slapped her gloves against her apron to clear dust away. "Just tinkering. A bit of clockwork, some sensors, punch cards, a bit of natural power. One never knows how it may prove useful."

Elif peered into the new face of the automaton. "What are punch cards?"

Jacqueline held up a large brass ring holding hundreds of tiny metal chips, each pocked with a pattern of holes. "Machines operate on a series of decisions," she explained. "On, off. Up, down. Left, right. A dear friend in England discovered that predictable patterns of decisions can be determined in a series of punch cards, in the same way Jacquard looms use punch cards to create a specific design. Ada didn't wish to pursue it, and her mentor Babbage disparaged her work, so their Analytic Engine never received the financing it needed." Jacqueline shook the ring to let the chips jingle musically. "I don't have a financing problem. I took Ada's work to an extreme. It's all just clockwork, but by using miniature punch cards, I can bring about a more autonomous machine, a mechanical intelligence." She smirked. "An *autonomaton.*"

Elif poked at the buttons along the torso. "That's how you created your housework machines?"

"Yes." Jacqueline turned, surprised to find it already evening. "And how have you spent your day?"

"Elsewhere. I have found your sister. As I told you, she has healed. And she seems to have formed an alliance with the man who took her."

"Alliance?" Jacqueline cried. Then she laughed ruefully. "Angélique. Yes, I know about her 'alliances,' as you say. But why that villain? Oh, mon Ange." She sighed again. "Shall we go then? The track to Paris is open. We can be at Montrouge before dawn, and I'll hire horses to take us where she is."

Elif slowly shook her head. "She is with the Count. And with Mirrikh."

Jacqueline's eyes narrowed grimly. "Good. We'll settle accounts with the Count once for all. I will not have him using my schematics to trap these souls, and I will not have him make war with my name on his weaponry."

"Then we will be heading in the wrong direction, kizim." Elif laid firm hands on Jacqueline's shoulders. "Your plans are in Paris, but they will most likely not be there for long. He will have the plans taken to his foundry in Czechoslovakia. You must disrupt their transference."

Jacqueline glared. "Angélique —"

"Does not need you just now."

"You don't understand. She's my sister," she cried. "My twin, my only sister! I can't let anything happen to her again. I can't let her be hurt like that again, and I don't know how I would hold on to my sanity if I lost her for good. And you tell me she's with the very men who —"

"She is safe," Elif insisted. "This, I swear to you. Others are not. Your friend at the university. He who would translate the spell on the skull. What happened to him? Who in Paris knows of your comings and goings and is working against you? Or have you forgotten?"

Jacqueline caught her breath. "Letronne. You're right. I should go to him."

"Who has secured your plans for you? Who is administering their transfer?"

"All right, all right, I'll go to Paris tonight," she cried, untying her apron. She dropped the apron and gloves on her worktable and headed to the door.

The autonomaton raised its head and followed a step.

Jacqueline whirled, and the autonomaton stopped. She exchanged long, uncertain looks with Elif. Reaching over, she raised the lever and lowered it again. This time she checked the gauges, but they remained steady even as the engine inside slowed and stopped. Jacqueline grinned.

"How about that? It works. Self-storing energy with limited emissions."

The mechanical man tilted its head as if trying to understand her speech.

Elif glared at her. "What have you done?"

"Just tinkering. No magic." Jacqueline patted the autonomaton's chest. "I'm just very good at this sort of thing. Thank you, Countess of Lovelace! Eh bien, Monsieur Claque. Come along, little tin-pot."

Claque followed easily despite his mass.

Shooting distrustful glances at the machine, Elif grumbled in Turkish the whole way back to the drive.

"One benefit is that Claque can load the coal hopper much more quickly than poor Luc," Jacqueline observed aloud. "And Claque won't require any more fuel for at least two days if I've calculated correctly. So, while you may complain—"

She turned to scold the Turque, but Elif had disappeared once more.

A puff of smoke popped from Claque's exhaust. "Zzzzt!"

Jacqueline scratched her head. "That's what I say."

Angélique sat up as soon as Llewellyn stirred. He reached out, wrapped his arm around her, rolled over, and grinned. Her tail wagged madly at the sight of his smile. Cotton fuzziness filled her ears, and she flopped down beside him, her skin tingling.

"I hope you've had a restful day as well," he said.

When she leaned over to lick his face, he chuckled and hugged her in return.

"Thank you for watching over me, ma'm'selle." He rose and reached for his trousers. "What do you say to some supper?"

Dinner! Yes!

She yipped and hopped off the bed to turn circles. The sounds of commotion in the château had wakened her hours ago, and the doings of Draganov and his ghouls worried her. The stink of the Count's pipe had masked any new scents.

Llewellyn yanked his trousers on and buttoned them. Then he tugged the bellpull before gathering stockings and boots to don. The servant knocked just as he finished dressing. Llewellyn unlocked the door and opened it a crack, then let the servant in. The man set down a fresh bowl of water for Angélique.

"My thanks," Llewellyn said. "Could you have a plucked chicken ready for her?"

The man nodded and left again with the empty bowl, and Angélique set to the fresh water gratefully.

"Let me see what I can do with that coat of yours," he said. Rifling through the toiletries from his trunk, he drew out a good boar-bristle brush.

Angélique stiffened and backed away, licking her lips. No one, not even Jacky, had ever groomed her as a wolf. And while she loved having her hair brushed as a woman, she had no idea what sensation she should expect in this form. She froze. Her ears flattened as he knelt beside her.

Llewellyn began at her ruff, pushing the fur up and firmly brushing it back down a little at a time. And again. Then moving over a little, and again. Then further down her back, and again. He pulled leaves and twigs and thorns from her, and again. He tugged a few knots away, but she couldn't protest. It felt wonderful. It felt *sensuous!* She dropped to the floor and rolled to her side with a contented moan. Llewellyn laughed but changed his strokes to languorous brushings, leaving Angélique panting in ecstasy.

"Well, my lady, I think you're ready for society to behold. Now it is my turn."

When he stood, she sprang to her feet and licked his hand. His lovely sweet-salty flavor blended with the taste of her fur on his skin. The commingling aroused her so much that she longed to change on the spot and take him there and then. Being human, Llewellyn was utterly unaware of the scent of her ardor as he went about his own toilet, pausing to examine his head in the mirror.

"Your mistress delivers a powerful punch," he told her, and Angélique couldn't help feeling a pang of guilt. "The swelling is down, but I have some vertigo and a bit of the collywobbles yet, so please don't let me tumble down the stairs, eh?"

As they left the room, Angélique's hackles rose, and she balked. New scents hung on the air, some of which she knew but couldn't place. She descended cautiously and pressed to Llewellyn's flank as he entered the dining hall.

"Ah, brigadier," Draganov greeted him. "Feeling better, I trust?"

"I am, thank you."

"And your *dog*. Is she well?" Mirrikh asked.

Angélique licked her lips and turned her head away at the sound of his voice. She strained, trying in vain to identify the new scents that set her on edge. She couldn't see the faces of all those around the table, more than were there the day before. Backing slowly out of the room, she glanced left and right for escape options. Llewellyn turned to her, questioning with his eyes. How could he stand so calmly amid the ring of malevolence? Angélique lurched away, trotting to the courtyard where she might listen at the open windows.

"...thoroughly. It was not in her workshop, nor in the château so far as I could ascertain," Llewellyn was saying. "That is, before I was discovered."

"Discovered and drubbed," a new voice said with a snort. "Clumsy oaf."

Draganovich!

Angelique panted, her unease solidifying into rage. Pacing, she tried to keep herself focused, swallowing her urge to snarl. How dare he call Llewellyn an oaf?

"I freely confess my failure, as I have from the start. But my point remains. The skull was not in the machine when it was delivered to Duval's château. I was there when it was brought in, and I watched her work on it. I watched her leave without the skull and slipped in after she left. The skull was not there. I searched the ground floor of the house before I was caught."

Angélique loved how easily he lied, but why did he feel compelled to do so? Once again, she wondered how he had come to be in the backwaters of Bellesfées. How could Llewellyn have known the machine would be there? The puzzle annoyed her, but she had no time to ponder it.

"And yet, *you* said it was clearly visible." Draganov seemed to direct this to one of the others. "Isn't that why you sent Llewellyn after the machine?"

Aha. Puzzle solved.

"Yes. And I will add if you had told me to retrieve the skull and abandon the machine —"

Angélique knew the voice but couldn't place it. It must have been someone on the Paris-Orléans, but who? It didn't sound like Delacroix. Wait… Was it de Guise? A growl rose in her throat.

"Yes, yes. It is done."

"There is another possibility," Mirrikh suggested, "one which I hope is not so: that the skull shattered during its rampage or transport and lies in pieces within the machine itself."

"And how long would that set us back?" Draganov demanded. "Days? Weeks?"

A heavy silence signaled the gravity of Mirrikh's comment. Angélique felt a spark of hope catch within her. She knew the skull rested in Jacqueline's safekeeping. But if these men believed it to have been destroyed, they might abandon their search and leave her sister in peace.

"Then start again," Draganovich said. "You can use the brigadier's thick skull."

Voices rose, but over the clamor, Angélique heard Mirrikh respond.

"It is not so simple as having a ready skull. You have no idea of the powers I must invoke or the means by which I complete these tasks. It would take months of preparation and —"

"That is not my concern. I expect you to fulfill your obligations to me. I don't want excuses, and I cannot accept failure. I'm too close to the completion of this endeavor to stop now."

The protests quieted. Finally, Mirrikh said, "There may be a more accessible path."

A general shuffling of papers and chairs was followed by the announcement, "Dinner. We'll continue after."

Plates rattled. Angélique's stomach rumbled at the thought of the plucked chicken Llewellyn had commanded, but she didn't dare return to the hall with Draganovich in there. She took off once again for the parc, where she knew she could find something to bring down, following a different path from her previous jaunt in case Llewellyn tried to find her. A few kilometers into the forest, she sensed a sounder of boar, so she pursued it. She drew nearer until she heard their grunts, then crouched for a while upwind to observe.

Suddenly, her nose twitched. A new scent assailed her. Musky and forest wild. Another wolf. She suppressed a whine. She had no desire for a confrontation, especially so soon after recovering from a musket ball. Yes, she was stronger and more powerful than natural wolves, and in the past, she had held her own against the ones that roamed the parc at Bellesfées. But here she was embroiled in far too much already and could not risk adding to her peril.

She stayed quiet and waited. Soon the swine began to squeal their alarm and broke, heading straight for her. Not willing to lose a free meal, she snatched a shoat so quickly it made no sound. Gripping its throat in her jaws, she remained still, waiting for the other wolf to show itself. A second later, it sprang upon the frantic sounder.

The unnatural size of the dark wolf stunned Angélique, and she knew it in a heartbeat for Draganovich. He seized the largest boar in his claws and dove for its throat. Hot salty blood sprayed everywhere, and Draganovich thrashed the animal in a taunting display.

Mon Dieu, he hasn't changed!

While Draganovich delighted himself in tearing his catch apart, Angélique slunk away with her shoat until she could no longer smell his scent or the blood, then ran deeper into the woods. She finally came to a heavy thicket, where she crawled in to settle down with her meal. Still, her close brush left her too anxious to eat. Her skin tingled. Her stomach spasmed. The shoat lay in front of her, teasing her hunger. Though she settled her head on her paws, she couldn't help panting.

How long could she stay out here? Llewellyn would probably come searching for her eventually, although it sounded like the Count had plans for a long night of further strategies and plots. How late was it, anyway? Dark. Likely after midnight. She saw no stars from her hideaway.

But if Draganovich was here, and changed, then either the war council had ended, or the boy played no significant part. If he had stayed at the château for dinner, he wouldn't be hungry enough to bring down a boar. He had done it for amusement. Self-indulgence.

Or perhaps a show of his strength for her benefit? Had he followed her?

Night noises filled the forest: the high-pitched yowls of foxes, warbles or hoots of owls, the delicate call of nightingales, chittering insects, and gulping bullfrogs. Nothing else. Despite the cover of the thicket, she worried she should have returned to the château rather than staying in the woods. Draganovich could easily find her here. She doubted he would be able to get at her, but to be safe, she pulled the thorny brush closer around her.

If, if, if. So many ifs.

Jacky, where are you? I'm not like you. You look at knots and know how many threads there are. I'm no engineer; I'm no problem solver. I can't see my way out of this.

Jacqueline slept while Monsieur Claque stood silent sentinel during the ride to Montrouge. They arrived hours before dawn, and Jacqueline remembered belatedly her MacMillan remained back at Bellesfées. She stood bewildered, looking down the hill to Paris, shaking her head. "A few kilometers. Not far."

Before she took a step to begin the trek, Monsieur Claque picked her up in his huge arms like a child cradling a poppet. Gasping, she clung to his arm as he trotted down the road to Paris. They arrived at the Barrière d'Enfer in less than half an hour. Monsieur Claque set her down gently, and she patted his chest. "Nicely done, Monsieur Claque. I think you're going to prove very useful."

He bowed and popped a contented puff.

She hailed a fiacre to transport them through the gates, thereby avoiding the agents who doubtless would have made her pay a tariff on Claque. This way, he was merely her companion. The fiacre took them to the hospital, where they arrived as the sun rose. She escorted Monsieur Claque to the bar-tabac she had fled not two days earlier, taking a table in the dark corner at the back, ordering her usual: café-au-lait and croissant chocolat. Claque watched, his head tipped as if curious. As he reached for her cup of coffee, she slapped his hand.

"That's *my* fuel, not yours."

He retreated and lowered his head. She grinned.

"That's right. Go pout while you poot."

The patron chuckled around the cigarette that dangled from his lower lip. "Glad to see you feeling better. That's an interesting companion you have there. Where does one find such a toy?"

"They find you." She sighed, then shook her head. "But in fact, I built him. Or rather, rebuilt him, so I suppose you could say he's unique."

"Well, he's quite a piece of work. I enjoy good clockwork myself." He nodded toward the end of the bar where sat an intricate box of brass with numbered pearl buttons. "My son made it for me. Tallies. Stays locked so no one can dip a hand in. Very handy."

She smiled her appreciation. "Clever boy! He should patent it."

"That's what I told him, but he's busy working out some big project." He scratched his grizzled red head. "Keeps himself busy, my Rémy."

Jacqueline snapped her fingers. "I wonder. If you're comfortable, may I leave my Monsieur Claque here while I visit the hospital? I doubt they would let him inside."

The patron laughed. "You're right about that. Certainly, if he's well trained, he may stay. Might be Rémy will have a chance to see him that way."

"Hmm." She frowned. *Well trained?* She hesitated, then told Monsieur Claque, "Sit here and don't move. I will be back."

The autonomaton blew a puff, shifted a gear somewhere inside, and powered down. She patted his hand. "Good Monsieur Claque. Help Monsieur—?" She glanced up.

"Brodeur."

"Help Monsieur Brodeur."

"He obeys orders?"

She shrugged. "I have no idea."

And she was off to the boulevard before the man could protest.

There was little foot traffic at this hour, and the hospital was quiet as Jacqueline entered. She waved to Sister Donna Marie as she entered the ward. The cheery sister had kept vigil with Jacqueline when Letronne arrived at the hospital, offering assurances between recitals of the rosary, recounting the many instances of recovery she had witnessed.

As Jacqueline moved through the ward to Letronne's bed, the good sister followed. The bed was empty, stripped. Panic choked Jacqueline, and she turned to the sister, stricken with fear.

"Professor Letronne—" she said, unable to form the question. "He—he isn't—"

"Oh! I'm so sorry no one told you," Sister Donna Marie's beatific smile brought Jacqueline no assurance as she clasped Jacqueline's hands. "But he is in a much better place." The sister crossed herself. "God hears our prayers and answers, madame. Always," she murmured as she bustled off.

Jacqueline sank slowly to a chair, the weight of Letronne's death crushing her. So much difference in a day. What started as a curious adventure had evolved into an intrigue both paranormal and political, and now fatal. But Letronne—he had hurt no one, had sought only to help her. And now he was gone because of her foolish prying into a mystery she could have easily ignored. She should have ignored it. An engineer was not a detective.

She blinked back tears, not because Letronne did not deserve them, for he did, but because they were tears of shame, not grief. She needed her shame to fuel her, not enfeeble her. Letronne would have justice.

She hastened from the hospital, uncertain of her next steps but anxious to take them, nonetheless. She leapt the sewage trench and crossed the boulevard, but she stopped short as she turned toward the café.

Walking toward her, oblivious to the gawkers around him, was Angélique's bohemian friend Charles, an aspiring poet if she recalled correctly, a slender fellow with a dandy's sense of fashion, disheveled black hair, and a full beard and mustache. He staggered down the boulevard covered in Paris yellow mud, obviously drunk (*still? already?*) and juggling three skulls.

12.

"CHARLES!" JACQUELINE RAN TO INTERCEPT HIM. HE STOPPED, AND THE skulls clattered to the pavement. "What in the world are you doing with these?"

Charles hiccoughed as he bent down to gather them up, then began juggling again. "I thought it was obvious." He tossed one to her, chuckling. "Death, while in life, should be no less a part of it."

She examined the skull, but it was unmarked. "I mean, how do you come to have these skulls? Where should they be? Surely your delight in the Empire of the Dead doesn't extend to grave robbing?"

He leaned a hand against her shoulder, grinning into her face. "You wound me, Mademoiselle Jacky. But I forgive you. For I am in love, and when I'm in love, no one goes unforgiven." He took back the skull. "No, I found these upon the ground near a slight aperture that most likely leads to the developing ossuary below us, to speak of the Empire of the Dead. The Catacombs."

"But they're closed to the public."

He set a finger to his lips. "Which is not to say how these three escaped."

Jacqueline drew a sharp breath. *Skulls from the Catacombs! Six million skulls, at least!*

"Charles, can you show me this aperture?"

He drew himself up, wiped a finger across his mustache, sniffed, and burped. "I'm not sure. I can try to retrace my steps once I remember where last I drank."

Jacqueline snatched his lapels and shook him. "Charles, I need—I *need* you to remember!"

"Easy, easy." He brushed her off. "I remember. There was a dead crow in the road. Near … the Toreau Noir."

"Up this way, then." She headed north, dragging him with her.

"Yes. A dead crow. Legs in the air like a whore."

"Charles!"

"But pulsing with life. Don't you know? Full of maggots. I think it was crushed by a cart. It looked like it was breathing, the way the maggots swarmed within, pulsing and writhing. The irony upon irony quite fascinated me. A carrion bird, itself carrion, dead but appearing to be full of life. Much like this city. Modernité, my dear Jacky. Life goes on not despite, but because of the rot."

Jacqueline wagged her head. "You are one morbid soul, Charles."

"I? I'm not the one looking to climb down into the Empire of the Dead." He pointed at a streetlamp as they passed it, swaying to that side with the motion. "You'll need light."

"Yes," she agreed. "Probably more than just a candle or two. I'll work that out."

He turned her off the boulevard to a side street and then a narrower closed alley. "Here," he announced with a dramatic flourish. "Le derrière d'Enfer."

The buckled pavement had tilted up and separated from the street. Where they had once met, a long opening had caved inward, just wide enough to let a slender body pass. Jacqueline stooped to examine it and found the yellow earth worn smooth.

"Someone comes through here regularly. It must be fairly usable then." She stood and wiped her gloves. "I'm almost willing to hazard there are candles and lanterns stowed just inside the entrance, but I won't wager my life."

She went back to the boulevard to get her bearings and pointed west. "Rue Saint-Georges it is."

Charles held back and bowed. "Not I. I have a rendezvous to keep with my beloved. I wish you good fortune on your hunt, Jacky."

She hurried back to him and kissed him on the cheek. "You have been an invaluable help to me, Charles. Thank you."

He blushed furiously but grinned as he saluted her and walked away. He began to whistle, indulging in the shocked glares of passersby.

Jacqueline headed back to the Barrière d'Enfer and hailed a fiacre. She stopped first at her house to change into clothing more appropriate for exploring the tunnels below the city.

Suitably attired, she then took another fiacre to Rue Saint-Georges, number 10. No more than a run-down barn, really. The temporary home of the "Adolphe Sax Musical Instrument Factory."

Entering the factory redolent of mineral oil, solder, and burnt brass—all the fiery, bitter, metallic smells of a comfortable workshop, Jacqueline moved past the many worktables crammed into the small building, each occupied by three or four workers assembling saxhorns. Like a veritable brass band in waiting, one table held basses, both E♭ and BB♭, another held euphoniums, baritones, each to its own space in various stages of assembly. She barely had room to pass through, there were so many tables. Briefly, she lingered beside the worktable containing her personal favorite, flügelhorns, daring to trail a finger along the scrollwork on a bell, recalling the sensual effect the instrument had evinced in her when the virtuoso Jacques d'Île had rendered several nocturnes and preludes in concert one en-chanting evening *chez* Liszt. Her lips quirked in a faint smile as she moved forward past the cornets and a particularly crowded table filled with the bells of Sax's pet project, the darling of the more radical composers, the saxophone.

Fortunately for her, due to the current conditions of his workshop, Adolphe Sax was willing to interrupt his work on musical instruments of his own design to cast brass tubing and sheets for her to bring in extra funds, hoping to soon buy himself a real foundry.

As she moved through the factory, she could hear Sax on the far side, engaged in a lively discussion with an older man. They broke off as Jacqueline approached.

"Duval!" Sax greeted. "Meet Hector Berlioz. Jacqueline Duval."

Berlioz kissed her hand perfunctorily, then took a second look at her, assessing her odd habiliment. Shrugging, he returned to Sax. "In any case, do not be surprised by commissions from Germany as I complete my tour. Will you be able to handle them?"

Sax waved him off. "Of course! Absolutely! By November, I'll own half this block, I'm sure of it."

"Good." Berlioz shook his hand enthusiastically. "Until my return then, my friend."

He strode out of the factory while Jacqueline shook her head. "Sax, you know you can't—"

"Tut!" Sax stopped her. "You have no idea what I can and cannot do."

She smiled wryly. "I know you're broke." She reached into the inner pocket of her coat and brought out a wad of francs, which she pressed into his hand. "I hope this helps."

"Every sou, each écu," he replied with a grin. "Where shall I deliver your order?"

She gave him the address. "One more thing, if I may, Sax. I need a lantern. A Mueseler, if possible. Do you have one to lend?"

He wagged his head, chuckling at her. "You are the strangest woman, Madame Duval."

But he did indeed have a safety lantern for her, and she came away satisfied, more so because she had managed to leave his shop before he started playing some new incarnation of his saxophone for her. She much preferred his flügelhorn.

Jacqueline debated returning chez Brodeur to retrieve Monsieur Claque, but she realized the huge machine wouldn't fit down the gap in the street. Crossing her fingers that her mechanical friend wouldn't cause any chaos, she headed back to the alley and the furtive entrance to the Catacombs.

The night dragged. Angélique had no way of marking time. Her ears flicked forward and back, and she paused in her panting every few seconds to sniff the air. No sense of Draganovich as a wolf, nor the scent she had picked up back at the dinner party, assuming that was the familiar odor that had pricked her memory. Unless that was the mysterious train passenger? She pawed at the piglet and finally gave in to her hunger, eating slowly, deliberately holding onto her focus. Still, though nothing disturbed her meal, her anxiety kept her from settling, and she vomited much of it up again. Now she was stuck in the thicket with a stinking puddle in front of her.

Don't whine! Don't whine! Don't let him —

"Anyel!"

She froze.

"Time to come in," Llewellyn called. "It's almost morning, and I need to sleep."

He was close. How had she missed that scent?

"And I'll not sleep without you on watch, Blaiddast Da."

Angélique inched her way through the thicket and emerged just as Llewellyn came into view. The sky was pale indigo; dawn approached. She stood and shook out her coat, trying to get circulation back into her joints.

He halted, fists on hips. "You're a mess. What have you gotten yourself into?"

She snorted and *whoofed*. *That's what I keep asking myself!* Not that he didn't look just as bedraggled. His hair had come loose from its ribbon, he was jacketless, and his shirt hung open. He looked and smelled absolutely ravishing.

"And I spent all that time grooming you." He clucked. "Come on, let's go back to it. We have a long day today. Heading to Paris."

She sat and whined, looking about. No sign or scent of Draganovich. Llewellyn came forward and knelt, embracing her head and rubbing her ears. She laid her muzzle on his shoulder. It was like coming home to something familiar, warm, and safe.

Today. I'll tell him today. We'll go back to his room, and I'll change and tell him everything!

Llewellyn brushed away the debris from her coat and checked her for ticks. Then he rubbed down each of her limbs and her ribs to assess any injuries. "No worse for the wear," he declared. "You had me worried, though." He embraced her again and roughly scratched her back. "I've lost too many things these past few days. I don't want to lose you too, my beauty. What would your mistress say if I don't bring you home?"

He patted her hindquarters and stood. She jumped up on him and licked his lovely face, rubbing against his wonderfully scented chest hair. He laughed.

"You're going to spoil me, ma'm'selle. Let's go."

She trotted easily at his side, eager to get back to his room with him so she might reveal her other form and speak to one another at last of their roles in this larger-than-comfortable plot. Among other things. These hopes were dashed when they left the forest to discover a coach-and-four waiting on the lane, the door open and the steps lowered for them. Angélique grumbled her dismay, then growled when she sensed Draganovich within. She halted.

"Hmm. I thought we'd have more time." Llewellyn held the door for her. "Ah, well, so much for sleep and a good shave. Up we go, girl."

She balked and snarled at him. Nothing could induce her to get in the carriage with that monster, even in his human form.

"Hurry it along, Gryffin. We've too much to do in Paris."

The sound of Draganovich's voice put her hackles up. As Llewellyn reached for her, she backed away, baring her fangs.

"Leave it. Father will get suspicious if we don't make the rendezvous. If we're caught in Paris traffic, we won't have enough time to search for the damned skull."

"She comes with me," Llewellyn answered. He turned to her again and met her accusing gaze with a calm but firm regard. "We must. Please."

Words spun in her head. *Father will get suspicious.* What could he mean? Was Draganovich working with Llewellyn against his own father? But he had sneered and called the Welshman a clumsy oaf just last night. Was that an act? *I don't want to lose you, my beauty.* Llewellyn would keep her safe. *We have a long day today.* Was the plot finally coming to fruition?

While her thoughts distracted her, Llewellyn caught her by the ruff. She wriggled and fought to get free, but he forced her into the carriage and climbed in behind her, hauled up the steps, and shut the door. The coach took off. Angélique hopped on the empty bench and stood, glaring at Llewellyn and then at Draganovich beside him.

In the five years since St. Petersburg, Draganovich had lost some of the attractiveness of his adolescence. His shaggy head of black hair framed a full, squarish face, still with the fringe beard and sparse mustaches. Even seated, he rose taller than Llewellyn, but he was heftier, broader in the chest. He still wore those foppish octagonal sun-glasses. When he fixed them upon her, his frown deepened. She looked away and panted.

"Gryffin, that's not a dog."

Llewellyn grinned. "I know. I told you she was stunning."

"She is indeed." Draganovich turned to the window.

Llewellyn switched over to Angélique's seat and coaxed her to sit by him. She kept her eyes on Draganovich, growling low under her breath. Llewellyn wrapped his arm around her and pulled her head onto his lap, smoothing back her ears and scritching lovingly under her jaw. Still, she remained tense.

"So, what did Brodeur have to say?" Draganovich asked.

"Nothing substantive. He hasn't been able to figure out how the prototype turned rogue and destroyed the others in the batch at Orléans."

"I'll remind you we haven't either," Draganovich replied, "although I have my suspicions. No… my beliefs."

"And I don't dismiss those. With all I have seen that ghoul do, it makes sense one of those poor souls would rebel. I'm surprised it's not more."

Draganovich closed his eyes. "You should have known her. Wise. And kind. But she didn't tolerate fools, and she didn't tolerate Mirrikh. Or what he'd done."

Is that regret in his voice? Sorrow? For whom?

"How the machine ended up on the Paris-Orléans tracks is another mystery."

Draganovich glanced back to Angélique. "A mystery that's becoming clearer. Blood calls to blood."

"What do you mean?"

"Nothing." He turned away again. "Gryffin, you have to leave the wolf behind."

Angélique rumbled a warning, and Llewellyn renewed his petting to try to calm her.

"What are you keeping from me?" Llewellyn returned. "Because I won't leave her without reason."

"Mirrikh will take her head."

"What are you talking about?"

"Tell me you haven't noticed the bastard's keen on her."

Angélique's ears pricked up and flicked.

"You mean he wants to use *her* skull instead of the other?" He hugged her again as she growled at Draganovich. "Why would he want a wolf?"

"And tell me you haven't noticed she is unique. Tractable. Intuitive. Empathic."

Llewellyn remained quiet. Draganovich stubbornly refused to look at him or Angélique, though his hands knotted, and he knocked lightly against the window.

"I tried to frighten her away. Last night. Mirrikh kept pushing and pushing about her, and I assumed she was merely a dog you'd picked up along the way. That would be just like you, wouldn't it? Stray dogs and damsels in distress. So, I thought I'd chase her off. Any dog or ordinary wolf would have run. Long gone from here. But your wolf is not ordinary, is she?"

Draganovich suddenly turned and looked deeply into Angélique's eyes. Voiceless words filled her head.

Did Mirrikh make you?

She recoiled and whined. How was he doing that? His voice *inside* her? She shook her head furiously. *No! How dare he!*

I don't know how this happened to you. I don't know what sorcerer made you this way, but I'm so very, very sorry, you can't stay with us. You're in grave danger if you remain.

Not only the words but the depth of compassion in the young man's expression shocked her. She panted, confused but at ease at the same time, seeing his weakness.

I know this existence is wretched. I hope you have found peace in your life. I wish I knew how this hap —

Ah, that was the Draganovich she remembered. *I, I, I.* She lunged. Llewellyn caught her back before she reached her nemesis. She hoped she had the same mental powers he had demonstrated as her thoughts flew up in a tsunami of rage.

It was YOU! You did this! You ripped into me. You tore me apart. You slaughtered me. You raped me and left me to die. But I didn't die, did I? Are you saying you didn't know this would happen? Are you saying you're sorry for making me? I don't care what your aims are now; I will never forgive you, and I will have my revenge.

Draganovich's eyes widened, and his swarthy skin, grey to her eyes, yellowed as he paled. He slowly sat back again, his clenched fists trembling. "Where did you find this wolf?"

Before Llewellyn could answer, Angélique sent a howling scream into Draganovich's mind. He cried out and doubled over. He covered his ears to no avail. Her scream intensified, and he writhed in agony.

Ah, the sound I could not make when you ripped my throat out!

"Good God, Toma, what's wrong?"

The sound I made when I discovered what you had done to me!

Draganovich grunted and banged his head into the back of his seat. Angélique kept screaming.

You've never made that sound, have you, little dragon? Little serpent? Little worm?

Draganovich curled to his side, clutching his head. "All right! You can stay! Stop! Stop!"

The coach jerked and slowed, then halted. Angélique broke off her attack. She lay her head down on Llewellyn's lap again, satisfied with her results. She couldn't stop licking her maw and menacing Draganovich with low growls.

"Are you going to explain?" Lewellyn asked after a tense moment.

Draganovich groaned. He rapped on the transom and told the driver to ride on. The coach pulled away again. He took several slow breaths before he could speak. Angélique panted happily, pleased with the effect she had inflicted on her first try.

Yes, little worm. Explain.

Draganovich sighed. "Very well. Be ready to hold her."

He peeled away his travel coat, jacket, and waistcoat. Angélique watched with growing anxiety as he made clear his intentions. She whined and scrabbled away, but Llewellyn pulled her close and held her more tightly. When Draganovich unfastened his pants, Llewellyn cleared his throat.

"Patience, my dear friend." Draganovich covered his nudity with his coat. He looked to Llewellyn, then to Angélique. "No one else but my father and, of course, Mirrikh knows of this. And until today, I did not know it went any further."

He changed.

Llewellyn tensed at the first spasm. He tried to reach for his friend, but Angélique nipped his hand to stop him. As he watched the familiar face distort to animal grotesquerie, Llewellyn's heart skipped a beat, then thudded in alarm. She snarled in anticipation when Draganovich slid to the floor of the coach. Beneath his coat, muffled growls and groans accompanied his transformation. Llewellyn made incoherent noises, wrapping his arms around Angélique and trying to hold her away from whatever was happening before his eyes.

"Tell me this is a dream," he murmured.

Draganovich, the wolf, rose up.

Angélique lunged at her nemesis. She bit his ear. He yelped, but he didn't snap back. She then gripped his throat and pushed him into the corner of the carriage. She held him there, snarling and digging into his neck, ignoring Llewellyn's efforts to rein her back. Draganovich growled, but Angélique pressed until he yiped his surrender. She released him, satisfied with the taste of his blood. He changed back, and

Llewellyn threw the coat over him again as he regained his human form.

Llewellyn trembled. He watched Draganovich dress himself and mop the blood that streamed from his torn ear and the light punctures along his neck with his shirt sleeve. They rode in strained silence for several kilometers before Llewellyn spoke up.

"Mirrikh did that to you?"

He nodded.

"And to her?"

"No." Draganovich groaned. "I made her."

"You — *made* her? What do you mean, *made* her?"

"I don't know how or when. And I never knew that could happen. I was too young to realize —"

Angélique growled again.

"I mean, I was too young to know what could trigger my change or how to manage my instincts. And I never believed I could pass this along."

And he still didn't know her? That could only mean he had attacked others and left them for dead. Had they also turned?

Angélique took up the corner away from the two of them, satisfied she had made her position clear. Llewellyn — well, he would have to accept her or not. If not, she had only to leave the pair of them, as Draganovich had suggested. But she would still have to get to Paris somehow, and a coach-and-four was as easy a means of transport as any for avoiding the entry tariff. Besides, she would need clothing if she was to be out and about in the city. She couldn't change here, and she wouldn't leave without knowing the outcome of their plot.

Llewellyn watched her, probably trying to decide what to make of the stunning revelations. She yawned anxiously and looked away from him, licking her lips with a soft whine. Was he disgusted, having slept with a freak of nature at his side? Horrified? Sickened? Angry? She glanced back at him, then looked away again.

Finally, Llewellyn began to stroke her head and ears, and she almost dared to relax. He pursed his lips. "Does this — metamorphosis hurt?"

"No."

"What was that pain you experienced, then?"

The other shrugged. "Shared thoughts. We can communicate. I tried to apologize. She doesn't forgive me. I don't blame her. I don't forgive myself. There can be no forgiveness for what I've done to this girl. Subhan Allah wa bihamdihi. Allah is all-compassionate and all-compassionating. But I am not worthy of such compassion."

"I don't understand how—"

"Nor do I. It likely has to do with mingled blood. When I was a boy, I was very ill, very weak, all the time. Healers had no idea what they were dealing with. My governess kept me alive through prayers and healing tinctures and ointments, but my father wasn't satisfied. He wanted me strong. So, he brought in Mirrikh. The next thing I knew, I was this — *thing*. And it ruled me. I was a boy. I didn't understand. And I don't know how—she—I—"

He continued to stare bleakly out the window, avoiding the glares of the other two.

"Mingled blood," Llewellyn repeated. "You blooded her?"

Draganovich squeezed his eyes shut. When he didn't answer, Llewellyn nodded. "Well," he said slowly, "she must have her reasons for remaining in this form. Don't you, Bleidd-ddyn hardd?" He kissed her head.

Angélique breathed easier at last. She licked his hand, wonderfully salty and moist. She wanted to show him, wanted him to fully understand her, but not here, in this coach with Draganovich. She wanted Llewellyn's first look at her to be his alone, intimate. And if Draganovich couldn't figure out who she was, then damn him thrice, *the little worm*.

"Does she understand what we say?" Llewellyn asked. Draganovich nodded. "I thought so." He chuckled and tousled her ruff. "No, I knew it."

He gathered her up in his arms and hugged her. Angélique melted against him, tipping her nose up to his to lick him gently. He kissed her in return. "My lovely Anyel. I'm going to hate saying goodbye when this is all over."

She whined and nuzzled his neck. Perhaps they wouldn't have to say goodbye at all. If he could accept what she was, could he not accept her in his life? Angélique was certain she could convince him. If only she'd been able to tell him in her own time, her own way.

Another complaint against Draganovich.

13.

SURPRISINGLY, ONCE JACQUELINE SQUEEZED THROUGH THE NARROW opening beneath the sidewalk, she sat in a much wider shaft, well paved, sloping gently down into darkness. There was a handful of candles along the dirt ledge, confirming her thought this was a well-used access. She ignited the safety lantern and leaned back to enjoy the slow slide, intermittently digging her heels into the paving blocks to pause and read some of the graffiti left by miners, gendarmes, and other interlopers across the centuries from the era when this neighborhood of Paris was nothing but mines or mire. She was far enough from the celebrated ossuary that she might not encounter illicit tourists, but she knew of those like Charles, whose fascination with the macabre led them to explore the more remote corridors of the old quarries. Further, she was aware of the colonies of troglodytes who had carved themselves homes down here and of the dens of Paris's demi-monde who had made the literal underworld a convenient hideout.

When she finally reached the bottom of the shaft, which she estimated at thirty meters, she found herself in a corridor. She looked left and right but saw no clear indication of direction. Moving to the right, her foot slid into a gentle rut. She stepped back and tested the ground to the left: No rut. No wear.

"Right it is," she murmured.

The passage was amazingly clear of debris. It was an ordered world she hadn't expected. Neatly constructed arches reinforced the intersections, and the names of the streets or landmarks above marked the masoned walls, enabling her to note the route and avoid getting lost in the labyrinth. Along the cold, dank corridor, a few gated and locked niches branched off, filled with piles of bones dumped from above, down chutes similar to the one she had employed in her descent. These remains of various closed cemeteries hadn't been incorporated into Monsieur Guillaumot's original designs for the great ossuary. Otherwise, there was no indication these old quarries were connected to the Catacombs proper.

Uncertainty marked her every step. At times she was forced to double back on her route and try another direction, and eventually, doubt gnawed at her sense of purpose. Perhaps this undertaking was a mistake. Of course there would be skulls littering these tunnels. Hadn't she passed plenty of them in the niches along the way? Why presume the Count's necromancer frequented *these* particular dumping grounds to collect them for his arcane purposes? But then again, where else would he find enough skulls to power an army, as Elif had suggested he planned?

Jacqueline came to another intersection, and she paused to read the marker: "Val de Grâce." *Merde!* Only a little over a mile traversed in what felt like hours. With a groan, she leaned heavily to the wall and knocked her head against it a few times, debating her next step. No sooner had she decided to turn back when the sound of metal reverberating on metal echoed from just ahead. An angry shout followed. In a few seconds, there came another clang, this time metal on stone. And again, another shout.

The noises came from a chamber further on. Jacqueline crept forward. If she squinted, she could just make out the archway. She lowered the flame in her lantern, and when she saw a dull glow lit the arch, she closed the lantern all the way. As she drew closer, the angry shouts clarified into obscenities. Sidling along the shadows, she stopped with her back against the wall beside the archway. Here she set down the lantern and inched closer to peer around the corner.

Monsieur Claque sat on a workbench, surrounded by the tools and machinery of a foundry. A redheaded young man stooped to retrieve a wrench from the floor of a cavernous room lit with gas lamps along the wall. Beyond them, scores of bronze automatons filled more than half the hall.

"La vache!" the man cried, raising the wrench. "I made you, and I'll unmake you!"

Claque batted the wrench away; Jacqueline interpreted his puffs of steam as chuckling at the man's rage. Again, the man retrieved the wrench, but Jacqueline cleared her throat and stepped into the chamber before he could make another futile attempt at assault.

"You may have shaped his casing, monsieur, but *I* made him," she said.

Claque stood immediately and strode toward her.

"Oh, no, you don't, you—" The man hurled the wrench at Claque's head, but it simply bounced off.

Jacqueline set herself in front of Claque and faced the man. "Why have you stolen my companion? Were you thinking of taking him apart?"

He shifted his weight from one foot to the other, uncertain what to do with her or his anger. He ran a hand through his greasy hair and rubbed the back of his neck. "You? Built him?"

"No. I rebuilt him. He came to me empty. I just gave him some purpose." Jacqueline nodded to the bronze figures, recognizing their form. "You designed these for Count Draganov?" She nodded at his surprise. "And you're Rémy Brodeur."

"How'd you know that?" he demanded.

"I left Monsieur Claque here with your father, who is exceedingly proud of what you can do." She waved at the army he had built. "But then, he doesn't know everything, does he?"

He sneered. "Now I know you. Duval. Mistress of the forge at Bellesfées. Think you're so clever?"

She approached one of the automatons and peered into the face plate. The black sockets of a skull returned her gaze. "I think you're disgusting, Brodeur. Graverobber. Filth."

"Those skulls were in the shafts, not the ossuary. Unsanctified. Just rubble, really."

"They were sanctified at one time, or they would not be here at all," she argued. "All of these bones, at one time, were people. Don't you realize that?"

"They're dead. Anyway, what business is it of yours?"

"At Val de Grâce, no less. 'The Vale of Mercy.' You're horrid. Your father would be ashamed to know what you do. And I will put a stop to this."

Brodeur rushed forward, his fist raised to strike her. Monsieur Claque blocked him, wrapping his metal fingers around Brodeur's wrist and slowly hauling him up to dangle like a toy he offered to Jacqueline.

Jacqueline laughed. She poked Brodeur's chest. "It's not just the forge I master. Remember that."

Monsieur Claque released Brodeur and shoved him to fall on his backside. Brodeur glowered, pouting like a petulant child.

"Go on, get out of here. But leave that machine. I built it. It's mine."

"He was never *yours*." She turned back to Monsieur Claque and stroked his arm. "He was commissioned by Draganov, and he escaped Draganov with good reason. He's mine now."

Monsieur Claque pooted more steam and took Jacqueline's hand to lead her from the cavern.

"Putain!" Rémy shouted after her. "The Count will hear of this!"

"I hope so," she muttered.

Collecting Sax's lantern, she lit it and held it up to survey their options, but Monsieur Claque chose a direction for her and strode off confidently. She followed, equally confident in his choice. Brodeur's son must have brought him through tunnels he could navigate.

The path he chose was more cluttered than the corridors she used to come in, with un-masoned walls and uneven flooring often submerged beneath sludge and water. Jacqueline stumbled and tripped along, soaking herself and sloshing up her pants and coat. A few chutes had spilled their grisly contents into the tunnels, and she could not avoid stepping on crumbling bones and slipping on the mud of their dust mixed with lime water.

Though the water levels rose, Monsieur Claque never slowed, un-aware of Jacqueline's worsening struggles as lime covered the surfaces with a slick finish. Twice she stumbled and nearly dropped the lantern. Soon the water flooded her boots. Holding the lantern aloft threw her balance off, and every step became treacherous. Eventually, Monsieur Claque moved so far ahead that she feared she would not be able to follow should he make a sudden turn. Realizing the danger that freighted their route, Jacqueline was about to call him back when she stubbed her toe on an uplifted slab, falling headlong into the filthy water.

Submerged and swallowed in darkness, Jacqueline floundered, unable to regain her footing. Her boot soles, designed for long hours in the workshop, found no purchase. When she grasped along the floor, her hands slewed along the débris of bones. Twisting about only trapped her coat on something she could not find, no matter how she slapped for it. Muddied water flooded her ears, her nose. The burning in her lungs meant, at any moment, she would either pass out or be forced to suck in water.

Suddenly, someone seized her collar from above and yanked her up. Jacqueline exploded out of the slime and roared a deep breath, falling back against her rescuer. An arm closed tightly around her neck. Panicked, she struggled to free herself, fighting to breathe.

As a silken-soft hood covered her head, she inhaled a faintly sweet gas. Her whole body went lax. Dream-like euphoria overtook her. Then she knew nothing more.

"But now tell me, how does this put her in danger with Mirrikh?" Llewellyn asked.

Yes, good question!

Draganovich's lip twisted wryly, showing a pronounced scar. "Oh, it's always about the blood," he said. "Blood magic leaves a mark, a link. The skull in the prototype had a blood spell on it."

"Yes," Llewellyn said, nodding. "Engraved in gold at the back."

"Mixed with Mirrikh's blood. All of his spells cost him blood, including the one that made me."

"You mean he's looking for a skull imprinted with his blood, or his magic, or his—I don't know what."

"Exactly. I thought he might turn to those things he reanimated, but he said reanimating dead bodies required little effort while harnessing souls required blood and something more, a life."

Llewellyn's face darkened. "So—the prototype. She was alive when…" Again, he hugged Angélique closer. "Blackguard! I'm so sorry, Toma. Well, he can't have my Anyel."

Draganovich didn't reply.

"It occurs to me that we should return to Bellesfées and see if we can't persuade Madame Duval to surrender the skull to us now that we've turned your father's gaze to Paris."

"Yes, I thought of that. But Father expects us to join him in Paris to collect the first wave. He still believes there is severe animosity between you and me. We dare not give him cause to question that belief."

Angélique perked up and whined. She didn't want these conspirators anywhere near Jacky, but the recovery of the skull was paramount, and if she could help keep it out of Mirrikh's hands, so much the better.

The skull is in Paris, she told Draganovich. *At the Collège.*

Draganovich straightened in his seat and met her eyes. "Which school?"

"What?" Llewellyn looked confused at the silent exchange.

Antiquities.

Draganovich grinned. "Beautiful you are indeed. Gryffin, she says the skull is in Paris. How would she know that?"

Llewellyn scritched the base of her ear. "Angélique is from Forge-à-Bellesfées. She's the house sentinel and security. I suppose she heard her mistress discussing it, or perhaps she was there in the workshop at the forge."

Draganovich snorted. "Mistress! Think. This is not a wolf nor a pet. The only thing Duval is mistress of is the—"

The color drained from Draganovich's face.

"Oh, God, the forge. Laforge!"

Angélique whined, then gave a low moan. He had found her out after all. It probably took him so long because he had thought her dead.

"God help me." He faced her, trembling. "Angélique Laforge."

She curled her lip, baring her fangs. Rage surged inside her once more. She fought to contain it lest she leave the carriage a bloody mess. Hackles raised, head high, ears out—she just wanted to sink her teeth into his throat.

Yes! Murderer! Monster!

Draganovich fell to his knees on the carriage floor in uncontrollable weeping. "My God, I am so sorry! I am so sorry! I was a fool! I am so sorry! I—I—"

Yes, I, I, I. Little worm.

He lifted his head and, with trepidation, kissed her chin. Her lips curled back over her fangs, and he ducked away with a quiet groan. Llewellyn gripped his arm and helped him back into his seat. They stared at one another for a long moment. Then Llewellyn again put his arm around Angélique. He stroked from head to hindquarters with deliberation.

"So, you do know her." It was an accusation.

Draganovich wept into his hands. "No forgiveness. Atonement, restitution, maybe. No redemption. What I've done—I can't—"

His misery satisfied a measure of her thirst for revenge, a small triumph, but enough to tame her rage. Draganovich was remorseful, but he feared her, wary of her retribution. Ashamed of what he had become and in horror of the consequence of his actions. She was surprised he had the mettle to defy his father's machinations.

"Angélique Laforge," Llewellyn murmured. "Well, well. I am a lucky fellow. Set it aside, Toma." He handed Draganovich his own handkerchief. He leaned forward with a grin. "She didn't eat you, so let's move on."

Then he gently rubbed the inside of her ear. Content, she allowed herself to relax, molding herself to him, mingling his scent with hers. She finally felt things were going the right way. They would soon be in Paris, they would catch up with Jacky, and —

And then he would be gone. She wasn't ready to let him go. Not until he had seen her as a woman. Not until she could tell him how she felt. How he made her feel. She nosed his chest, and he hugged her. In that moment, she knew she wanted this in her life. Maybe all her life.

"We have an advantage if Angélique knows where to find Miss Duval. While your father inspects the new design, we can get hold of the skull."

Draganovich sighed. "It is what comes after I fear more, now that I know—" He clenched his jaw. "If we turn it over, we must find yet another way to stop my father. I had planned to smash it, but now we know Mirrikh will just seize Madame Laforge, a live body already imbued with his magic."

"Not if we run. The world is wide, Toma. Angélique and I can flee to any of the French colonies or to the Americas or to India."

"I have tried. It is the blood magic. He'll find you."

"But would he bother to do that, given your father's demands for immediacy?"

"I don't know."

"I believe it is an advantage nonetheless to have it in our possession rather than Mirrikh's," Llewellyn argued.

"I concur."

Llewellyn looked down at Angélique. "Should we do this, Anyel?"

Yes, by all means! She licked his chin and whined.

He chuckled. "That's three of us. Ask her where we find Miss Duval."

14.

Jacqueline giggled.

"Güzel-kizim, don't stay in your dream!"

But Jacqueline wanted to stay! What better place to be than a pleasant dream where she danced in de Guise's arms and swayed with the rhythm of his heartbeat? He had such strong arms and broad shoulders. In his arms, she felt dainty and delicate. Her hip pressed firmly to his as he led her dancing down a corridor of bones, bones, and more bones.

"Oh, Oh, les os!" she sang without a melody.

She pushed against him teasingly and set herself off laughing. An old love song filled her thoughts, but her tuneless humming couldn't approximate it, so she gave up and leaned her head on his shoulder. The almond fragrance of his soap—Savon de Marseille, the richest!— and the faint scent of his neck so close dizzied her. Steadying herself by pressing her nose to the smooth texture of his fine wool jacket, her chin barked against a large hard object in his inner pocket. A pistol? A very large one at that. She caressed it lovingly.

"Never wanted a man so much." With a longing sigh, she plucked at his cravat. "Never had time. Never thought I would. Never never never never..."

"Güzel-kizim, don't stay in your dream!"

Jacqueline giggled again and breathed a contented "Aaaaah!" Her body buzzed with warmth as if she were part of a Leyden jar circle, except the sensation filled her rather than running through her.

"Wake up, Jacqueline," de Guise urged her. Or was it Elif? "Breathe!"

"Mmmmm. Mmm-hmmm."

She leaned back in his arms and spun around and around. "I don't want to wake up," she cried, and her voice echoed in her ears. "Never never never never! I feel like—I feel like a flügelhorn sounds when Jacques d'Île plays. Ah, Jacques d'Île, so sweet. He hold the flugelhorn like—a lover."

De Guise tried to slow her spinning, and but she tripped, laughing when he caught her up. She stood tiptoe to whisper to him, "I've never held a lover." Then she giggled. "I suppose I shouldn't have said that! But Jacques d'Île, when he plays... Everything inside me is hungry and full of colors! Ah, I heard him play Chopin's *Prelude in E minor*, and oh, my! If I did have a lover, it would be the way Jacques d'Île sounds so warm and deep and soft and—"

She threw her arms around his neck and kissed him. So warm and deep and soft. Don't let it end. *"Please, sir, I want some more!"* Yes, that was it. Hunger. A hungry little orphan who had never been kissed. Why did kissing make her hunger for more? Kissing ever deeper, desire mounting, terrifying and wonderful. Warm and deep and soft. Then de Guise floated away from her.

"Oh. My." Again she spluttered a laugh. She could not stop laughing. Why was she laughing? "Alain, don't go. I apologize. Have I affronted you? I'm—I'm—" No, she could not speak the lie. "I'm not sorry!"

Jacqueline lost herself again in paroxysms of giggles, unable to catch her breath. A cold, sopping wet cloth settled on her forehead, and she calmed enough to rein in her hilarity.

"Alain. Sweet Alain. *My* sweet Alain."

"This won't do," de Guise said. "Jacqueline, you have to wake up."

"Güzel-kizim, don't stay in your dream," she murmured. "But I want to. I want to stay in my dreams with you and climb to the bell tower of Notre Dame and fly away forever! Maybe in an airship. I'll build one! I can do that. For just you and me. Stay forever, Alain. I'm in love with you! I—I love you!"

She pulled him down to kiss her again, but the wet cloth slipped and came between them. De Guise pulled her up to sit, then hoisted her to her feet.

"Whoop!"

Her body was not hers to control, slipping sideways until he propped her against something and held her. Uncomfortable in his gaze, she gaped about in wonder. They were in the center of a low-ceilinged cavern with lit corridors leading away in two directions. As far as she could see, the walls and the ceiling were a mosaic of skulls and long bones laid in elegant patterns.

"Look at all these bones!" she said in a hushed voice. "They're so beautiful!"

Her shoulder rested uncomfortably against an empty eye socket, part of a huge pillar, as round and as large as the Heidelberg Tun but constructed entirely of skulls and the joint ends of long bones. She looked up at de Guise.

"They're all dead, aren't they?"

He peered worriedly into her eyes. "Yes, Jacqueline, they're all dead."

Giddiness waned. "That's sad. And yet, they're so beautiful. I didn't realize there could be such beauty in the dead. Modernité, modernité. Charles was right."

"Let's make sure there's not one more beauty among these dead." He slipped his arm around her and helped her to walk forward.

"You think I'm a beauty?" She blinked in amazement. "No. My face. My eyes. My arms, mon Dieu, my arms are hideous. My hands are like leather. I see myself in the mirror and... Not beautiful. I'm just—"

"As I have told you, you are never 'just' anything," he assured her. He kissed her head, pressing his lips to her hair almost reverently. "Come, you need to move about. Walk with me."

She gazed up in adoration. "I'll walk with you."

It was all she wanted to do. They walked on air. On clouds. On soft cushions. The damp air of the corridor enveloped her like a waterfall. Lifting her chin, she stuck out her tongue to catch the drops that tasted of sunrises and the color eleven.

"I'll walk with you I'll sing to you I'll go with you I'll kiss you I'll love you entirely and I'll never let go."

De Guise grunted some words. Something about a miserable f—

Jacqueline gasped, shocked. "Language, Alain! Do you work in a forge?" But when she squeezed her hand around his biceps, a kind of hunger she had never felt before moved in her. "Oooh. I bet you do. Oh, hold me in these arms!" She looked up at him longingly. "Your eyes are so lovely. I noticed that the first time we met. Your big brown eyes and your golden curls and your beautiful mouth. Kiss me again? Please?"

He responded with more vehement muttering. Why was he in such a foul mood when the world was so wonderfully funny? She leaned in closer, her body melting into his. He held her as if she would break, as if she might float away from him. And she might have if she had so desired, but what she desired more shocked her and made her giggles resurface.

After a while, she could walk on her own, suddenly full of boundless energy despite the morbid decor of their path. A step at a time, her world became more real as the surreality of it pressed upon her. She threw him off and ran ahead.

"Jacqueline!"

She halted, then ran back to him, huffing indignantly, "Someone attacked me."

"So, it would appear." De Guise reached for her. "With nitrous oxide gas."

Eluding his grasp, she trotted back the way they had come, halted, then returned to meet him. "Hence the hysteria."

"Yes. They do call it the laughing gas."

"A silk hood covering the face in the mirror... Oh!" Her hands flew to her throat. "Water! I drowned, and strangled, but then... I danced? Elif."

Conflated images confused her. Limewater still plastered her clothing to her body. How much time had passed? How far from that tunnel had she been transported? And Claque, what happened to him?

"But you found me?"

"I did. Thank God."

Faint gaslight cast double and triple shadows of their figures. Where they overlapped, eerie silhouettes mocked Jacqueline's efforts to sort facts from illusions. She set her head to his chest. His heart thumped against her cheek, steady, strong, providing a continuo that grounded her. Her hands slid around him, trying to draw him closer, but he held back, resisting her.

"You're here. How? How did you find me?"

His pulse raced, then skipped a beat. "I found you unconscious, Jacqueline. I was afraid you were dead. It took so long to wake you!"

"No, how—how did you *know* where to find me, how did you guess I'd be here, how did—"

"You lead a charmed existence, Jacqueline."

He patted her back, not a gentle gesture. More like a mother burping a well-fed baby, a sensation that soured her stomach and brought a pout to her lips.

"I happened to cross paths with your newest creation in a faubourg where I was scouting a property for the railroad. I almost didn't recognize him with all your alterations, but he seemed to know me. He was quite agitated, and he insisted I follow him. I could hardly believe it when I found you. Down here! I only left Bellesfées a day ago, and here you are amid the blessed bones of Paris."

"Claque!" She clapped her hands against de Guise's lapels. "Is he safe?"

De Guise calmed her, finally drawing her into an embrace. "Quite safe when I left him at the tunnel entrance."

And his heart raced again, ever so quickly. The gaslight shadows froze in place, defying her.

He's lying to me. Why is he lying?

Nitrous oxide may have put her to sleep, but to have the gas administered to keep her asleep very long might have killed her. Certainly, the time for Claque to make it out of the tunnels, stumble so fortuitously into de Guise, and lead him to the entrance, and how long for de Guise to figure out just where in the labyrinth she had been abandoned?

Time and the total didn't tally.

No. The facts refused to reconcile for her. She gave de Guise one last hug and pushed herself away from him, hoping to hide her awakening suspicion that de Guise himself had abducted her. It made no sense he would, but nothing else could explain her condition and his presence there.

"Home," she said. "I must get home."

"Which home? Bellesfées or Paris?"

"Paris. My—"

Her breath caught. He had found her on the train. He had found her at Bellesfées. How much more did he know about her? What did he want from her?

"My house. I have a small home here. In the city."

"Then I shall escort you thence, once we make our way from this ghastly place."

She let him wrap his arm around her waist and feigned more weakness than she felt. Such happiness only moments before, spoiled forever. Instead of dancing, sullen staggering. Instead of euphoria, only anger and emptiness. Failure colored all her thoughts a Paris limestone yellow. She hadn't secured her plans, she hadn't learned who attacked—no, *killed*—Letronne, she was unable to stop Rémy Brodeur, and she hadn't figured out how to derail the Count.

That de Guise himself might be working against her dispirited her more than her grief and fear.

There were times she envied Angélique's ability to change and leave her passions behind to follow instincts of survival and self-indulgence.

It was early evening when they emerged from the clandestine tunnel de Guise followed, which indeed led to the land newly acquired by the railroad where Monsieur Claque awaited them stolidly, so perhaps that much was not a lie. De Guise hailed a seedy-looking fiacre to take them all back to the Barrière d'Enfer, where he procured a higher-quality coach to take them to her home. A pang of regret deepened her grief as she gave the coachman her address—one more intimate detail given over to the enemy. They rode in silence, and she felt his gaze upon her the whole time.

Finally, he cleared his throat. When she glanced up, he smiled his dazzling smile. "I will not pry. It is beyond my comprehension to know how you came to be where I found you, as I found you. But I swear to you, dearest Jacqueline, I am grateful beyond words that you are so brilliant as to rebuild that automaton, which truly saved you in the end."

Tears pearled in his eyes and gleamed by the gaslights of Rue St. Jacques.

"I'm ashamed of my behavior," she countered, turning away to stare out the window. "Please consider I was not myself."

He leaned forward and took her hands in his. Drawing a handkerchief from his pocket, he wiped away the caked mud and lime from her skin. "And I am thankful you came to yourself before I was tempted to behave shamefully in kind," he told her. "I confess, I thought for a moment I too had been transported in the euphoria of the laughing gas." He drew her hands to his lips. "A happiness I hope I can experience once again, freely, in the light of day, with no shadows or fears."

Her eyes flashed up as she freed her hands. "What shadows? What fears?"

"I'm not a fool, Jacqueline. I know there is some grievous intrigue surrounding you." Bending closer, he lowered his voice. "The mechanical man, the mysteries of the Orient, and the attack on Letronne. I should have questioned the comings and goings from Bellesfées to Paris but did not. Of course, I know of your private rail. I *am* a railroad agent. But a split lip. Your sister missing. And now this, you, drugged and abandoned—"

"Monsieur de Guise—"

"Madame Duval!" His urgent tone cut her off. "Don't pretend otherwise. I'm in a position to help you if you would let me."

"You are in the perfect position to hurt me as well," she retorted.

Her accusation struck him like a blow. She thought he would protest his innocence, but he didn't. His fierce look frightened her for a moment. Then her resolve hardened to match it.

"I am likewise not a fool, de Guise. Don't pretend you are not part of the 'grievous intrigue' I have had to put up with the past three days. Did I foil your plans for this automaton when I appropriated it? Thus, you followed me to Bellesfées to investigate further? Having Luc take your clothes and the porter your boots was most inconvenient for searching the château, n'est-ce pas? I suppose it was the skull you were looking for, just like everyone else."

"Who else?" he demanded.

Her lips twerked. "No, monsieur. I am owed far more than I owe right now. A man gave his life for that skull. I want to know why." She crossed her arms and gave an indignant *Bof!*

They glared at one another in an interminable silence until de Guise relented. "I wish to God you hadn't interfered," he said. "I should never have let you take the damn thing." He grinned ruefully at Claque and shook his head. "And look what you've done with it. It's no good to us now."

"That's a comfort," she snapped.

He shook his head again, more serious. "You have no idea what you've become involved with here."

"But I do. Count Draganov is creating an army of automatons to gain some sort of power in Moldovarabia."

His eyebrows rose. "Yes."

"And he purchased my designs to complete his project."

"Yes, he did."

"I'm not going to let him do that."

"Jacqueline—"

"Who are you?" she cried, her voice sharp enough to rouse Monsieur Claque, who straightened, puffing and pooting indignantly. "Why should I trust you?"

De Guise gazed back at her steadily, his clenched jaw revealing the conflict within him. The carriage slowed and stopped at the locked port-cochère. She waited a few seconds more. Then she reached for the carriage handle. He set his hand on hers to stop her.

"Invite me in. I'll tell you what you want to know."

Angélique reached Paris by noon. The carriage passed windmills, farms and vineyards, forges and markets, lumber yards, and a few factories. Traffic and poor paving slowed the carriage to a walking pace, allowing Paris time to inflict its noisome airs on Angélique's sensitive nose: manure from stables and barns, rancid meat from abattoirs, the stench of decaying swamps and marshes, and the sewage trenches along the boulevard. Angélique whined until the carriage finally stopped in front of the double gates of a port-cochère that opened to admit them to a well-swept courtyard with a large garden and an alley of stables and mews.

Angélique burst from the coach to relieve herself in the garden, then returned to Llewellyn's side. Together, the three of them entered the house while four liveried men fetched their bags and trunks, and a fifth closed the gates and barred them. Inside, a butler took the men's coats, staring impassively at Angélique, evidently accustomed to his master's eccentricities.

"Three of us for dinner, Broz," Draganovich informed him as he directly mounted the stairs without a backward glance at his guests. "Water right away for the wolf. And, of course, for the brigadier. In the sitting room. I'm not to be disturbed until Salah is complete."

Panting nervously, Angélique kept watch until he vanished from view and closed himself into his room. With servants out of the way, she pawed at Llewellyn's leg.

"He's late for his prayers," he told her, rubbing her ear until her eyes closed. "This way, ma'm'selle. Or, I suppose it's madame by now?" He led her to a sitting room toward the back of a central corridor. When the door closed, she yipped at him and growled.

"Yes, yes." He locked the door before drawing all the curtains. "Is this what you wanted? Ah, one more thing." He opened the privy screen in the corner near the commode, then cast about the room. "I suppose... You'll want..." Snatching a throw from the back of a chair, he folded it over the top of the screen. "Is this enough?"

Anticipation had set her whole body to aching throughout the journey, but now, confronted with the moment, she yawned and whined. This was not the intimate setting she had hoped for. Meeting his anxious gaze, she didn't know how to read the light there. He smelled hungry, and his pulse pounded the same way hers would just before pouncing on prey. She paced a circle, whining again.

He stooped and caught her in his arms, wrapping them around her and burying his face in her ruff. "You don't have to," he said. "It makes no difference to me except — well, I'm curious to meet you, is all."

Curious!

Snorting an indignant *whoof*, she wriggled free and glared into his eyes until he averted his gaze.

"I'm sorry. Fy nghariad. Be who you are, who you want to be."

Another pretty apology. Angélique's tail swished as she bowed an invitation to play. His chuckle set her to chasing her tail in delight before she abruptly broke off to trot behind the screen to change.

As she straightened up, she debated bothering with the throw; but then she realized he had provided it as a token by which she could trust him as a gentleman, and she should honor that. However, covering herself only made her more self-conscious, as if she were ashamed of who she was, of what she was: an animal. A she-wolf with no pack. No laws beyond animal instincts and bestial appetites.

A modest wrap asserted her womanhood, her existence in the world of men and women, a society with its own pack rules and limitations of behavior, implicit laws she had shunned since returning from St. Petersburg. Not in protest of these social standards, like the Decadents' or Incroyables', nor in the defiance of the revolutionaries. Only that she had observed those niceties and refinements, and they had not saved her life. Her lupine blood had. She transcended mere woman, with heightened senses and strength and powers that served her even in her human form.

But with Llewellyn, Angélique became so much more than an animal. Until now, her beauty gave her power. Men desired her, not for who or what she was, but as a bauble, a thing to be owned, like Prince

Abadi's ruby. She had turned their empty lusts to her own purpose. She had always taken what she wanted whenever she wanted.

Llewellyn gave. Care, concern, trust, affection. Even when she had taken advantage of him in his helplessness, he had forgiven her. Her sexual arrogance would not serve her at this moment. Could she honestly stand before him as a woman, with nothing to offer him but who she was—a dissolute, profligate, self-indulgent grotesque?

"No," she whispered. Or at least she thought she had whispered.

Llewellyn stirred. "No?"

She clutched more tightly at her wrap. "I—I can't—I mean—"

"Then don't. It's all right. Angélique, please don't feel—"

He set his hand against the screen as if to comfort her. She placed her hand against his.

"Your voice. It's lovely," he murmured.

"So is yours."

Their fingers molded against one another. Then he pulled away.

"Wait here. Please, don't—don't change back, Anyel. Yet. Unless you want to."

Before she could answer, he left the room.

Stunned at his departure, she stumbled from behind the screen and flopped into a bergère to hold her head in her hands. She hadn't eaten a 'decent' meal, as Marthe would say, in almost two days, and she needed a good night's sleep, maybe even in a bed. And she was so close to reuniting with Jacky. The ninth arrondissement meant she was only a few kilometers from her friends and the homes that would welcome and succor her.

But right now, here, in a strange house, with only Llewellyn and that monster… she felt trapped, uncertain of her next step, and—well, she was naked. And she had never been a wolf loose in Paris before. How would she navigate the streets?

She groaned and sat up, brushed back her hair with her fingers, and heaved a long, deep sigh. Pouting never accomplished anything. Or, at least, not much.

Back behind the screen, she poured water into the basin on the credenza and plunged her face in to wash, using the cloth to scrub behind her ears, her underarms, and her feet. Rose powder and lavender oils she found by the ewer restored a sense of femininity, and with that returned a sense of self and power. Inside the credenza cabinets, she found table linens more suitable for covering herself than the Jacquard throw. Two of them she draped like a half-sari and choli from India. She had just finished arranging these when there came a timid knock at the door.

"Yes, come in."

She braced herself to meet Llewellyn, but instead, a woman entered, a cook judging by her smell of onions and cabbage and the stains on her apron. Like Marthe, she had a weathered face and red-raw hands, and she walked as if her legs had far too much weight to carry about. The woman took one look at Angélique and chittered.

"Not sure about this! Trews and stockings and sabots and a workman's cap? Man don't have eyes if he thinks these 'propriate!"

Oh, but they were! Angélique accepted them with a laugh, and when the woman left, she switched into the habiliments of a stable boy or a youth of the street. As she adjusted the cap, a second knock came, more timid than the first. At her reply, Llewellyn opened the door but stopped without entering.

"Iesu mawr! Anyel?"

She lifted her chin proudly and made a little bow, touching her cap. "H'oui, m'sieur!" In perfect Parisienne patois. "Work the stables, no? Or sweep out the coach? Any sou'll do!"

Then she shuffled and danced a little clog dance, knocking her wooden-soled shoes together. Llewellyn didn't laugh as she'd intended. He simply stared. Angélique cleared her throat uncertainly, hoping she appeared neither teasing nor coy.

"I hope this means you like what you see."

Llewellyn came to her and bent to one knee, taking her hands and kissing each one. "I am honored. Angelique Laforge, the brilliant pianist. I saw you perform in Vienna. I never thought I would— May I introduce myself?"

"Brigadier Gryffin Llewellyn," she said, "how much grief would have been spared us both if you had done that in the first place."

He leaned his cheek on her hands. "You're right. I was wrong. I can only ask you to forgive me."

She knelt, too, gazing into his eyes. "If you forgive my interference. And my violation of your trust and intimacy."

"You have beautiful sun-gold eyes."

No one had ever called her deformed eyes beautiful. Warmth beyond the July heat blanketed her as her heart raced. Then his lips brushed hers. She leaned hesitantly into his kiss before surrendering to her desire. Gladly she let him pull her into an embrace she had longed for since first he had aroused her senses. Grateful and eager, they fell together on the carpet in the delight of a never-ending kiss, the kind of kiss that requires no other gesture, no caress, no teasing, no demand, and no yielding, only the taste of one another, new and unique and delicious.

15.

Angélique ate ravenously. She saw no point in maintaining the airs of a lady of society when the two men at the table with her knew who and what she was: she was a conspirator like they were. She felt their gazes, the one admiring, the other longing and regretful. All she could focus on was the fine roast of lamb, heavy sauce, and root vegetables. And wine, thank heavens, a good solid red from Pays d'Oc.

"Father will set the airship down near the Moulin Moque-Souris around midnight," Draganovich explained. "There are still tunnels from the old limestone mines that lead to the Catacombs. We are to meet him there and proceed to Brodeur's workshop to inspect the devices he's put together. Mirrikh plans to animate them at that point, then lead them back to the ship. We have until midnight to find that skull."

"And if we don't recover it?" Llewellyn asked. "Would Mirrikh really take your head?"

"Or mine?" Angélique put in.

"Or hers?"

Draganovich leaned back in his chair. He contemplated his plate for a few moments before answering, "I believe he will not take my head, although he has suggested it to Father. He would indeed have Madame Laforge's head. But failing that, I fear the most expeditious plan is that he would find a way to trigger my change and feed someone else to me. I would prefer not to have that happen."

Angélique's lip curled. "You still can't fight it? Are you that weak?"

He cleared his throat. "It is an art I have learned, but I have not yet mastered."

She glared. "I once offered to teach you restraint. Imagine if you had listened."

He threw down his napkin and stood. "You'll excuse me. Be ready to depart in ten minutes."

"To go where?" Llewellyn asked.

"To my home," Angélique cut in. "Here in Paris. Jacky may have left the skull in our safe."

Draganovich nodded. "That sounds like a reasonable place to begin." He turned to leave.

"Otherwise, she may yet be at the Collège with her professors working on the translation."

"What!" Draganovich whirled about. "*Translation!* Doesn't she realize what—Oh, God! We have to find her."

Angélique gaped at him. "What is the matter? Is it dangerous?"

Draganovich shrugged off his dinner jacket and reached for his coat. "It's more than dangerous. It's obscene. And who knows what she can summon with even a portion of that spell? All the demons of hell!" He slapped his forehead. "Of course! That's what de Guise was referring to when he spoke of the chaos in that professor's office."

"De Guise!" Angélique drew a sharp breath. "So, he is part of this plot! He was there at the start, flirting with Jacqueline. I will devour him!"

"No, no, he's true," Llewellyn reassured her. "One of us, trying to stop this madness. He was on his way to Orléans to track the rogue when it intercepted the train."

"And now we know why it intercepted *your* train." Draganovich wagged his head. "Allah has brought us all together. Allahu akbar."

She relaxed again, grinning wryly. "And here I thought Paris was all revolutionary words and no beneficial deeds."

"You're an habituée of the wrong cafés," Draganovich replied. "Mark my words: Paris will no doubt erupt in the next decade at the least. That, however, will be someone else's problem."

"And with good fortune, they will not have this infernal army to engage," she answered.

"Or enlist," Draganovich added. "Come, make haste. We have a skull to find."

When he left the room, Angélique smiled shyly at Llewelyn. He took her hand, but he didn't return the smile.

"I don't like the idea of your coming with us. I'd rather you ran off and hid somewhere safe."

She bent to kiss his fingers. "There is nowhere I can go now that Mirrikh knows of my existence. He's a necromancer. He tracked the skull to Bellesfées. He'd find some occult way to track me down." She shook her head. "I'd rather stay with you and make certain you are safe from any retribution should they discover your little cabal."

He pushed back a lock of her hair that had slipped from the cap, and he gazed at her lovingly. "Then stay a wolf. Be my Anyel for just a little longer. You have a better chance of defending yourself than I have of defending your presence with us, although I will give my life if I have to."

Angélique grinned. "I will confess, I rather enjoy being a wolf. I don't see it as a curse, like Draganovich. But then, I have never—"

She halted suddenly. She was about to say she had never killed anyone, as Draganovich had. Before two days ago, that was true. Angélique had often annoyed her oh-so-proper sister with facetious threats of savagery and slaughter. But the ruffian at Bellesfées—she had torn out his throat. Of course he was dead. But was he still? Had he taken wolf form because of her bite? The Benets—were they safe?

"Angélique, what is it?"

She stood abruptly. "Draganovich. Where is he?"

"I believe he went to check the horses."

Her heart pounded as she ran from the room, out of the house, and into the mews. She found Draganovich talking with the stable boy. He turned in surprise.

"Madame La—"

"How did you create me?" she cried. "How is it done?"

He held up a hand to silence her. "Nico, be certain three horses are ready within the hour. Go."

Angélique quaked, her fists clenched. "Is it because you shed my blood, or because you spent your infernal seed inside me, you animal?"

Draganovich took her arm, but she shoved him off. He raised his hands in acquiescence, then indicated the doorway and escorted her from the stable to the alley. Here he seated her and took a place beside her.

"I have been pondering that question since I realized who you were. I believe I now know the answer."

She glared all the more fiercely at his calm response.

"Mirrikh works dark magic," he began, "requiring blood. His blood, the blood of his victims, the blood of his subjects." He tapped his lip and the scar where years ago she had bitten him for his forceful kiss. "You drew my blood. No doubt you even swallowed some of it. Or perhaps that blood fell upon your open wounds. In any case, our blood has mingled, as mine once mingled with the wolf's."

The memory rushed back to her, and with it, disgust. Her lip curled. "So, it wasn't enough to rape my body. You had to poison my blood as well. Mon Dieu, how I despise you."

Draganovich nodded in resignation. "I despise myself. I have committed the most unforgivable atrocities, and at the time, I felt justified. I was angry at Father for making me this thing. I blamed Mirrikh. I took out my anger in selfish debauchery and, yes, in slaughter. I have killed others."

"Monster!"

"I am indeed. But you, Madame Laforge, were the only one who also drew my blood. When my father dragged me home from St. Petersburg, Mirrikh spent months training me to avoid my lower appetites for violence. And I recalled then the teachings of my governess about living in the Light of Allah. I confess I am no devout, but her words have brought me peace and a way to find better peace. For such crimes as mine, there can be no forgiveness. I can only try to atone. No, I cannot always control the shape of my skin, but I can fight to control what I do within that skin."

He laughed quietly. "If only Father had known he was raising his nemesis. I don't want this war any more than I want to be this accursed *thing.*"

Llewellyn appeared in the stable doorway, joining them. "You are a force for good, Toma. I don't accept your belief that tampering with God's creation has removed your soul. Your actions — Angélique's actions — there is redemption in them. You are both messengers of a better nature."

Toma looked to him in gratitude, but Angélique bowed her head. "So, it's the mingling of blood. Your man. Szolt." Her voice caught as she recalled the shambles she had left on the salon floor. "I think — I may have been bleeding when I —"

Draganovich assured her, "When we have finished this night, we will go together to Bellesfées and find him. I will take full responsibility. You couldn't have known what could happen any more than I. I sincerely had no idea."

Llewellyn pulled her to lean on him, and she nodded reluctantly. She reached for his hand. Their fingers laced. Toma headed back into the stables.

"You're right," Angélique said. "I will go as your Anyel once we have finished searching my home. Who knows? Perhaps Jacky is there. She'll find a way. I know she will."

"Together we will," he reassured her. "We found one another in all this. We will find a way out of it as well."

"I never understood Jacky's predilection for trousers until now," Angélique said as the three made their way through the Faubourg Saint-Germaine. "No ridiculous corset or crinoline. Just freedom. And no one ogling me. I may grow quite fond of them myself."

Draganovich snorted. "Until you try to free yourself from them to become the wolf."

"I've never become a wolf while clothed but the once, the first time," she replied. "I had only a chemise."

"Please!" Llewellyn's face turned a deep color. "Angélique, you are positively decadent sometimes."

She grinned. "I don't have much choice, dear Llewelyn."

He wagged his head and smiled. "I love the way you say my name. 'Lu-el-leen.' It's lovely on your lips, that pretty French accent."

"But is that wrong?"

"Not from you. I love it."

"And how do you say it?"

When he gave its proper Welsh pronunciation. She burst out laughing.

"How is there a *k* or *h* in there? What is that noise?"

"You lift the middle of your tongue and sort of blow around it."

After several failed attempts, she laughed again.

"'Gree-fan Lu-el-leen' is fine with me," he assured her.

They arrived at Rue Cler, and the housekeeper Agnès didn't seem surprised to see them. "Mademoiselle Jacqueline was here already," she explained. "I knew you wouldn't be far behind."

"Do you expect her back this evening?"

Agnès gave her a wearied look that said, *Since when do you girls do anything I expect?* and headed off to the kitchen.

Angélique removed her gloves but paused with her riding coat half off her shoulders. "It's not here," she declared. "I can't smell it."

Draganovich nodded agreement but still perused the room and hallway. "Upstairs?"

"Or the shed."

She opened the safe, finding it empty. She and Draganovich searched the rooms, their senses open to the specific scent, while Llewellyn visited the atelier and gardens. They had to concede the skull was not on the premises. She left a note on Jacqueline's dressing table in case her sister returned in time.

"Rugère will be closed," Angélique reflected. "If we go to the Collège and she's there, I could find her. But at this hour, I can't think why she would still be there." She shrugged. "All I can suggest is the cafés in the Quartier Latin. Some friend or other may have seen her."

Llewellyn embraced her. "Here's hoping these will be the right cafés."

Agnès had left the argands lit in the front windows. A clockwork porter greeted Jacqueline and de Guise as they entered. Jacqueline promptly shed all but her chemise and drawers and dumped them into the porter. De Guise's astonished look annoyed her. As if, after all this, she should worry about modesty!

"Allow me to wash and dress," she told him. "I'm sure there is something in the larder and wine in the pantry. Claque, can you start a fire for me?"

The autonomaton turned to search for the drawing room. De Guise chuckled and placed his own coat on a hook. Jacqueline noticed his clothing wasn't soaked with lime or mud, clearly exonerating him as the one who had assaulted her in the flooded tunnel. That fact mollified her somewhat.

She padded barefoot up the stairs, followed by a clockwork scrubber that mopped up the splatters from her steps. She didn't have the luxury of a bath in her city house, so she settled for wiping herself down as best she could. She didn't even bother with her hair; drenched in lime, it would take too long to wash. As it was, the longer she dallied, the more time de Guise had to devise a plausible explanation for the events of the past three days. Jacqueline stripped down and dug out a peignoir to throw around a fresh chemise. Sitting down at her dressing table to comb knots from her hair, she found a small, folded note addressed to her in Angélique's hand.

Her heart thumped. She unfolded it quickly and read,

Darling Jacky,

I am safe for now, but you must return the skull to Count Draganov in order to keep me safe. Please meet us at the Moulin Moque-Souris tonight at 23h. I need you.

A.

Jacqueline couldn't catch her breath. Angélique in the hands of Count Draganov! "*I need you.*" She raced down the steps to find de Guise in the kitchen.

"Are you in league with Count Draganov?" she demanded.

He paused in the midst of arranging two plates of charcuterie, his face a mask of equanimity. "I would not say so," he replied, "but I am working beside him."

"Who are you, de Guise?" The catch in her voice annoyed her. She didn't want him to see her fall apart, but she felt her world spinning out of control. Even her body betrayed her as she trembled in fury.

Rather than answer, he carried the plates toward the drawing room, Jacqueline snorting fire as she followed. After setting their plates on a small side table, he took a seat and pointed, indicating she should sit as well.

"If I am right, you haven't eaten a bite since a mere croissant chocolat this morning. After all you've suffered today, I recommend you have some nourishment while I tell you as much as I am permitted."

"Monsieur, I've been caring for myself and my sister since we were seven years old."

"Then you must learn to be cared for," he answered, "as I care for you."

She waved him off. "Just tell me—"

"I am an agent of the Sûreté Nationale, in the service of His Majesty Louis-Philippe. I am here to beg you to surrender that skull you took from the automaton to prevent a war between France and Russia."

A security agent. A spy. With Romantic curls and big brown eyes and lovely lips. Now there was a design whose specifications she could not have imagined.

"France and Russia? But I thought Count Draganov—"

"Draganov is fighting for the control of Moldovarabia, which he hopes to rule as its liberator and pass along to his son."

"So, how does that concern France?"

"Her Majesty Victoria Regina of Britain wishes to establish an entente between our two countries. Russia now controls Moldovarabia. Due to the details of international treaties, should any army from the Ottoman Empire attack Russia, our two countries will perforce become engaged as belligerents."

He leaned forward, his tone urgent. "Security agents from all the European powers have been following his actions for several years. So many secret societies looking to overthrow Ghica's rule in the area, but Draganov counts the loss of Moldovarabia as a personal attack on his family, his history."

"A son of the Dragul."

"Exactly." He stopped abruptly and leaned back, studying her. "You seem to have a bit of knowledge in all this."

She answered evenly, "A bit. Keep going."

"*Hmm.*" He smiled and gave a quiet chuckle. "You are an astonishing woman."

"Yes, I am. Continue."

"In Moscow, the Count met a young polytech."

"Rémy Brodeur."

Once again, her foreknowledge surprised him. "Brodeur's designs were clumsy, but he was the only one interested in automatons as a military force. His were inefficient, but the Count's advisor convinced him to buy nevertheless."

"That would be his sorcerer, Mirrikh." She threw down her serviette. "De Guise, I asked you to tell me what happened tonight."

"You got too close, Jacqueline. Brodeur panicked when he saw you in his workshop. I'm thankful he didn't drown you in that sludge. He keeps a store of nitrous oxide with him everywhere. Claims it gives him visions for designs. Certainly nothing as elegant as your Monsieur Claque. I was to meet him in his workshop to gauge his progress, but when I found Claque at the tunnel entrance I feared the worst."

"So, it was a petty act of pure temper. He should hope I never encounter him again."

"Did he realize who you were? He's furiously jealous your containment plans were selected over his."

"Yes, well, the Count is not getting them. I'll return his funds and burn my designs if I have to. You can be my courier if you like."

"I *am* his courier. I already have those plans in my possession, but so does Rémy."

"Then you can give them back to me. And the Count is to release my sister at once."

De Guise looked truly nonplussed. "Your sister? There's no one— I don't understand. He is holding your sister captive?"

She slapped Angélique's note on the table. De Guise read it, but his confusion remained. "I swear to you, I know nothing about this."

"She's in the company of a British officer, Brigadier Gryf—"

"No! Llewellyn would not have done such a thing."

"I don't know what he has or has not done, but there is the proof they are in league."

He perused the note. "I sent Llewellyn after the automaton once I realized I couldn't dissuade you to leave it. I wired him from Orléans, and he took his boat down the Loire. He was to recover the skull and hide it. We hoped to delay the Count's plan as long as possible until we could find a way to stop him completely. I had no idea your sister was any part of the issue."

"Issue!" she cried. "And the janissary?"

"What janissary? Jacqueline, you're not making any sense."

She rose and stomped around the room. "It would appear you didn't get as close to the Count as you needed to learn his secrets, like how those automatons are fueled. Or how Mirrikh turned the Count's son into a slavering beast who, in turn, changed my sister into a wolf."

De Guise didn't protest as she thought he might. As she watched for his reaction, she could almost see his train of thought chugging sluggishly from the station. She smirked. His head tipped to one side as his eyes followed an invisible trail of facts.

"Your wolf. Is your sister. And you say Toma—"

"Mirrikh created Toma. Or rather, re-created him into a shapeshifting wolf. Toma raped Angélique five years ago and left her for dead, clawed to pieces, her throat torn out. If he had not been bleeding himself, she would have died. But the mingling of their blood gave her the power to live. Only as a shapeshifter."

"I saw her. At Beauville, the Count's château. She isn't held captive at all. Unless the Count has divined who she is—"

"Mirrikh already knows. And if I understand the janissary, if I do not return the skull, he will use Angélique to complete his work animating the souls of the dead to drive his automatons."

Jacqueline paused at the hearth where Agnès had left a cauldron of bouillon on the hob. She stared at the bubbling pot and felt like one of the bones in there. "What do I do? I don't have the skull. The janissary took it."

She pressed her head to the mantelpiece. *Elif! Where are you, Effendi?*

De Guise set gentle hands on her shoulders. "I am not your enemy, Jacqueline. I am your friend and ally, and would that I could be more than that to you. If I hadn't found your automaton, if I had taken any longer to find you—I'm just glad Brodeur had the sense to leave you somewhere you could be easily found. Mon Dieu, if you had stayed hooked up to that gas, I—" His voice trembled slightly. "Dearest Jacqueline—"

"No." Shying away, she shook her head. "I'm not suffering the effects of nitrous oxide any longer, and I cannot help seeing what I took for affection is mere affectation. It's the skull you want. Not me."

He turned her about and searched her face, his brown eyes wide as a puppy's. "I protest. I'm not given to outbursts of passion, I admit, but, my dearest Jacqueline, I have grown very fond of you, and that can't be undone. Nevertheless, our task now is to give Draganov what he needs to save your sister and yet prevent this invasion. Where is the skull?"

"I don't know." Fear sparked tears. "It was taken from me."

"By whom?"

"The janissary."

He shook his head. "I have no idea who that is. Where is he?"

"*She.* I don't know. She comes and goes. Didn't you see her in Letronne's office—?" She gasped suddenly. "Letronne! Oh, de Guise, he's dead!"

"What? No!"

His stricken expression echoed her own grief. Jacqueline buried her face against his chest. Exhaustion, hunger, and an emptiness more than hunger had drained her for days. Having this much more of the puzzle completed, she gave in at last and wept. De Guise held her stiffly at first, but then he surrendered, caressing her back and combing through her knotted hair. He kissed her head over and over. Jacqueline clung to him and poured her soul out in tears that soaked his lapel.

"How did Draganov find me in Letronne's office? Has he been following me that long? And why would he attack the professor? He hurt no one!" The whine in her voice sounded like a child complaining, and she hated herself for her weakness in de Guise's presence. But when she tried to push away, he embraced her all the more tightly and murmured in her ear.

"I don't believe he has followed you. I don't believe he even knows you're here in Paris. The last I reported to him, you were in Bellesfées. But I don't understand. I visited Letronne myself before I met you in the market that morning, before the attack on him. I needed to consult him on—never mind, another matter. After you left the next day, I had Letronne moved to a private hospital to keep him from being found."

"He's in a much better place." The sister's words.

Hope filled Jacqueline's heart. She blinked up at him, sniffling into the sleeve of her peignoir. "You? Moved him? He's not dead?"

His eyes twinkled when he recognized her mistake. "I'm so sorry to have scared you."

With all the deceptions surrounding de Guise, Jacqueline hardly dared to trust him. "He's safe? You're certain?"

He kissed her brow. "Letronne is far too important a figure to the government on too many issues to allow him to be endangered. I thought—"

Jacqueline smacked his chest with both fists. "You frightened me! Why didn't you tell me?"

De Guise gently took her wrists and wrapped her arms around his waist. "And why didn't you tell me about the skull?"

She bit back a retort as de Guise chucked her chin.

"There are many truths I won't tell you, Jacqueline, but I will never lie to you. Never. I will tell you this: I will stop Draganov and do what I can to rescue Angélique. Please, trust me."

"Alain, I'll trust you, but—"

He put a finger to her lips. "You called me Alain," he said with a smug smile.

16.

Darkness shrouded the streets and alleyways of the Quartier Latin, but noisy crowds packed the Boul'Mich. Raucous music of guitars, accordions, and sour pianos poured from open doorways, and laughter and shouting rained from upper rooms where the various coteries met for pretentious philosophical discourse and political declamations. Angélique, Llewelyn, and Draganovich nudged their horses through the crowds as Angélique stopped at this café and that, asking for word of her sister. Finally, someone told her where to find Charles, who spoke wild tales about dancing with Jacky, a dead crow, and some skulls: at La Mère Cadet, naturally. She bid the two men wait in the street and headed upstairs to the gathering that called themselves the ExCréateurs, thinking themselves quite witty.

"Ah, the golden angel arrives! Angélique Aurélie!" Charles cried out, unceremoniously dumping two grisettes from his lap as he stood and exaggerated a bow. The crowd about him laughed and cheered, welcoming her. He snatched her and put *her* on his knee. "Join us! You know the fellows, yes? Heinrich, Karl?" He pointed his beard at his companions. "Tell me why you haven't slept with me yet, O goddess of the dawn with the golden eyes."

"Charles, my love!" She kissed his cheeks. "I haven't allowed you to enter the chambers of glory because I don't want to end up in your poetry as a skeleton or a vampire. You are most unflattering to your mistresses!"

"Ah, but I am in love now," he replied, "and I can hate no woman while I am in love. My love blooms!"

"Yes, but afterward, those lovely flowers rot to produce your evil rhymes." She tweaked his nose.

"Flowers of evil—I like that!"

"Tell me this tale of my sister I've heard you've been prattling."

"Oh, your sister, your sister, the other divine Duval." Charles leapt up and waltzed with her clumsily. "But first, taste this most excellent eau de vie." He snatched a glass from one of his companions and pressed it to Angélique's lips.

It was no more than rotten peach vinegar to her mind, but Charles' senses were addled with dawamesc. She could smell the cloves and cardamom on his breath.

"Now—" Charles covered a burp, then slung his arm over Angélique's shoulder. "You keep promising me a poetry recital at Bellesfées, my golden angel. When?"

"Charles—"

"Give me a date, and I'll give the tale," he teased.

His compatriots took up the taunt and thumped the tables chanting until Angélique surrendered and named a week in August. Charles planted a sloppy kiss on her mouth and began an embellished account of his meeting with Jacqueline.

The tale finally told, she kissed his brow and bid the cenacle of socialists and *so-called* poets adieu.

"He said she descended to the Catacombs sometime this morning or afternoon," she told the other two when she regained the saddle.

The men exchanged worried looks. "Brodeur's workshop," Draganovich said.

"We may be hunting needlessly if Brodeur has that skull."

The clock at the intersection of Boulevard Saint-Germain said ten-twenty.

"We haven't enough time to get to the underground before meeting the airship at Moque-Souris." Draganovich cleaned his spectacles, frowning. "What shall we do?"

Angélique fretted with the reins. "I don't know. I just—need—"

"Time we do not have. Paris may be a city, but in essence, it is the largest village in the world. Word will get to your sister. I am certain of it."

"But will it reach her in time?" Llewellyn argued. "And failing that? Will you sacrifice Angélique?"

Draganovich set his jaw. "I will defend her with my life. I can do no less after all the horror I have inflicted. We will find a solution."

Jacqueline quickly donned work clothes suitable for the night ahead. As she reached for her gogglers, she halted with a start. Elif sat in the corner bergère, holding out the coveted skull.

"Elif!" she cried. She hugged the janissary in relief and anticipation. "By all the mummies of Egypt, how do you do this! You heard my cry! You know, then?"

Elif stroked her head like a doting nursemaid. "Kizim, I would not abandon you or your sister to Draganov. Can you place this into your re-creation?"

Jacqueline cradled the skull and examined it anew. "I would rather not. It's such an offense to treat it so barbarically. Besides, I wouldn't know where to install it in such a way any power could be drawn from it."

"Simply let it reside within. Do not fear any sacrilege: I have — *altered* — its function. This will not summon the powers Mirrikh hopes to invoke."

"You can do that? But how?"

Elif smiled. "Do you forget I am master of laws you have not yet learned?" She stood and smoothed her uniform, straightened her hat, and rested her hand on her kilij's pommel. "You will present your Monsieur Claque to Draganov, the skull fully integrated into your design. It is imperative you do this. He must recite his spells over *this* skull."

"No!" Jacqueline held the skull away. "No, I won't allow it."

Elif frowned with determination. "You must to put an end to his plot for all time. Kizim, trust me. Trust to the One God. I will not fail you."

"Trust! I trust you to keep disappearing when I need you."

"As I have trusted you with many secrets. Bismillahi, I came to you to save this poor soul, and you did not fail me. Now you will see I repay your generous spirit with my very being." She gathered her cape about her. "But only if you are willing to obey without question."

"But there's no time! I can't —"

"My life is in your hands. The work must be completed. Will you have faith?"

Jacqueline searched her face and weighed the determination in the janissary's eyes. With a sigh, she nodded.

Elif whirled and vanished once again into the folds of her cape, which spun itself out of existence.

Jacqueline wasted no time cursing or questioning. She had the skull. Monsieur Claque waited downstairs, and she kept a small atelier behind the house. She fairly flew to the drawing room.

"Claque, with me!"

De Guise followed her. "What is it? What's happened?"

"A solution!"

Out the back door and across a small garden stood a small shed. They entered, and Jacqueline pointed to the workbench. "Sit," she commanded as she began gathering tools. Both Monsieur Claque and de Guise obeyed. She took her leather apron down from its hook and tied it on. Then she positioned her welding gogglers and took up a torch. She chuckled when she turned and saw them sitting side by side watching her with suspicion.

"Just Claque, thank you. I'm resetting his operating parameters."

She brought the skull to the bench. De Guise snatched it up. "You found it?"

"It was returned to me with changes in its specifications."

She reached for it, but he held it from her. "No! You can't let him have this. Did you not understand me?"

She snatched up her welding torch and sparked it to life. "The janissary claims to have altered the spell. Give me the skull, Alain."

"Who is this janissary you talk about?" he cried. "Jacqueline, I'm committed to destroying this thing, now that I know it is the key to Mirrikh's magic and Draganov's ghastly army."

"Then you sentence my sister to die by Mirrikh's hand." She brought the torch close. "You demanded my trust. Now I demand as much. This is not the skull Mirrikh expects. Don't ask me how I know that."

Indeed, she couldn't explain it to herself, but she had to believe Elif would not have returned it without undoing the spell that bound the soul to the skull.

Monsieur Claque turned his head to watch the struggle and decided it for them. He closed his hand around de Guise's wrist and removed the skull with the other. He presented it to Jacqueline with a bow of his head.

"Jacqueline, please! This is no time to be stubborn."

"No, it's time to be right, and this is right." She directed the torch to the rivets at the side of Claque's faceplate and began. "I have faith."

Angélique worried the reins as they passed the Luxembourg Gardens and followed the Rue d'Enfer toward the gates of the city. She tried to console herself. After all, Jacky was the engineer, the planner, the solver of riddles. Surely by now she had winkled out the skull's filigreed secrets. Her bags had not been repacked, so she was still in Paris somewhere, but not down in the dark corners of Paris's Bohemia. Prie Dieu, that she was not somewhere even darker!

They left the city and headed east. The windmills that had lent their sobriquet, "Moque-Souris," no longer dotted the hill some now called Montsouris. No moon lit the night. The canopy of stars spread above them like a ragged, moth-eaten curtain. As they turned from the little pond, the forest enveloped them in a deeper night. One could well believe the tales of the giant ghost of Isauré haunting the little lake and its environs. The trees opened up finally to the hill where the airship would put down near the observatory.

Angélique halted before they left the shadow of the forest. "A third horse can't be explained away. If I become wolf, what excuse can you give for it?"

Draganovich took her reins. "Go. I'll tell Father we had hoped to find your sister and bring her with us."

She dismounted and headed into the denser woods, where she undressed and changed. As she emerged, she caught the sound of others on the road along with a metallic tromping. Jacky's scent was unmistakable. Elation filled her. Angélique leapt down the hill to greet her sister in a tumult of relief and joy.

"Mon Ange!"

Jacqueline stooped down to receive her sister in her arms as Angélique licked her face and throat and danced circles around her. "Oh, mon Ange, how glad I am to see you, my love!"

De Guise grinned, while Monsieur Claque continued on. "Hurry now," he said. "We are complete. I see Llewellyn and Toma Draganovich."

They followed Monsieur Claque, and as they reached the hilltop, Llewellyn and Draganovich dismounted. They greeted de Guise solemnly and bowed to Jacqueline. Angélique took up beside Llewellyn, whining and sneezing her excitement.

Draganovich studied the automaton with some doubt. "Is this the rogue?"

"I made a few modifications," Jacqueline replied. "You are Toma Draganovich?"

When he nodded, she drove the heel of her hand into his nose.

He fell back as blood poured across his face. He gave a cry that might have been a snarl, and Jacqueline kicked him. Twice. She flexed her fist, but her hand didn't hurt enough to detract from her satisfaction.

"If I could kill you, I would, but as I understand it, we are to be allies. So, you live."

Draganovich pulled out a handkerchief to stanch his nose. He had the decency not to look her in the eye. "Madame Duval, your anger is well deserved, and I hope to atone for all my past wrongs this night."

He cast about and retrieved his sun-glasses. As he struggled to regain his feet, Claque extended a hand and gently helped him stand. He stared back at the automaton, a curious smile on his face.

Llewellyn also bowed. "Madame Duval, I beg you forgive me. The last time we met—"

"Calm yourself. I won't break *your* nose. Your head's already cracked." She pointed to Angélique, who was fawning over him. "My sister trusts you. For her sake, so will I."

He grinned and reached down to scritch behind Angélique's ears, who grunted in delight.

"Tell me," Draganovich asked Jacqueline, "do you have the skull?"

She pointed to Monsieur Claque, who tapped his head in answer. Draganovich peered up into the faceplate of the automaton. Monsieur Claque nodded.

Angélique yawned, suddenly nervous. Familiar vibrations set her hackles up, and she nosed Jacqueline. Then she howled as a portion of the stars seemed to vanish. Llewellyn knelt down and embraced her, and she pawed at him to make him pay attention. The airship was coming. Soon the horses also stamped and nickered, then whinnied and ramped as the stench of the airship's contingent reached their nostrils. They looked to the sky, and the airship could soon be distinguished from the night.

Draganovich straightened. "Mesdames, perhaps you should take your leave at this time. My father will have all he needs, and you—"

"We are staying," Jacqueline insisted. "I've put too much effort and desperation into this monstrous endeavor, and I will see it completed."

"But what can you gain?" Llewellyn argued.

"It's not what I gain, Monsieur Llewellyn. It's what Draganov loses." She indicated Angélique, who pressed close to Llewellyn's thigh. "I know she will not leave you until she sees you safely through. And I will not leave her with Mirrikh. Yes," she answered his surprised expression. "I know what he is and what he's done. I will have satisfaction."

"Madame, you are putting yourself and your sister in the gravest of dangers," Draganovich said. "We have the skull. Father will be satisfied with that, and we will continue our plan to thwart his efforts. But I cannot ensure your safety once my father realizes he has no further use for you or your work."

Llewellyn knelt and held Angélique by her ruff. "I think he's right, my darling Angélique. I'll return to you once this nightmare is over."

Angélique growled and pulled away, her eyes narrow.

Jacqueline chuckled. "Oh, I know that look. She's not going to leave your side. And I'm not going to leave hers."

De Guise slipped his arm around her waist. "I don't suppose I can convince you either?"

"No." Then she grinned. "Besides, I want to see how this airship manages to be invisible in the dusky skies. Don't worry, chéri. I will charm the good Count, I promise."

He kissed her brow. "Once again, you manage to get your way."

Nevertheless, he trembled, and Jacqueline took that as an indication of his concern for her. She was surprised by the sudden awareness he genuinely cared for her welfare. That he cared for *her*. And that this awareness aroused her whole body and almost overwhelmed her thoughts.

Not now! Not yet!

She shook out her arms and stamped her feet, anxious for the night to be over.

The ship descended. Jacqueline took in the scope of the design of both the pretentious gondola and the envelope. She discerned the envelope was made of a reflective material, nothing magical or mysterious, and a similar material covered the ship itself. Perhaps a silver or aluminum coating? Otherwise, the ship had no unique element of engineering at all. De Guise had already told her the thing was driven manually by revenants controlled by Mirrikh. She wondered if the envelope was filled, not with hot air, but with the souls of the dead, like the automaton? A literal ghost ship. Her revulsion toward the Count deepened.

The ship put down and drop lines flew over the railing to land. A handful of men leapt down to secure the huge aerostat by pounding large stakes into the ground and tying off the dock lines. A gangplank was placed, and the Count disembarked with Mirrikh. In the dark, Draganov's pale face contrasted sharply with his hair. He held a pipe in his teeth. Mirrikh waddled at Draganov's side, his jowls waggling with each step. Angélique shifted her weight, straining to keep from pouncing. Both men scowled at the sight of Jacqueline, but she forestalled their wrath with a hurried curtsy as she cried out in elation.

"Count Draganov! I am so pleased to meet you at last, Your Excellency. And I beg your forgiveness for having caused you any concern or inconvenience with your exquisite automaton. Please let me congratulate you on this achievement."

She proffered her hand with a coy smile. Draganov pulled the pipe from his mouth and kissed her hand in reflex.

"And what a magnificent dirigible," she continued in the same delighted voice. "So vast and original in its elegance. Brilliant in execution. You cannot imagine how excited I am to make your acquaintance once Monsieur de Guise explained my egregious faux-pas. Oh, I do beg your forgiveness."

Draganov looked to de Guise, taken aback, then made a short bow to Jacqueline. "You are Domnişoară Duval?"

"Oh, I am sorry, I thought you knew. I assumed you had seen the presentation of my plans at the Institute last month. Jacqueline Marie-Claire Duval de la Forge-à-Bellesfées." She curtsied again. "But please, Madame Duval is fine."

She brushed past him and walked up the gangplank, gesticulating with exaggerated enthusiasm. "What a beautiful envelope! I thought it was star-studded at first, but I see now how it reflects all around it, rendering it invisible at night. Such brilliance, Your Excellency. Did you design this? If you did not, I would so love to meet your engineer."

She kept up the mad babbling, smiling broadly in delight or cooing in fascination as she explored the deck of the vessel. The others hurried to keep up with her, but she continued blithely, commending the artistry of the capstans, the battens, the masts; wrinkling her nose and joking obliquely about the stench of the crew and their shabby attire being out of place on so magnificent a ship — both the revenants and the minions, n'est-ce pas? — and complimenting the system of gas canisters while ascertaining they were indeed hydrogen. All the while, her heart raced and every nerve burned like electricity through her. The shambolic corpses so infuriated her that she wanted to seize Draganov with her bare hands and wrench his scrawny neck until he faced his own derrière.

"Ooh, is that a musketoon?" she said to one of the men, coquettishly caressing the short-barreled gun tucked into his belt. "They are ever so much handier than a musket, no?"

Jacqueline's eyes slid askance to her sister, who answered with a low growl to confirm this one was the one who had shot her. Jacqueline made a mental note to make him pay, but for now, there was no time. She had to focus on the airship and how it maneuvered.

"Oh, I am so grateful you have allowed me this tour, Your Excellency," she said at last, clasping her hands. "And I have brought my designs for you in practice, as you can see." She indicated Monsieur Claque. "I hope you forgive me for making adjustments to the casque, but I thought it advantageous to give the automaton senses for its surroundings. And my reconfiguring of the fuel systems will prevent the disastrous rupture that caused it to malfunction. Your former engineer should be dismissed for such a calamity and lack of foresight. He is a clod and does not deserve whatever you are paying him."

Claque nodded his agreement. Draganov looked Monsieur Claque over, frowning. "You've replaced the skull?"

"Replace? Well, I put the same skull back where your engineer had placed it. I confess I was doubtful of its efficacy, but—" She shrugged with a small laugh. "In this age of industrial and spectral wonders, wonders will indeed never cease."

Mirrikh leaned to the Count's ear and murmured quietly in Persian.

Jacqueline's brows rose. "Really? You have more of these? How exciting! May I watch?"

The two men were startled when she understood Mirrikh. The Count's frown deepened. "No, domnişoară. My business here is concluded. De Guise will escort you on your way. I'm sorry to disappoint you."

She made a pretty moue. "Alas, I had so hoped to better make your acquaintance."

"Another time, perhaps. For now, we must be on our way. De Guise."

De Guise bowed. "Excellency." He offered his arm to Jacqueline. The tension in his expression eased.

Jacqueline sighed. She had rather hoped for more information, and to come away with her sister in tow.

Angélique rumbled to herself. Jacky was never so gaie-à-la-folie. Nor had she ever affected that falsetto that reminded her of Baronin Spransky. She shook herself. The scene would be laughable had their circumstances not been so desperate, but Angélique was certain Jacky was mapping out a takeover of the ship.

Jacky knelt before her and stroked back her fur from her face. "You be a good doggie, now," she said, gazing into Angélique's eyes and giving a quick, reassuring nod.

Angélique licked Jacky's cheek and whined. Knowing Jacky, some convoluted, steam-powered rescue plot brewed in her sister's head. She trotted after her twin as Jacky took de Guise's arm and disappeared down the gangplank, following their retreat as they mounted horses and vanished into the forest. She howled a mournful farewell before returning to Llewellyn's side.

The Count waved his Czech bulldog at his son's twisted and swollen nose. "What is this?"

Draganovich shrugged. "We were assailed by a band of Roma near the gate. You know how bad that faubourg is. I might have been quite battered if your brigadier hadn't stepped in. It would seem the oaf has some use after all." He adjusted his sun-glasses. "It'll heal soon enough."

Angélique snorted. Between Llewellyn and Draganovich, she had never heard so many lies spouted so easily in her life. The air was rank with the acrid smell of deception.

The Count then turned a dark eye to Llewellyn. "And you. How long will you pretend that animal is your bitch?"

The revelation struck Angélique like a blow. She dropped to a crouch, ready to pounce on Draganov. Mirrikh sneered at her. Llewellyn returned the Count's gaze but said nothing.

The Count smiled grimly. "I see."

He signaled to Yorg with a quick nod of his head. "Don't ruin the skull," he said.

The henchman drew his musketoon and loaded the breech. With a snarl, she lunged across the deck. Yorg hurriedly snapped the chamber closed and took aim as Angélique leapt straight for his throat.

Behind her, Llewellyn shouted, "No!" She cursed as she heard him charge forward.

Yorg fired just before the two brought him to the deck.

The bullet slashed the side of her neck. Angélique screamed. Searing pain blinded and deafened her. Yelping, she scrabbled to cling to Llewellyn. Together, they rolled away from Yorg. Llewellyn didn't move. His pulse began to fade. Angélique laid her head on his chest. The warm wetness of his blood soaked into her own bloodied ruff. His arms lay useless at his side. She tried to hold on, but consciousness ebbed. Her last sight was Draganovich, watching solemnly, a slow smile spreading across his face.

The Count clapped his son's back. "Keep an eye on her, Tomica, until we return. We may need her."

Draganovich nodded, his sun-glasses fixed on Angélique. "She is safe with me," he said.

17.

JACQUELINE STOPPED AT THE SOUND OF THE SHOT. "WHAT WAS THAT?" She reined her horse around in a panic, but de Guise blocked her.

"Angélique! I have to go back!"

"No. Jacqueline, you can't."

Terror blinded her. "But I can't just leave her! My God, my God! Mon Ange!" She tried again to urge her horse.

De Guise took her arm. "We don't know if it is Angélique in peril. We don't know who fired the shot. But Mirrikh has his precious skull, and they will finish their task as quickly as possible. We must get there before they do. Jacqueline, she will live, I promise you!"

She threw him off. "You cannot promise me that! She's not safe. Draganovich raped her and tore her to shreds, do you understand? The Count let him slaughter her and said nothing. How can she be safe while she's in the hands of that ghoul Mirrikh?"

Once again, he blocked her from turning. "That ghoul is planning to resurrect the dead to animate those automatons this very night. He must hurry to do so if he is to march them back to the ship before dawn. He will not interrupt that plan for anything. Your engineering has been installed in these models, and he can ill afford their being discovered."

Jacqueline's heart ached, and she felt she couldn't breathe for grief. She choked back a sob. She could hear Elif's words reassuring her, "*Your sister will heal,*" but she could find no way to draw comfort from them.

De Guise said, "I promise you will see your sister again. Alive. As you saw, the ship cannot leave without Mirrikh, and I swear Mirrikh will not survive this night."

"You men and your promises. You can't promise me that."

"But I do."

She trembled with a desperate ache but surrendered, falling in beside him. Still, she couldn't stem her tears. De Guise gave her his handkerchief, but he said nothing further.

Jacqueline expected they would return to the city, but de Guise turned aside just past the observatory grounds and before the retreat house. They followed a small rill until they came to a mining adit, a narrow access tunnel long fallen into desuetude.

"We go on foot from here," de Guise said, dismounting.

Jacqueline followed, and they hitched the horses to a rusted railing at the entrance. "Another way into the Catacombs? All the way out here?"

"Eventually, yes." He felt around inside the entrance and found a lantern and igniter. "I'm afraid these tunnels are almost as bad as the ones you were in earlier, but they are at least clearer of débris and above water level. They have the advantage of being parallel to the route the Count will use, so he won't overtake us. And I know the way, so we'll be able to move more quickly. Please, Jacqueline, trust me."

Jacqueline nodded. She barely felt her limbs anymore. Her world seemed upside-down. Her head understood Angélique would survive anything shot from a gun, but how long would it take her to revive? What if Llewellyn was the target? Was Angélique now in Mirrikh's hands, unprotected? Jacqueline shivered, unable to still the doubts in her heart. De Guise wrapped his arm around her, and she leaned on him as they descended into the underworld.

They followed a set of rail tracks through a tunnel so low they both had to hunch down to pass. While the groundwater at times came over her shoes, it was not so deep as where she had fallen that day. Still, she was exhausted, and the day's exertions had taken a great toll, as had her encounter with Draganov. She hadn't known what to expect of him. Certainly not that he would be handsome and charming and polite. She had played the gaie fillette, but inside she'd been terrified the Count would slay her at any moment, having secured what he was after.

Yet, she had to steel herself against what lay ahead. If she had understood all Elif had intimated, Mirrikh would recite a final incantation to activate the spell inscribed upon the skull, powerful blood magic that transformed it into a vessel of necromantic forces that would imbue the skulls installed in the automatons with the spirits of their dead, which Mirrikh would then control so long as they did not burst their containment, as Monsieur Claque had done. She supposed Brodeur had reinforced the tubing in the machines in his lair. But with Elif's interference, would the same powers be invoked? Would her machinations transcend the new constraints? Jacqueline fervently believed Elif herself would meet them in the Catacombs to see the execution of her plan and the culmination of her war against Mirrikh.

The corridor soon widened, the waters receded, and Jacqueline realized there was light ahead of them. They approached the Catacombs proper, now closed off from the public but still lit by gas fixtures for the workers reinforcing the unstable areas. She roused herself to match de Guise's pace. Plaques on the wall told them they had reached the Place d'Enfer, a good thirty meters above them. Further on, a macabre welcome sign warned them:

"ARRÊTE! C'EST ICI L'EMPIRE DE LA MORT."

"Not yet, it isn't," Jacqueline muttered. "And not if we can stop it."

The bones of six million dead defied her.

Tunnels whose walls were piles upon piles of long bones and skulls stretched before them. Skulls formed patterns and shapes against the bones piled and packed into the lime: a heart, a cross, an arabesque mosaic. Jacqueline folded her arms across her breasts, unwilling to brush too closely.

"So much death," she whispered. "So many."

Thousands of skulls mocked her. She shuddered. De Guise turned with a smile. He took her hand and pointed to an engraved marble block set into a break in the wall of bones. *"Death is always future or past,"* he read. *"Once death is present, it is gone."* He squeezed her hand. "Unless, of course, it's resurrected in profanity. We won't let that happen."

They pressed forward. Black eye sockets, gaping jaws, cracked crania, and withering joints swallowed them. Jacqueline only drew a comfortable breath when the endless remains were interrupted with more epigraphs, memorials to sepultured notables, or various pillars of historical reference. As they plunged deeper into the ossuary, overwhelming dread eased to grim acknowledgment and, eventually, acceptance. Oddly, Jacqueline felt a peaceful acknowledgment of mortality that resonated more with life than death.

The tunnel opened to a wide, comparatively well-lit room. From each side of the chamber, a corridor branched off. Before them, the opposite wall opened to a section six meters wide where two stone pillars supported the low ceiling to either side of a granite bowl upon a short plinth in the center of the room. More long bones and lines of skulls formed the walls. Beyond the plinth, the osseous wall opened into a small alcove at the far end of the narrower section. The whole chamber held the aura of a house of pagan worship.

Jacqueline halted. She had seen this dry fountain before, in a dream. Was it only three days ago she dreamt Pasha Elif Effendi had sat atop that same brazier and called her to waken in the steam coach?

"What is it?" de Guise asked.

She shook her head. "What is this place?"

De Guise took in the small cavern. "They call it the Crypt of the Sepulchral Lamp. An overly romanticized name. In former days, miners used this brazier to gauge the oxygen flow in the corridors. When the fire guttered, the workers evacuated until the next day."

"How far is it to Rémy Brodeur's workshop?"

"Not far at all." He pointed to the left corridor.

A rush of clarity swept over her. "This is it. This is where it will happen. Not in the workshop."

"What do you mean?"

Jacqueline set her hands on the rim of the Sepulchral Lamp. "This bowl. Mirrikh needs to do a blood ritual, and this will be his altar."

He looked skeptical. "How do you know?"

She pursed her lips. "Don't ask me how. I don't know how I know this any more than I know how Mirrikh is able to animate those poor creatures to do his bidding aboard the airship. Any more than I know how Angélique can be— Angélique. I just know this is where the final step will take place. This is where I need to be to observe and, if possible, help disrupt his handiwork."

De Guise grimaced. "I don't know where we could possibly hide here. The corridors are all gaslit. We would be seen no matter where we stood."

Jacqueline made a tour of the cavern and finally came to the alcove behind the Sepulchral Lamp. "Up there," she said, pointing to the half-meter gap between bones and the low limestone ceiling.

De Guise scratched his head as he surveyed the possibilities. "You're mad. Do you mean to use these skulls as stepping stones?"

"Not if I don't have to. If I boost you up, can you pull me after you?"

"Boost *me* up?"

She rolled her eyes at his incredulity. She pulled off her coat. "De Guise, I have machinery that weighs far more than you." She tossed her coat up into the niche. "It's not even two meters. I think I can hoist your leg up, and once you're up there, if you lend a hand, I can swing myself up and in."

De Guise wagged his head. "I have a better plan. I can tuck you in there and head to Brodeur's workshop. I don't actually have to hide at all. I've nothing to fear from the Count."

"Truly? Do you suppose Llewellyn also had nothing to fear from the Count once they shot Angélique?"

"We don't know for certain—"

"And you will take that chance?"

"Yes!" He caressed her face. "To keep you safe, I would."

He stooped to wrap his arms around her legs and lifted her high enough to climb into the grisly crypt.

"I hope you don't regret this," she grumbled.

"And I hope you don't have long to wait. Use my handkerchief as a mask so you're not breathing the dust of these remains."

She reached down to him, and he took the opportunity to kiss her fingertips. Then he gripped her hand and pleaded one last time, "Please. Stay safe and hidden."

Jacqueline watched him retreat down the tunnel leading off to the left until the darkness swallowed him.

She covered herself with her coat and tucked back against the stone wall of the cavern. De Guise's handkerchief masked her nose and mouth, but she hid her face behind the sleeve of the coat for added cover. It took her a few minutes to settle her nerves and lie still enough not to rattle her bed of bones. She did not have long to wait. The clomp of Monsieur Claque's metal tread echoed down one of the corridors, followed by voices. Soon she could see them coming. She ducked further down.

Mirrikh and Count Draganov led a small group of about a dozen men. Her heart sank when she saw that neither Llewellyn nor Draganovich accompanied them. She held on to the fragile hope they and Angélique were still alive aboard the airship or would soon follow.

"We'll leave you to your work," the Count said to Mirrikh as they halted by the stone lamp. "The men and I will lead the machines out once you have animated them."

"Leave one man with me, I beg you," Mirrikh replied. "I may need assistance."

"Of course. Yorg."

The Count nodded to one of the men from the deck of the airship, the one who had shot her sister. Yorg leaned back against a pillar behind Mirrikh while the Count and the other men headed up the tunnel de Guise had taken.

Monsieur Claque, hunched over to fit into the room, slowly scanned the cavern. He paused when he spotted Jacqueline but made no sign Mirrikh might read.

The fakir set down a small bag beside the plinth. With pudgy fingers laden with rings, one by one, he removed items Jacqueline couldn't make out. He pronounced solemn words over each object and kissed it before arranging them with deliberation around the rim of the brazier. Jacqueline's heart stuttered and her scalp tingled when the items emanated a crimson glow in the dusk of the cavern. Finally, he signaled to Monsieur Claque. Jacqueline held her breath as her autonomaton approached him. Mirrikh examined the faceplate of the casque and cursed when he saw it had been welded shut. He set his hand against the rivets and mumbled inaudibly. The rivets popped away, and the faceplate swung open.

"Huh. Good trick, that," Yorg said.

Jacqueline could not argue but did twitch in annoyance. She had worked for almost an hour to secure those rivets.

Gingerly, Mirrikh removed the skull from its setting. Monsieur Claque slumped. Jacqueline chewed at her cheek; her punch cards and fuel system should have kept the autonomaton active. Elif's tweaking of the spell must have overridden his system of programmed chips.

The sorcerer chuckled as he cradled the skull in his hands.

"You have led a merry chase, you old witch, but at last we bring this to an end."

Placing the skull in the bowl, he circled the plinth, chanting in a language Jacqueline didn't know. Yorg shifted uneasily as he peered at the sorcerer's work. Mirrikh paused and turned to him, smiling.

"Come, see," he invited.

The man leaned closer to look into the brazier. In a swift movement, Mirrikh sliced his throat. Jacqueline winced as blood spurted across the pillar and poured into the bowl to cover the skull. She pressed her jaw tightly closed to keep her breathing even. Mirrikh gripped the man by his hair until a pool of blood drenched the skull, then let his lifeless body drop to the floor. As the sorcerer resumed his chants, the items along the edge of the bowl glowed brighter.

The wall beneath Jacqueline quaked. She thought back to her dream, the bones of this chamber collapsing, the skulls crying out, rising up to smother her.

Perhaps I should have found a better hiding place!

Mirrikh lifted the skull in his right hand, and with his left, he began to trace the gold filigree. As soon as his thick finger touched the lettering, a wisp of vapor rose from each eye socket. The slight tendrils grew as he proceeded until the vapors flowed down to cover the floor of the cavern. There they roiled and billowed, deeper and deeper, rising to Mirrikh's knees, to his waist, to his chest.

Above the resonance of Mirrikh's voice arose distant noises from the tunnel de Guise had taken.

Mirrikh finished his invocation. He held the skull aloft above the mists that had all but swallowed him. He gave a final cry, a command. As a wild cyclone, the mists gathered and spun crazily around the cavern, around Mirrikh, sweeping past Jacqueline with a cool touch both formidable and somehow reassuring enough to convince her Elif, not Mirrikh, controlled the spell.

As the whirling mists swept by, more ghostly vapors poured from the skulls adorning the wall, as if the enchanted skull called on its friends to come to play. Mirrikh frowned and repeated his final command. The cyclone settled upon Monsieur Claque, and the automaton lifted his head. The mists danced up and were swiftly drawn into the casque. The faceplate slammed shut.

Far, far down the tunnel, cries turned to screams.

Mirrikh glowered. "What? What has happened?"

From the shadows of the tunnel, Pasha Elif Effendi emerged with slow, deliberate steps, raising her bullwhip.

18.

Jacqueline's heart leapt to see Elif at last.

Mirrikh backed away. His eyes bulged and he stammered, "How — how are *you* here?"

The janissary grinned in wicked delight. "You summoned me, O master." She followed him around the Sepulchral Lamp. "You called, and I answered."

She cracked the whip to send three of the glowing artifacts off the Lamp. Mirrikh wailed in pain. *Crack!* The rest of the artifacts fell.

He shook the bloodied skull at her. "I command you to protect me! You will not harm me!" he cried, fear breaking his voice.

More shouts came from the tunnel.

Jacqueline dropped from her perch. Mirrikh whirled on her. His eyes bulged. "You?"

She fumbled in her pocket for a weapon, but all she found was a protractor. She brandished it en garde.

The whipped cracked. Mirrikh snapped his attention to Elif, backing up to take in both women.

"This is not your war, kizim," Elif warned.

"Maybe, but you're my friend." Jacqueline inched closer to Mirrikh.

Laughing, Mirrikh clenched his left fist. With a cry, he waved it in Jacqueline's direction. An unseen force slammed her into the alcove. She slid to the floor, momentarily stunned. A second later, Elif hit the ground beside her. The kilij slipped from her sash as she tried to rise. Jacqueline, on all fours, crawled to the blade and recovered it. She got to her feet, holding the unfamiliar weapon awkwardly in both hands, waiting for her vision to stop spinning. Her head wobbled as she tried to find her balance.

The sorcerer cackled and called out more words in his necromantic tongue. The ceiling groaned. A chunk of limestone struck Jacqueline, driving her to the floor with her hands over her head. More pieces of the ceiling dropped on her, then larger blocks crashed beside her. The whip cracked, and the avalanche ceased. A metallic taste filled Jacqueline's mouth. When she lifted her head, blood dripped from her chin. Mirrikh barked another command.

Jacqueline coughed lime dust from her throat. "Elif," she rasped, "release Claque!"

Elif grunted. She lay curled to her side at the other side of the alcove.

"Stupid witch." Mirrikh spat on Elif.

He went back to the Lamp and reset his talismans. Above his incantation, a distant roar like a locomotive rumbled up the corridor from Brodeur's workshop. Jacqueline got to her feet and stumbled over to Elif.

"We have to go," she urged.

The janissary gasped. "The spell—has not yet—completed its task."

Jacqueline lifted Elif's head into her lap. "What can I do?" she whispered.

A shriek of rage interrupted them. Eyes wild, Mirrikh raised the skull over his head and smashed it into the brazier. He gathered the shards and hurled them at Elif.

"Miserable witch! What have you done?"

A wall of mist thundered into the cavern. De Guise emerged brandishing a Colt Paterson revolver. Slewing on blood, he halted to assess the tableau, then fixed his gun on Mirrikh. When he spotted Jacqueline, he hastened to her side and took her hand, keeping the gun trained on the sorcerer.

"We must run," he urged

Jacqueline pulled back. Elif rolled from her lap and got to her knees. "Go with him, kizim."

"No!"

"Jacqueline, those things are coming," de Guise said. "Something has gone terribly wrong. They attacked the Count's men. They're berserk."

"They are doing what I invited them to do," Elif said with a fierce smile. "Exactly as I rewrote the spell. See!"

Amid the dust of the alcove, more spirits issued from the skulls to join the mists rolling into the chamber from the tunnel.

"I will kill you!" Mirrikh cried.

De Guise fired, but the bullet ricocheted as if Mirrikh were made of metal. A second bullet pinged into a pillar. Mirrikh clenched his fist and spoke. Elif smashed against the alcove wall.

"Elif!" Jacqueline reached for her.

Cursing, De Guise shoved his revolver back inside his jacket and pulled Jacqueline to her feet. "Come now!"

As they turned to flee, the mists separated into individual streams. At the head of each formed a ghastly face like Jacqueline had first seen in the rogue automaton, pre-Claque. They shot up to the ceiling, dove to the far corners of the chamber, and rushed back to dance around the mortals invading their realm. De Guise set Jacqueline behind him defensively, but the spirits ignored them to surround Mirrikh.

The sorcerer crossed his arms before his face. The streams circled the Sepulchral Lamp, spiraling in a braided helix upward. Howls rose from their gaping mouths, a dizzying hurricane of souls roaring their fury. Mirrikh began to chant but managed a single word before one of the haunts dove into his chest and out his mouth.

Mirrikh screamed. As he tried to speak, the spirits roared. One of the ghosts tore through his body. Blood poured from the side of his mouth and streamed from his eyes and ears. He writhed in agony. Again, an avenging spirit assailed him. His sobbing cries grew weaker.

Still, Elif remained crushed against the wall. Jacqueline edged toward her. She froze when the Count's men tumbled into the wider room from the corridor and tripped into one another. The maelstrom of spirits regathered themselves. Jacqueline covered her ears as their howls redoubled.

In a single wave, the spirits flew into the men and through them. Wails of terror became tortured shrieks that rose above the howling. Over and over, the spirits assailed them, pulling entrails behind them, thrusting eyes from their sockets, ripping men's jaws apart, and flinging offal across the floor.

"Elif, Elif, please!" Jacqueline wailed. She found the kilij in the rubble.

"Jacqueline!" De Guise pressed her against the alcove, shielding her from the horror with his body.

"It's done," Elif said. She closed her eyes.

Monsieur Claque jerked his head around. He seized Mirrikh by the collar of his cloak and lifted him off the ground. The sorcerer struggled in vain.

"Kill—me—you die." Mirrikh choked on his words, blood bubbling from his lips.

"Yes. In peace." Elif lifted her eyes heavenward and prayed again, "Inna lillahi wa inna ilayhi raji'un."

She grinned at Jacqueline. "Now."

Immediately, the assailing ghosts abandoned Mirrikh and flooded the alcove. They shoved de Guise away from Jacqueline, surrounding him in a cyclone of mist. He flailed, hemmed in by the ghostly horde. He called for Jacqueline, barely audible above the wails of the spirits, but he couldn't press through the veil to reach her.

Jacqueline hesitated, her heart pounding. She didn't know how to use a scimitar. Stab? Chop? Perhaps pound down like a sledgehammer. It wobbled in her shaky grip. What was she to do with it?

Mirrikh wheezed a mocking gurgle.

His sneer enraged her. She shrieked, "Putain!" and swung in a blind fury. Her arms jolted with the shock of severing the head from the spine. Blood spurted across her face and drenched her coat. She stepped back with a gasp and stared at the fallen head, Mirrikh's bloody sneer still defying her. Monsieur Claque released the limp body. It fell atop Yorg's corpse.

From far down the tunnel came a reverberating thunder of metal on stone—the army of now-inanimate automatons crashing down— followed by a distant roar that shook the foundations of the Catacombs and collapsed the ceiling of the tunnel to the workshop, burying all evidence of the infernal work.

The sudden silence overwhelmed Jacqueline. She dropped the kilij and stared at her bloodied hands in horror, then at the shambles around her. Bodies lay ripped open, Rémy Brodeur among them. Jacqueline retched as the mephitic odor of ruptured bowels across the smeared floor filled her nose.

De Guise was suddenly beside her. He held her close, and she let him, burying her face into his shoulder until his spicy scent erased the stench of death. When she opened her eyes again and looked about, the ghosts had vanished. And Elif with them.

"Wh—where is she?"

De Guise shook his head. "Who?"

"Elif."

"You keep saying that word. What does it mean?"

"Pasha Elif Effendi. The janissary!" She stamped her foot and pointed to where Elif had stood moments before. "The woman who fought Mirrikh! The Turque! Elif!"

"What woman? What Turque?" He peered into her eyes, looking for clarity. "Jacqueline, are you all right? I think Monsieur Claque decapitated Mirrikh. He must have closed that metal claw of his and—" He nodded to the grisly evidence.

She shoved him. "You mean you didn't see her?"

"There is no one else," he insisted. He retrieved her coat and put it on her. "Come, let us leave this butchery and get back to the ship. Toma and Llewellyn didn't come with them, and Draganov is not among these poor souls. He must have fled by another way. I must stop him."

Jacqueline looked around the cavern wildly, but the janissary had once again vanished along with her kilij.

"But she was right there. She told me—" She stamped her foot. "*Zut!* She's done it again!"

"Jacqueline. Please, hurry. We must get back to the airship. Your sister!"

Stunned, Jacqueline didn't fight him as he pulled her along through the tunnels. Every step juddered her body and spirit as she tried to piece together what she had just witnessed. How could Elif simply abandon her after the turmoil they had faced? Jacqueline could not reconcile her relief with her anger. Nor could she shake off the horror at what she had done. She had slain an enemy, stopped the army of clockwork revenants, and prevented war. She had no reason to feel ashamed, but she had never killed anyone. She literally had blood on her hands. And her face.

Monsieur Claque clanked behind them. Otherwise, the silence of the subterranean corridor felt like a vacuum pulling thoughts from her mind. De Guise gripped her hand; he was her only anchor to reality. Get to the airship, save Angélique, keep the Count from leaving France. Keep going, keep moving. Newtonian laws, those laws she had mastered, would take care of the rest.

When they got to the horses, de Guise asked, "What of Claque?"

"He'll keep up. You know he can run. He ran from Draganov, remember? That *is* how we met."

She urged her horse forward, and they both took off at a gallop toward Moulin Moques-Souris. Monsieur Claque kept pace with them, tiny bursts of steam popping up from his head every few minutes.

"I would think," de Guise shouted, breathless from their run, "you might find His Majesty would pay handsomely for an army of Claques."

"I'm sure he would." Jacqueline frowned. "I'd prefer he didn't know about Claque."

"Nor about Angélique, I would guess."

Setting her jaw, she leaned forward in the saddle. *"Hue! Hue!"*

Her horse gathered speed, and she outpaced de Guise and Monsieur Claque.

19.

As Jacqueline and de Guise emerged from the woods at the gallop, she saw the airship silhouetted against the vespertine sky. Occasional bursts from the hydrogen tanks flashed like lightning. By their light, she saw a coach pull away from the hillside and a tall, slender man stride up the gangplank.

"No. No! Angélique!" Jacqueline cried.

"That's Draganov. He must have exited the Catacombs in the city and taken a coach. Damn the man!"

Draganov ran across the deck of the airship and vanished. By the time he reappeared, Jacqueline and de Guise had reached the ship. Jacqueline flew from her mount and ran as the Count and one of his lackeys attempted to withdraw the gangplank. She threw herself flat on it and crawled. With de Guise right behind her, the two of them made too much weight for Draganov to thwart them. Monsieur Claque then stepped up, and the plank settled, secure. Draganov retreated, his cloak flapping behind him like the wings of a bat.

Jacqueline regained her feet and lunged at the lackey, clawing at his face, shrieking her rage. "Where is she? What have you done with her?"

The man squeaked and ran down the gangplank. He leapt before Monsieur Claque could reach him and rolled down the hillside. Jacqueline watched him flee, then turned to take in the grisly deck strewn with the rotted bodies of the revenants, deprived of reanimation when Mirrikh died. She stared about wildly, but she didn't find Angélique among the grey, crumpled heaps.

"Claque! Get these bodies off the ship. Into the lake."

The autonomaton clomped up onto the deck.

Jacqueline ran to catch up to de Guise in pursuit of Draganov, who had fled to the forecastle. As de Guise gained the ladder, the Count kicked at his head, missing him but striking Jacqueline's shoulder. She tumbled backward down the steps.

"Putain!"

She sprang up again just as de Guise caught Draganov's boot and wrenched it sideways with a satisfying crack! Cursing, the Count staggered back until he was cornered at the prow.

"You and Llewellyn!" he rasped. "When Mirrikh gets here—"

De Guise shook his head. "Look around you," he said, indicating the corpses befouling the deck. "Mirrikh is dead. Your army is defeated. Go back to Chisinău, by order of His Majesty Louis-Philippe."

Draganov bellowed with rage. He fumbled at his pocket, but de Guise was quicker. He pulled his Colt Paterson from inside his jacket. Draganov froze, then slowly raised his arms.

Jacqueline threw herself at Draganov and beat his shoulders. "Where is she?" Jacqueline cried, trying to punch his face as he held her off. "Where is Angélique? Where is the wolf?"

Draganov curled his lip. "Dead." He spat in her face. "Along with Llewellyn, shot for a traitor. Their bodies are below if you wish to bury them, but I think my son may have eaten them." He laughed when her eyes widened.

The sky had turned from violet to auroral lavender. Now a shaft of daylight pierced the clouds along the eastern horizon. For the first time in days, hope swept in to banish Jacqueline's fears for her twin:

The Count didn't know his son had turned against him as well.

She gripped Draganov's collar, shook him one final time, and then shoved him away.

He rebounded off the rail to knock Jacqueline into de Guise. As the two fell together, Jacqueline's head struck the deck. Stunned briefly, she watched in dismay as Draganov scudded down the steps and hobbled toward the ladder to belowdecks. Her heart sank.

"Toma! Tomica! My son, help me!" Draganov called. Then he halted abruptly, hopping on his good foot to catch his balance.

A huge black wolf crouched at the open door, snarling.

The Count's expression twisted. "Tomica! What is this?" he demanded impatiently. Then his eyes bulged in horror and he roared, *"What is this?"*

Sweet-salty musk. Bitter salt. Further away, urine, man-sweat. Rotting flesh.

Angélique sneezed and tried to paw her nose. Sleeves hindered her forelegs, so she gave up. A breeze crossed her face, carrying with it the florid fragrance of linden trees in bloom, erasing the harsher odors. Nestling down, she brushed against someone curled beside her. Someone nude.

Merde. Who did I sleep with this time?

Any memory of the night's bacchanal eluded her. Cautiously she opened her eyes just enough to peek at the man beside her in bed, but the room was dark, and her eyes clouded. She nudged closer to sniff around his neck, trying to identify the luscious aroma of his skin mingled with her own musky scent.

I must have enjoyed you, chéri. Such sweet flesh…

Another odor crept in, at first an awareness, then a panicking threat. Sensory recognition jerked her wide awake in darkened quarters. Four open windows to her right allowed no light, but she needed none to know she lay on a canopied bed beside Llewellyn's cold, silent body. Her efforts to sit up only entwined her hindquarters further in the chemise someone had dressed her in. Yelping, she tossed her head wildly to learn who held her captive.

A phosphorous match flared, blinding her, then ignited a lantern on a small writing desk. Seated in the corner beside the head of the bed, Draganovich replaced the globe and blew out the match.

"Allahu akbar. Welcome back." He indicated the chemise. "I covered you in case you inadvertently changed upon your revival."

She panted, glaring, but slowly her fear abated as the logic of his choice broke through her panic. How had they come to be here, in the great room of the airship? The last she remembered was Jacqueline disappearing into the woods of Moque-Souris. But then…

Draganov. Yorg. Putain!

The bullet nicked your carotid to strike Gryffin up through the heart as he tried to cover you. Draganovich smiled. *Quite heroic.*

His words in her head brought the entire memory into focus, ending with the two of them entwined on the deck, dying as Draganovich watched with satisfaction, his smile almost smug.

You! She snarled. *You let this happen! Salaud!*

I could not have stopped it, but I knew you'd live. My hope is that you have the same powers I possess, for Gryffin's sake.

His words gave her pause. Moreover, they brought a spark of hope as well as trepidation. If she could revive Gryffin… as a lycanthrope…

She shook her head. *He will despise me, as I have despised you without knowing you were to blame for my fall.*

Turning his gaze to Llewellyn's pale face, he answered, *I thought only of my friend and my promise to you.*

After another attempt to sit up, she begrudgingly asked, *Can you help me change?*

Of course. Forgive me.

He hastened to adjust the chemise along her limbs and smooth it out across her body. To her amusement, he turned his back to allow her to resume her human form in privacy. As soon as the last of her tail retreated into her spine, she lay a hand on Llewellyn's chest, willing his heart to beat again. Caressing him, she felt the bandaged wound. She shuddered.

"How long has it been?"

"A few hours." He checked his watch. "A little after three. The sun will be up in another hour. I removed the ball and treated him." Rubbing his brow, he blew a weary sigh. "It is a theory. Only a hope, really. But you lay so beautifully together in death, hope was all I had. Father was furious at Yorg for killing you. Mirrikh, enraged."

He resumed his vigil in the corner chair. "How do you feel?"

Still addled, Angélique pushed herself up to the pillows and tucked herself under Llewellyn's head to cradle him in her lap. "You believe I've changed him." More of a doubtful question.

Draganovich pursed his lips. "I am no sorcerer like Mirrikh. As I told you, I can only surmise how your change came about, but if I am right, the same will happen to Gryffin. At least, that is my prayer, in sha'Allah."

"In sha'Allah," she echoed. "God willing. Please, my love, please." So she prayed, caressing Llewellyn's face and fretting with his unbound hair as the darkened windows gradually took on the uncertain deep indigo of pre-dawn.

When the skies were light enough to make out all the details of the great room — the benches along the hull, the plain wooden dining table and six chairs, a privy hole to port and bathing hole to starboard — Angélique's prayers turned to doubts.

"Why is it taking so long?" she cried.

Draganovich, who had sat quietly, eyes closed, through the hour, leaned forward, elbows on his knees. "How long did it take you to revive the first time?" he countered. "In Saint Petersburg?"

His wolf-eyes pierced her soul, reviving the flashes of memory of the moment he had taken on his bestial form to rape and slay her. She couldn't look at him. Instead, she gazed down on Llewellyn's face, placid in death.

"I don't know. I awoke in the morning." Her mouth flooded with nauseous saliva. She breathed deeply to settle her stomach. "But you left me in much worse condition than a simple shot, if you recall that evening."

Draganovich accepted her accusation. "*Hmm.* And how long the *next* time?"

Her eyes flashed up at him. He removed his sun-glasses and answered her gaze calmly. She swallowed and looked away. "Not as long."

He waited silently as Angélique endured the flood of images his goading evinced. The second time: slashed wrists in a Montmartre garret a week after fleeing to Paris. The third time, an accidentally slashed throat in a tavern fight. Once she accepted her immortality, anger drove her to more reckless pursuits: Cholera. Pox. Syphilis. Opium. Morphine. Each death a mocking reminder of her grotesque condition, driving her to deeper depression and more savage self-destruction until she learned to pursue self-indulgence and take what pleasure she could find in life since clearly, she could not end it.

Draganovich replaced his sun-glasses. "When I failed in my efforts to end the curse, I struck out against the whole world in violence."

The ease with which Draganovich discussed his crimes so casually with his victim gnawed at her, and she suppressed a growl.

"Then I realized I had infinitely more time to help heal the world rather than destroy it. By the Light of the One God —" He salaamed. "I have found a measure of peace."

A measure of peace. Like the peace she had found so briefly in Llewellyn's tender kiss.

"Please," she whispered again.

Llewellyn's lips parted in a sigh.

Both Draganovich and Angélique gasped together. When Llewellyn's heart thumped, then beat evenly, Draganovich smiled and leaned forward to take his hand.

"Allahu akbar. Welcome, my friend, to endless possibilities."

Llewellyn's eyes twitched and flickered open. He beamed at Angélique and cupped her cheek. "I must be in heaven," he murmured, "for I would die before presuming to take you before our wedding night. Or is this another of your bewitching dreams? Ah, I would enjoy waking up to you every morning if you'll have me, fy nghariad Anyel."

Tears welled in her eyes. "My love!"

He moved to rise, then groaned and fell back. "*Hmm*. Something…"

Angélique caressed him. "Slowly. Yorg shot you. You were dead. But he killed me as well, and now…"

Llewellyn sprang up with a roar. "He what? Killed you!"

His body convulsed. He doubled over, then dropped to all fours. Angélique knelt beside him and held him as he transformed, speaking gently in his ear, stroking his back until she combed silvery fur.

My love. My love, she called to him, spirit to spirit. *Forgive me. Forgive me! I did this. I couldn't help it. We fell together. I could not stop it.*

Llewellyn barked, then whined and nuzzled Angélique. She lifted her chin to him, and he licked her throat as she rubbed his ear.

Cariad. Fy nghariad. I'm – I'm complete! Now I am truly yours!

Their reunion was cut short, interrupted by whinnies and nickers of horses outside. Draganovich peered out the window.

"My father," he said grimly. "De Guise failed."

Footsteps pounded up the gangway, followed by shouted orders. Draganovich turned to face Angélique and Llewellyn.

"It's up to us."

Angélique hugged Llewellyn closer. He whined in pain.

"He's not healed yet!" she cried. "We can't—"

"In my experience, a good meal will hasten the process," Draganovich replied. "Join me?"

He began to strip. Angélique's eyes widened as she realized his plan. She quickly ducked behind the privy screen to shed her clothes and transform. She joined the other wolves in greeting and scenting one another. When she batted Llewellyn's nose, he bowed to her, then rubbed his muzzle to hers while Draganovich gruffed and unlatched the door.

As soon as it was open, Angélique caught Jacqueline's scent. She heard her sister yell, "Claque! Get these bodies off the ship!"

The wolves emerged from the room and headed up the ladder, Draganovich in the lead. He stopped at the doorway and crouched, snarling. Tawny Angélique and silvery-grey Llewellyn took their places beside Draganovich, their lips curled back over their fangs. Drool slipped from their maws.

"*What is this?*" Count Draganov bellowed.

The three wolves pounced, Draganovich first, tearing into his father's face and dragging him down to the deck.

Yes! Ah, finally! With a triumphant cry, Angélique dove on top of the flailing Count. His screams only aroused her bloodlust. Her claws shredded his coat and shirt away, exposing the Count's breast.

You watched me die, you bastard!

She slashed the flesh along his ribs. Her quarry's shrieks and the sharp scent of blood and meat fed her rage, blinding her to all else. She bit into the mess of blood and muscle. Thrashing once, she tore away his flesh. Both wolf and vengeful woman, Angélique gnawed into him until she could bury her teeth in his beating heart.

The screams stopped.

Sated, Angélique sat up, panting. *Dead. Dead. You're dead!*

Jacky's voice broke through the euphoric buzz in her ears, though her words were unclear. Through a haze, she saw her sister with de Guise. She flashed them a drunken grin and slid down to wipe blood from her muzzle and lick her paws clean.

Beside her, Llewellyn ripped out viscera and flung it across the deck where Monsieur Claque impassively continued his task of collecting the long-dead corpses to dispatch in the lake. Draganovich gnawed through the Count's throat and tossed the head over the rail. As sunrise lit the summer clouds in brilliant flashes of crimson, vermillion, and gold against a bright blue sky, the wolves devoured the corrupt father, the would-be conqueror of Eastern Europe, this black-hearted boyar who had abandoned Angélique to rape and death.

The Czech bulldog clattered across the blood-slicked deck.

RÉSOLUTION

THE THERMAL AIRSHIP SAILED SERENELY ABOVE THE LOIRE VALLEY, ITS chameleonic envelope shimmering the full spectrum of the day's end: green, yellow, pale blue, sun-bright white. Cottony clouds flocked the early evening sky. The Loire, a golden ribbon below, wound away to the west, where the Paris-Orléans trundled north, its smokestack belching out black billows that quickly dissipated.

Jacqueline and Angélique stood side by side at the railing on the forecastle of the aerostat, their arms linked, their heads tilted together. Knotted honey-gold hair mingled with wild tawny in the winds. The beauty of the vale escaped Jacqueline, still raveled in too many unaccustomed emotions as she replayed the impossible scenes of the past week in her mind. Revenants, spirits, magic… Nothing in her years of science had prepared her for such supernatural encounters except, perhaps, her sister's saga.

Jacqueline nudged her twin. "Was he angry?"

Angélique shook her head, then sighed in dreamy wonder. "And isn't he just the most beautiful creature?"

"He is indeed."

"With beautiful silver-blue eyes."

Jacqueline grinned. "Well, deep olive green, in fact, but beautiful indeed, mon Ange." She kissed her cheek warmly, eliciting a shy, girlish smile. This was the sister she had lost in St. Petersburg.

"But no, not angry." To Jacqueline's surprise, Angélique actually blushed. "M'amie, he asked me to marry him. Me, Angélique Aurélie Duval de la Forge-à-Bellesfées. Not the prima donna, not the virtuosa, not the bohemian Angélique Laforge. He knows who I am, what I am, and I think he truly loves *me*."

She grabbed Jacqueline's hands. "And I said yes. I want this — what did you call it? Contentment."

They held one another then as they used to do as children, and they both laughed at the tears that spilled.

Then Jacqueline chuckled. "And who licked whose chin?"

Angélique feigned shock. "Can't you guess?" Then she grinned. "To tell it truthfully, I licked his. Absolute surrender. But afterward, with Draganov's blood all over both of us, it was a mutual surrender of absolute sensuality."

"Mon Ange, that's disgusting," Jacqueline cried, pushing her away.

Angélique shrugged, but her sly grin spoke of a lupine ritual Jacqueline didn't want to imagine.

Below them, the vineyards of Bellesfées spread out across a vast rolling expanse, and beyond that, the towers of the château gleamed rose-gold.

"Cutting the burners!" Jacqueline sang out. She yanked on a cable she had rigged to control the hydrogen tanks. One by one, they closed. "Full stop, everyone. Get to the crown lines, Claque."

Monsieur Claque lumbered from the capstan to the rail, where he pondered the task. He easily reached the steel mouth supporting the envelope's skirt. Somewhat less elegantly, he hauled his heavy form up to stand on the rail to secure the lines that contained the great envelope. The ship drifted down as gracefully as a blossom on the July breezes. Once it settled, Monsieur Claque pulled the crown lines to collapse the silken envelope.

"Bravo, my friends." Jacqueline clapped her hands and laughed. "Thank you, thank you."

She and Angélique embraced again. "It's so good to be home," they said in unison, then giggled, hooked their little fingers, and cried, "Twinicism!"

De Guise and Llewellyn came to the ladder to await the women, who eagerly accepted their hands to descend to the deck. De Guise pressed his lips to Jacqueline's fingers and caressed her arm. Llewellyn and Angélique kissed far more intimately. Jacqueline wagged her head and chuckled, but she didn't protest when de Guise lifted her into his arms and kissed her in kind.

Warm and deep and soft.

Draganovich strode away, head bowed. He unbattened the gang-plank and affixed it, then took possession of his horses and led them off the ship. When the others finally disembarked, he turned and bowed to the sisters.

"With your permission, I will take my leave of you," he said stiffly. With a rueful frown, he pointed to his nose, returned to wholeness, and said, "I am well aware my presence in your home would only insult you, Mesdames. I have no hope there is any apology I can make to atone for my past, but I offer it in all humility. I beg you to allow me to stable my horses here for the time. They're quite spent. If I may use a carriage—"

Llewellyn nodded sympathetically. De Guise offered his hand.

"Well done, Toma. I'm sorry it didn't end as you might have hoped, but war has been averted thanks to your efforts. You have the gratitude of His Majesty, the King of the French, and that is no small recompense. And you have your father's estate, which I know you will maintain with justice and mercy."

"And you have Elif," Jacqueline assured him. "She loves you, and I know she'll be overjoyed to be reunited with you now that Mirrikh is gone."

Draganovich's frown deepened, and he bristled. "What are you talking about?"

"Your governess, Elif. Pasha Elif Effendi. Perhaps she used a different name…" Jacqueline tilted her head, puzzled at his reaction. "She's responsible for our success. She took the skull from me that first night and rewrote the spell upon it. Didn't you know she was a janissary and a mystic before she came to your household?"

She looked to the others, but they were equally confused. De Guise patted her hand.

"Stop condescending to me, de Guise," Jacqueline said, pulling her hand away. "Draganovich, didn't you know she was working with me?" she persisted. "She used her powers to speak to Angélique. She led the assault on Mirrikh in the Catacombs. We could not have won the day if she had not been so determined to put an end to that monster's blasphemy. She loves you."

Llewellyn tapped her shoulder and set his hand there to silence her. De Guise shook his head. "Jacqueline, I keep telling you—"

Draganovich leaned to one of the horses trembling. She could not tell from anger or exhaustion.

"I— I am glad you met her," he said at last, his voice breaking. "I'm glad I will not be the only one to remember her with gratitude and love."

"Honor her memory, my friend," Llewellyn said. "Be the good and devout man she raised you to be, and you will see her again on the Day of Reckoning."

Jacqueline watched him head up the hill toward the stables, his shoulders slumped, his steps heavy with grief. "I don't understand. I thought he'd be—What do you mean, 'honor her memory'? Elif—"

"His childhood governess is dead, Madame Duval," Llewellyn told her. "The skull was hers."

Jacqueline searched her memory for the signs she had missed. "This poor soul," Elif had said. The disappearances. Her ability to speak to Angélique. Mirrikh's final words. Elif's final prayer, "To Allah we belong; to Allah we return."

"Oh, Elif," she murmured. Tears slipped down her face. "Allah ma'ik."

The bedraggled quartet halted at the doorway, confronted by Marthe waving her rolling pin threateningly, though her ruddy face revealed no anger. "No warning? How am I supposed to feed you all? You!" She smacked Llewellyn's arm with the pin. "How dare you leave this house an abattoir? How dare you leave at all? How's that thick head of yours? Get your hands off my girl!"

Angélique laughed and pulled Llewellyn away from the house-keeper's berating.

"And you." Marthe aimed the rolling pin at de Guise. "Behave yourself. You upset my girl leaving so early the other day."

Jacqueline beamed up at him, hugging his arm. "Don't worry, Marthe. He has since made up for it."

A voice boomed out from upstairs. "Are my wayward daughters home at last?"

"Papa!" the twins cried.

They rushed away, their beaux following, to meet their father in the hallway at the foot of a winding staircase. A tall, lanky man with twinkling grey eyes and a full head of ash hair still wet from a bath, Michel Duval welcomed them in a brocade dressing gown and slippers. He opened his arms wide and embraced his daughters with a jovial laugh.

"My girls! My girls! Have pity on a poor old man," he begged. He eyed Llewellyn and de Guise. "What's this? Have you finally found gentlemen brave enough to court you two? I'm not dressed for company, but then—" He grinned and winked at the men and squeezed his daughters. " —neither are my girls. Ever."

"Papa," Jacqueline began, "may I present Alain de Guise. He—"

"I work with the railroad," de Guise cut in quickly with a surreptitious nudge to Jacqueline, reminding her his true position was not for public knowledge. "It is an honor to meet you, Sir Duval de la Forge-à-Bellesfées." He bowed.

Duval guffawed. "*Mon Dieu,* that's a mouthful! Duval de la Forge à Bellesfées de Mon Cul sur le Pot de Chambre!" He shook de Guise's hand. "I am simply Duval, like my daughter. We're all citizens here."

"Gryffin Llewellyn," said the other, "Duke of Singlebury, Glamorgan, brigadier in service to Her Royal Majesty Queen Victoria."

"Duke!" Angélique clapped her hand over her mouth. She looked down at the filthy chemise she wore, pouting. She smacked his arm as Marthe had done. "You never told me that part."

Llewellyn chucked her chin. "We're in France, Anyel. We're all citizens here." He shook Duval's outstretched hand.

"My Lord Duke of Singlebury. An honor, Your Grace." Duval wagged his head, incredulous. Then he smirked and pointed to Llewellyn's lupine eyes. "And I see you and my daughter have much in common, n'est-ce pas?"

Llewellyn stammered, but before he could reply, Duval waved him off, laughing again.

"Come, let us sit and you can tell me your wild tales. Angélique will reassure me she has not been detained by the Paris gendarmes while I was away, and Jacqueline will explain the monstrous thermal aerostat on my lawn. Please tell me you didn't steal it."

"Say rather I appropriated it." Jacqueline hooked his arm in hers, her eyes full of mischief.

Angélique steered them toward the library rather than the salon, not trusting the scrubber to have erased all traces of the mess she had left behind. Jacqueline had reassured her the unfortunate minion had been dispatched, but she wanted her father to have no questions before the tale could be told. As they settled in, Marthe brought a board of cheeses, bread, and cold meats, and a bottle of dry vermouth and soda water for aperitifs, a habit Angélique had brought home from Venice.

"Well, gentlemen, I will warn you my daughters are not to be domesticated," Duval said as he prepared drinks. "Lord knows I would not have them so, nor, I guess, would you if you have suffered this far. I sincerely hope you know what you're in for."

"Believe me, Papa," Angélique said with a little laugh. "They know a lot more about us than you do."

She gazed up at Llewellyn, her whole body warming to the love in his wolf eyes. Jacqueline set her head on de Guise's shoulder. Their father shrugged in resignation.

"So that's how it is? My girls declare their womanhood, and well about time. I do hope you haven't outgrown presents."

He pointed to his desk where two packages sat. Jacqueline fetched them.

"This one weighs a ton!" she said, hefting a large box. "I'll wager it's for me."

"And you'd be correct, my little polytech," her father replied. He took the smaller, lighter box from her and handed it to Angélique. "And for my little angel—"

Llewellyn grinned at Angélique. "Anyel?" he teased.

The women untied the wrappings and cooed in delight.

"Frank Johnson scores!" Angélique caressed a stack of manuscripts.

"They cannot do justice to his performances at 'proms,' as they call those outdoor concerts on the promenades," her father said, "but I knew you would enjoy them."

Jacqueline opened her gift, a tool case, and lifted out a massive wrench with a turn-screw mechanism. "A coach wrench. But adjustable with a turn of the screw. This—this is ingenious!"

"It's called a 'monkey wrench,' although I don't know why. Americans seem to have their own language."

Llewellyn commented, "Sailors use the term 'monkey' to mean something small. That doesn't look small to me."

"But it is. Much smaller than a vise, say, and much easier to use!" Jacqueline's eyes glinted with anticipation. "And a whole case of them, different measures. Oh, Papa!"

She closed the case and kissed her father's cheek. Angélique kissed his other cheek.

Jean-Paul appeared and cleared his throat. "Father is caring for the horses. I'm to take the cabriolet again, mademoiselle?" he asked, jerking his head to the front door to indicate Draganovich had been to see him.

Jacqueline accompanied the boy to the entryway. "Yes, that's fine. Thank you, Jean-Paul. Have your mother pack you a good supper for the journey. If you must, stay the night at an inn and see that Bisou is well stabled." She sent him off to the kitchen.

Draganovich stood beside the carriage. He bowed to her and saluted solemnly, but a grateful smile appeared before he turned away. The boy soon headed his way. Draganovich climbed up to the seat at Jean-Paul's signal. He didn't look back as the carriage headed off.

The others joined her and watched him leave.

"A disappointed suitor?" their father asked.

Angélique shuddered. Llewellyn held her closer and kissed her hair.

"No, Papa," Jacqueline said. "No one we'll see again."

Their father gauged the air of melancholy that had so suddenly quelled their jocularity. He studied his daughters and the two men at their sides: exhausted, disheveled, and unkempt, their clothing blood-stained, their shoulders set defiantly.

"Well," he said, "It is obvious you have all been up to trouble. Nothing unusual for Angélique, of course, but you, Jacqueline? I look forward to hearing the tale. I'm sure it's nothing a fine dinner won't heal. Myself—" He rubbed the back of his head and stretched. "I've been on that brand-new train all day, which I greatly appreciate, Monsieur de Guise, but there were no post stops along the way. So, I'm going back to the library for a few more titbits. I hope you will all join me." He assessed them again and grinned. "It looks like at least two of you could use some repast."

He winked at Angélique and headed off.

Angélique snickered, and Llewellyn laughed out loud. Then they kissed. As they parted, Angélique grabbed his arm. Together they gamboled down the hillside, around the pond, and into the woods.

Jacqueline smiled to see her sister had finally —*finally!*— taken her advice. Perhaps it was time she took Angélique's. She clasped de Guise's hand, enjoying the grounded feeling the simple gesture lent. She was beginning to understand the mysterious quality of romance that gave strength where none was needed, and took nothing where all would be gladly given.

De Guise lifted her chin, his eyes filled with regret. Her smile faltered. Had she been wrong about him? Was it affectation after all? She trembled, her heart pounding.

He shook his head. "I won't deceive you, Jacqueline," he said. "I never will."

He caressed her cheek, sending a shiver through her. But his smile was sad, and her hope failed.

"I love you. Do not doubt it. But I belong to the king. I am not free to ask—"

Joy returned, filling her eyes with sparkling tears. She set a finger to his pretty bowed lips. "You don't have to be free, Alain. And you don't have to ask."

He searched her face. His smile dazzled once again. She kissed him. Warm and soft and deep.

Before he could respond, a shriek from the kitchen startled them. They hastened to learn what had caused Marthe's alarm this time. They found her standing on the preparation table, arms folded. She glared at Jacqueline and pointed her rolling pin.

Monsieur Claque stood at the sink, washing glasses as expertly as a Paris café patron. He whistled in tiny puffs of steam.

Acknowledgements

THE FIRST PERSON I NEED TO THANK IS MY HUSBAND JACK FOR HIS enduring patience—forty years' worth! I'm sorry the house wasn't always neat and clean, and I'm sorry for hours spent gazing off into the void. You have been my rock, my source, and my comfort. You are my de Guise.

Gregory Frost told me almost thirty years ago that I could write, and I should write. His guidance through the nameless workshop, various Penn Writers Conferences, con panels, emails, conversations, readings, and especially his own writing has been instrumental in making me the writer he said I could be. As a beta reader, he showed me my own story and made me dig deeper to write it. There isn't enough single-malt Scotch in the world to thank him enough for all he has been to me.

My other beta readers—my twin Sally Weiner Grotta and John Schoffstall—gave invaluable guidance and feedback, as well as catching the stupid I couldn't see right in front of me. More importantly, we talked writing, which kept me writing. Thank you, my dearest friends.

Thanks go out to Yann Matthieu for tips on historical accuracy and social customs, and especially for "mon cul sur la commode."

Thanks to the Bucks County Writers Workshop for helpful tips on engineering and characterization. Engineers write! Special thanks to Lindsay Allingham, who "got" Jacqueline, and Bill Donahue and Chris Bauer, whose storycraft skills are incomparable.

Part of the intrigue of writing historical fiction, particularly steampunk that isn't entirely based on handwavium or balonium, is rooting out anachronisms and remaining fact-based while creating a world of utter fantasy. Yes, there were automatons in the 1800s, but the work of Ada King, the Countess of Lovelace, whose designs would have given artificial intelligence to Monsieur Claque, would not be discovered for almost another hundred years. That doesn't mean Ada couldn't have discussed her work with someone as brilliant as Jacqueline, who would put it to good use. Of course, the aerostat had not progressed any further than the Montgolfier by 1843; that doesn't mean it couldn't have. Yes, people had a subconscious, but the word 'subconscious' had not yet been coined, so no one in the novel would use it in conversation; therefore, the narrator couldn't either. I can't begin to tell you how many words I had to edit out because they simply didn't exist in 1843, even if they were the perfect word for the situation—like "goggles"!

People who aren't familiar with history or the culture of European countries other than England often don't realize just how different life was in the 1840s in France. This isn't the Versailles of Louis IV. Nor is it Downton Abbey. You did not have trains departing every hour on the hour, zipping along at fifty or seventy miles per hour. In those days, nothing traveled more than thirty miles per hour. Dogs and other various domesticated animals often rode with their owners, so, no, it would not be a terrifying or even an unusual event to have a tame wolf seated beside someone on a train. Servants in a palace wouldn't scold a king, but in a citizen's home, the servants could be surrogate parents and treat the master's children as they would their own.

Walking that fine line between fantasy and historical fact makes steampunk that much more fun to write. It does, however, demand research. I did mine.

Along with simple Google searches, the following resources were of infinite value:

- The Rosny-sous-Bois Railway museum and the wonderful agents there.
- The SNCF Archives and their genial curator
- *Chemins de Fer d'hier et d'aujourd'hui* by O.S. Nock
- *Scènes de la vie de bohème* (French Edition) Henri Murger
- *ADOLPHE SAX 1814-1894: - his life and legacy* Wally Horwood
- *Les Fleurs du Mal* by Charles Baudelaire
- *Chopin in Paris* by Tad Szulc
- *Ada, the Enchantress of Numbers:Poetical Science* by Betty Alexandra Toole

Finally, I thank Danielle Ackley-McPhail for believing in the Twins of Bellesfées, bringing me into one of the finest publishing stables in the genre. I have admired her work for many years, as an author, publisher, and entrepreneur. I've since learned her editing skills are impeccable, and I've learned so much throughout this whole process that I cannot wait to apply to my next book.

Danielle, you are amazing. Thank you.

ABOUT THE AUTHOR

EF DEAL IS A NEW VOICE IN THE GENRE OF SPECULATIVE STEAMPUNK with her debut novel, *Esprit de Corpse*, but she is not new to publishing. Her short fiction has appeared in various magazines and ezines over the years. Her short story "Czesko," published in the March 2006 F&SF, was given honorable mention in Gardner Dozois' *Year's Best Science Fiction and Fantasy*, which gave both her and Gardner great delight. They laughed and laughed and sipped Scotch (not cognac, alas) over the last line.

Despite her preoccupation with old-school drum and bugle corps — playing, composing, arranging, and teaching — Ef Deal can usually be found at the keyboard of her computer rather than her piano. She is Assistant Fiction Editor at Abyss & Apex magazine and edits videos for the YouTube channel Strong Women — Strange Worlds Quick Reads.

Esprit de Corpse from eSpec Books is the first of a series featuring the brilliant 19th-century sisters, the Twins of Bellesfées Jacqueline and Angélique. Hard science blends with the paranormal as they challenge the supernatural invasion of France in 1843.

When she's not lost in her imagination, Ef Deal can be found in historic Haddonfield, NJ, in a once-haunted Victorian with her husband and two chows. She is an associate member of SFWA and an affiliate member of HWA.

About the Artist

Although Jason Whitley has worn many creative hats, he is at heart a traditional illustrator and painter. With author James Chambers, Jason collaborates and illustrates the sometimes-prose, sometimes graphic novel, *The Midnight Hour,* which is being collected into one volume by eSpec Books. His and Scott Eckelaert's newspaper comic strip, *Sea Urchins*, has been collected into four volumes. Along with eSpec Books' Systema Paradoxa series, Jason is working on a crime noir graphic novel. His portrait of Charlotte Hawkins Brown is on display in the Charlotte Hawkins Brown Museum.

The Patrons
of Bellesfées

Adam Nemo
Amanda Nixon
Andrea Hunter
Andrew Kaplan
Andy Hunter
Anonymous Reader
Aramanth Dawe
Austin Hoffey
Aven Lumi
Aysha Rehm
Bea Hersh-Tudor
Becky B
Benjamin Adler
Bess Turner
Bethany Tomerlin Prince
Betsy Cameron
Bill Kohn
Bill Schulz & family
Brad Jurn
Brendan Coffey
Brendan Lonehawk
Brian G
Brian Quirt
Brooks Moses
Carol Gyzander
Carol J. Guess
Carol Jones
Caroline Westra
Carolyn and Stephen Stein

Carolyn Rowland
Cathy Green
Chad Bowden
Charles Barouch
Charles Deal
Chris Bauer, novelist,
    Blessid Trauma series
Christopher J. Burke
Christopher Weuve
Cori Paige
Craig "Stevo" Stephenson
Cristov Russell
Dale A Russell
Dan Persons
Daniel Korn
Danielle Ackley-McPhail
Danny Chamberlin
Darke Conteur
Darrell Z. Grizzle
David Goldstein
David Lee Summers
David Medinnus
Debra L. Lieven
Denise and Raphael Sutton
Dennis P Campbell
Diana Botsford
Donna M. Hogg
Dr. Kat Crispin
Edwin Purcell

Ef Deal
Elaine Tindill-Rohr
Ellery Rhodes
Elyse M Grasso
Emily Rebecca Weed Baisch
Eric Slaney
Erin A.
Fantasy Supporter
Gary Phillips
Gav I.
Glori Medina
GraceAnne Andreassi
    DeCandido
Greg Levick
Heidi Pilewski
Hollie Buchanan
IAMTW
Isaac 'Will It Work' Dansicker
J. Linder
Jacen Leonard
Jack Deal
James Hallam
James Johnston
Jason R Burns
Jeffrey Harlan
Jennifer L. Pierce
Jeremy Bottroff
Jim Gotaas
jjmcgaffey
John Keegan
John L. French
John Markley
John Peters
John Schoffstall
Jonathan Haar
Josh Ward
Jp
Judith Waidlich
Jules
Julian White
Julie Strange

Kal Powell
Karen Krah
Kate Myers
Katherine Hempel
Katie
Kay Hafner
Keith R.A. DeCandido
Kelly Pierce
Kelsey M
Kerry aka Trouble
Kimberly Catlett
Kit Kindred
krinsky
KT Magrowski
Lark Cunningham
Lawrence M. Schoen
LCW Allingham
Lee Jamilkowski
Linda Pierce
Lisa Kruse
Lisa Venezia
Lori & Maurice Forrester
Lorraine J. Anderson
Lowell Gilbert
maileguy
Maree Pavletich
Marilyn B
Mark Bergin
Mark Newman
Mark Squire
Mary Perez
Matthew Barr
Maureen Lewis
Mauria Reich
Megan Murphy Davis
Melanie Ball
Michael A. Burstein
Michael Brooker
Mikaela Irish
Mike "PsychoticDreamer"
    Bentley

Mike Bunch
Mike Crate
Mike Zipser
Mina Ellyse
Miriam Seidel
Nathan Turner
Nathaniel Adams
Nicholas Ahlhelm
Pat Knuth
Patrick Purcell
Paul Ryan
Paul van Oven
Pepita Hogg-Sonnenberg
Peter D Engebos
pjk
Pookster
prophet
Raphael Bressel
RAW
Rich Gonzalez
Richard Novak
Richard O'Shea
River
Rob Menaul
Robert Claney
Rochelle
Rose Caratozzolo
Ross Hathaway
Ruthenia

Sally Wiener Grotta
Saul Jaffe
Scantrontb
Scott Elson
Scott Thede
Sheryl R. Hayes
Sidney Whitaker
Steph Parker
Stephanie Lucas
Stephen Ballentine
Stephen Cheng
Stephen Lesnik
Stephen Rubin
Steve Locke
Steven Purcell
Stuart Chaplin
Svend Andersen
The Creative Fund
The Reckless Pantalones
Tim DuBois
Tina M Noe Good
Todd Dashoff
Tom B.
ToniAnn & Kyle
Tracy 'Rayhne' Fretwell
Ty Drago
Vee Luvian
Will "scifantasy" Frank
William J. Donahue